The
Boy Who Talked
To Planes

Pitmeddan Castle School   James Edwards

by John RH Milne

This story is fiction, but placed within an historically accurate framework of time and events.

First published in the UK in 2013

by **J&J Milne**
storyofjames.tumblr.com

ISBN 978-0-9576035-0-9

Papers used in this book are natural, renewable and recyclable products sourced from well-managed forests and certified in accordance with the rules of the Forest Stewardship Council.

FSC
www.fsc.org
MIX
Wood from
responsible sources
FSC® C021018

Typeset in Adobe Garamond, designed and produced by Gilmour Print, www.self-publish-books.co.uk
Cover design by Brodie Milne

Part 1

The Thirties, a Time of Innocence

Chapter 1

Take offs were always exciting, the sports car like acceleration, the vibration of wheels on short grass, the transition from solid earth to fluid air and the slight wiggle as Dad corrected for the cross wind. There was always a cross wind.

Once clear of the trees, we skimmed over the lake drifting to the right to avoid the spray from the fountain and zoomed up in a climbing turn to the left. It was like being on the biggest fun ride imaginable. We levelled out and built up speed flying back towards the house.

"Come on Midge, let's make a really steep turn over the house and scare Papa."

Our left wing pointed at the terrace where Papa stood watching us. I waved from the side window and he took off his homburg hat and waved back. It takes a lot to scare Papa. We continued to the south east and quarter of an hour later we were heading into wind to land at Hatfield. Dad wanted the mechanics at the De Havilland factory to give Midge a quick check and service, so while he talked to them I climbed into the cockpit of an old DH4 and talked to him.

He had been a fighter bomber in the Great War and was full of exciting stories, like the time he shot down an enemy airship and sent it flaming into the North Sea. We chatted on all morning about great dog fights with famous pilots and their aircraft. I told him about Midge who he remembered for the sensation her innovations caused when she entered the hangar shortly after she was built. I could have stayed longer but it was near lunchtime and I was hungry. I climbed out and gave his wing strut a pat before leaving to find my father.

"Dad, is it lunchtime yet?"

"Yes James, but we'll have lunch at home. The mechanics are finished and Midge is fine, so we can go now."

"Dad."

"Yes James?"

"I was talking to the old DH4 and he was telling me what he did in the Great War and it sounded great. Now I know why it's called the Great War. It's because it was great fun. Can I tell you about it?"

He sighed and looked at the sky.

"No James, you can tell me later and never say it was fun. It was anything but."

So I told Midge on the flight home and she said they were the same stories he told her all those years ago.

Nettleton House was my home. It stood higher than the surrounding land, so we always took of downhill and landed uphill, no matter which way the wind was blowing. The front of the house faced north and a long drive lead to a turning area next to the main entrance. The large terrace on the south side looked on to a stretch of gently sloping lawn which also served as our airstrip. It was protected on either side by avenues of beech trees, beyond which lay the lake with its ornamental fountain.

I could see my bedroom window on the top floor of the east wing as we flew over the house, so announcing our arrival to the staff. We landed and taxied to Midge's usual spot below the terrace, where helpers were waiting to fold her wings and roll her into her small hangar.

Papa had travelled by train in to London where he worked at the Air Ministry. Dad had work to do and Mum was visiting friends, so I was left to have lunch in the nursery with Nanny. I was bursting to tell someone what the DH4 had told me about the Great War so I told her everything he'd said. Her reaction surprised me. Her eyes opened wide and she put a hand to her mouth.

"Ooh you are a card Master James and no mistake," as she ran from the room, howling with laughter.

"Er yes, if you say so Nanny. I didn't think the stories were all that funny."

At our evening meal, I asked again if I could tell them about the DH4 and his stories of the Great War, but Dad said I should wait until we were all finished eating. Once the plates were cleared away, he sat back in his chair.

"Now James you can tell us what the old DH4 told you about the Great War."

So I did, only this time the reaction was even more surprising. There eyes opened wide, and their mouths. My mother blushed. Dad was clearly offended by something I'd said and the butler appeared to be in great pain while staring fixedly at a point on the ceiling. I stopped mid sentence.

"James! Where on earth did you hear language like that? It certainly wasn't in *this* house."

"The old DH4 said . . ."

"That's enough James. I've had it up to here with your stories. It was someone in the hangar at Hatfield wasn't it. I'll have it out with them tomorrow. Using language of that sort in front of a child is really not on."

Mum looked utterly miserable.

"Honestly," I pleaded, "I was only saying what . . ."

"Just go to your room. Your mother and I have things to discuss."

I felt dreadful. I'd obviously hurt them in some way, so I got down from my chair and quickly left the room. When I reached the first landing I stopped and listened. Dad sounded so sad and Mum, ever the peace maker and voice of reason was suggesting sources of words I had never heard before and who's meaning I could only guess.

"Vicky, we have to get his story telling sorted out once and for all. It was tolerable when it was only with Midge, but when he uses any old aircraft as an excuse to swear like a trooper, it has to stop."

"Peter, have you considered the possibility that his stories may be true and he really can hear aircraft talk."

"Oh come on Vicky, you're not seriously suggesting that he hears Midge talking in words, in English."

"Be fair Peter, I've heard you talking to Midge; though you

usually call her 'old girl' and I bet she talks to you in her own way. She certainly talks to me."

"Well all right Vicky but that's different. Every pilot listens to the sounds and feels the vibrations that tell when things are right or wrong, but talking in words, that's just plain odd."

"It's certainly different. I never told you this, but before James was born, when I was flying Midge and he was growing inside me I was aware. Now you're going to think *I'm* a bit odd and that's probably why I didn't tell you at the time."

"Vicky, you're the sanest person I know. You were saying you were aware, of what?"

"All right, there's probably a bit of hindsight involved, but I was aware," and she took a deep breath, "of them conversing."

"Good grief!"

There was a long pause. I was afraid to breathe in case I made a noise. I could hear my father sigh.

"It's all right Vicky. I believe you. We'll need to talk to him. I wonder if your father could devise some gentle way of finding the truth. I'll write to him tonight and send it first post. You know, I was shocked at the swear words, but take them out and what was left had a certain recognisable ring to it. Do you think I should have a quiet word with him?"

"It's all right I'll talk to him and you can write to Papa. James will need a biscuit and something warm to drink."

I raced upstairs to my room, washed, brushed teeth, into pyjamas at lightning speed and dived into bed. A few minutes later my mother entered with a mug of malted milk and a plate of biscuits on a tray which she placed on a bedside table.

She then explained that the DH4 was a fighter and some of the words he used were like bullets and could hurt. She told me they should never ever be used in polite society and since then I have never used them and certainly not in company. They are far too precious for every day speech, but are kept in reserve, treasured like secret weapons, to be used only when attack is the best means of defence.

The Boy Who Talked To Planes

From the confidential diary of Sir James Nettleton

Room 407B,
Air Ministry,
Whitehall,
LONDON.

Wednesday 5th October 1938

A letter arrived this morning from Peter. James has
been repeating words no child of his age should
know, never mind utter. He claimed the old DH4 at
Hatfield had been telling him about the Great War. I
find it odd, as I know the foreman and bad language
is never allowed in the hangar.
Can James really hear planes talk? It sounds
unlikely, but if true, could be useful the way things
are going.
I contacted the Commanding Officer of 111 Squadron
at Northolt. He's a good chap and owes me the odd
favour. I hope we're able to devise some test. If we
use his latest Hurricane we should discover the truth.
I wrote a reply to Peter to say I've arranged a day
out for James at Northolt. The details can be sorted
out at the weekend.
If we're dragged into another war, we could be subject
to aerial bombardment. I'll need to find a safe school
further north. It's time he moved on from old Davies
and met folk his own age. I phoned Anderson at
Intelligence and asked him to pick out a suitable
minder for James. He may also know of a good
school, as I believe he comes from that neck of the
woods.
James may yet prove to be a valuable weapon. Lord
knows we have little else. What a dreadful business. I
only hope Munich buys us some time.

Chapter 2

Sir James Nettleton is my grandfather, but from an early age I called him Papa. He didn't mind. I believe he saw it more as a title than a pet name as it established him in all our minds as the paternal head of the household, which indeed he was.

His other life at the Air Ministry was less defined. His suit was invariably clerical grey and I believe said more about his role in government, than any rank or title. The most I was able to discover about his work was he advised. Who or in what capacity remained the same colour as his suit.

Through the eyes of a young child he looked aloof, a private figure, like a distant giant to be looked up to with due respect. As I reached school age we drew closer. He often came home at the weekend and we would sit together on his couch. He listened to me chatter on about the lessons from my tutor, Mr Davies and was especially interested in what Midge, our beautiful white Puss Moth, had been telling me. I wondered why he didn't ask Midge. Couldn't everyone hear her? Realising I was the only one who could hear aircraft talk was a nasty shock. It made me feel uncomfortable; different.

Perhaps that was why I had a tutor, instead of attending the local primary school. To me, the only difference between people talk and plane talk was the planes talked inside my head with the words echoing between my ears. It may sound odd, but I thought that was normal. My mother Victoria, also a skilled pilot, accepted it without question, but Peter my father, was harder to convince, which was one of the reasons we paid a flying visit to RAF Northolt.

We flew in Midge, piloted by my father, with Papa sitting in the back, as he said, 'just for the ride'. Whatever his position in government, he was without doubt, the key that could open all doors.

This was my first meeting with a modern fighter aircraft, but I was the one on test. I wasn't aware of any exam pressure, it was simply fun, an exciting game.

After landing at Northolt, we taxied and parked near the main building complex. We climbed out as a tall officer came smartly towards us. He was dark haired with a neat moustache, similar to my grandfather's. He approached, putting on his hat and smoothing his uniform. He stopped in front of my grandfather, saluted and they shook hands.

"Good morning Sir James. I trust you had a pleasant flight."

My grandfather smiled and nodded, put his arm round my shoulders and ushered me forward.

"This is my grandson James, the one I told you about."

The officer stepped forward and bent down to shake my hand.

"Good morning Sir," I said.

"And good morning to you young fellow, I believe you have come to examine my fine new fighter plane. It's called a Hurricane."

"That would be splendid Sir. Can I sit in the cockpit?"

"Indeed you can young man, indeed you can."

My grandfather turned to my father.

"I believe you've already met my son-in-law Peter, when he came to enlist, unsuccessfully I gather."

The officer looked slightly embarrassed and made to speak, but was waved to silence.

"There's no need to apologise. Before long there'll be work for everyone in the country, service personnel and civilians alike."

We were walking towards a modern streamlined aircraft, unlike any I had seen before. Looking at its smooth curves, I didn't realise it had been doctored to see if I could find out the faults. I was only aware of the excitement of meeting a front line fighter.

The officer climbed onto the wing, slid back the cockpit canopy, lifted me up and helped me into the seat.

"Just the one circuit now, try not to bend it," he quipped.

Even with a cushion I could barely see over the edge of the cockpit, but that didn't matter, I had found a new friend. I started chattering right away without being introduced; very rude.

"Hello, I'm James. I'm here with Dad and Papa. That's our Puss Moth over there and she's called Midge. You're enormous. Is this the button that fires your guns?"

"Please don't touch that. Oh dear, someone else who talks to me. It would be nice if someone listened for a change."

"But I am listening, honest. I'm sorry for being rude. Perhaps we could start again. My name is James, what's yours?"

"Not that you can hear, but it's Tommy." He sounded rather bored. "You can tell by the big 'T' on my side, but my pilot says it's 'T' for Tailwind."

"Honestly, I *can* hear you. Why does he call you Tailwind?"

A shocked silence followed as the Hurricane realised for the first time that his thoughts could be heard.

"You really can hear what I'm saying. Can everyone hear?"

"I don't think so. I certainly don't know of anyone else. Why are you called Tailwind?"

"Tailwind, I'll try and explain. This *is* fun talking to you. You will come back and see me again won't you?"

"I'll try, but please, why Tailwind?"

"It was in all the newspapers. We broke a speed record flying from Scotland to here at over four hundred miles an hour."

"That *is* fast."

"It's absolutely true if you take it as speed over the ground, but we didn't tell the press we had a gale force tailwind pushing us along. So you see that's why I'm called Tailwind."

"That's a great story. Wait 'til I tell Papa."

"Oh I think he already knows. Anyway, there are more important things which you should tell him."

"You mean like, no don't tell me. Give me a moment."

I sat for several minutes holding the control column. Starting on the left of the cockpit, I moved my hands over the various levers switches and dials. I could feel the Hurricane 'T' for

Tommy watching me. All felt normal until I touched the engine temperature gauge. There was a sensation of heat.

Moving my right hand down, I felt an even greater reaction as I touched the lever used to raise and lower the undercarriage. The sole of my left foot went numb and I felt a bubbly flutter above my right hip. Tommy couldn't stay quiet any longer.

"This is amazing. Can I tell you what they did?"

I flopped back into the seat, exhausted.

"Please do, but I think I can guess, at least some of it. You see, I've no experience of a plane with a liquid cooled engine or retractable wheels. Have they let some of the air out of your left tyre?"

"Spot on, absolutely correct. They also drained some of the cooling stuff from my engine to see if you would find that."

"That makes sense."

"The most important thing is I'm bleeding from my right landing gear. I don't know what it's called, but I'm losing some vital fluid, especially when my engine is running. You must let them know because it could be dangerous."

"Don't worry. I'll let them know right away."

I stood up on the seat cushion and waved. The officer walked over, climbed onto the wing and lifted me out, passing me to my father who was waiting on the ground. I ran my hands along the fuselage and could hear Tommy.

"Please come back and see me soon."

"I'll try," I said

"That's the spirit," said the officer, who thought I was speaking to him. How could I persuade them to act in time to save Tommy?

"There are things I must tell you," I said.

"How about some lunch first and then we can have a nice chat."

"No, please, it may be too late then."

This was awful, but my grandfather could see I was upset.

"Let's have a seat in your office while lunch is being prepared, and let James get what ever is worrying him, off his chest."

"Good idea," replied the officer, who was unlikely to disagree with my grandfather.

Once in the office they sat down, leaving me standing in the middle of the floor. I had my arms stretched out like wings. I pointed to my right side about waist level.

"He's bleeding from here."

"You're bleeding?" said my father.

I felt so exasperated, why couldn't they understand?

"Not me, it's Tommy Tailwind. He says it's dangerous. I think he could die."

Questioning glances passed between my grandfather and the officer. He pressed the intercom button and was answered by a metallic voice.

"Sir?"

"Get my airframe fitter at the double."

He stood up and walked over to the door. In a short space of time an airman in service overalls appeared. He had clearly been running. They talked quietly for a few moments before the airman left and the officer sat down next to my father.

"Now don't you worry young man. We'll make sure that no harm comes to Tommy. Is there anything else you could tell us," the officer asked in a much gentler tone.

"Yes Sir," I said. "He needs some air in his left tyre and is rather low on cooling stuff."

"Very good," said the officer, looking at me thoughtfully.

"Why did you call him Tailwind?"

"He said that's what you called him after your record breaking flight from Scotland."

My grandfather looked over at the officer.

"Now do you believe me?"

The officer looked up and nodded.

"Yes Sir, I certainly do."

There was a gentle knock at the door, which the officer answered. He talked quietly to the fitter before returning to sit down heavily at his desk. His face was ashen. We were all looking at him expectantly.

"The fitter says a seal has gone in the hydraulic jack that operates the right hand undercarriage leg. It may have retracted in flight, but it certainly wouldn't have come back down again. The jack is being replaced now."

He looked at me in a quite different way from when we first met.

"James!"

"Yes Sir"

"You have my sincere thanks. But for you, it could have been, shall we say, embarrassing. I think we can go to lunch now."

"Great, I'm starving."

"And quite suddenly, I'm not," whispered the officer.

Chapter 3

I'm constantly surprised how adults underestimate the sensitivity of a child's hearing. Add to that my ability to hear plane talk and my hearing becomes several grades above super sensitive. I'm also able to filter out loud noises and pick out the small important ones. I hear many snippets of conversation that I shouldn't and most of the time it doesn't matter. However, there are times one overhears talk of a personal nature and it can shock and hurt. I've had to train myself not to react, difficult, but I'm getting better.

On the way home in Midge, I was sitting in the rearmost of the three seats, my father in the front piloting and grandfather in the middle. Normal conversation is difficult due to engine noise, but I saw Papa lean forward and whisper in my father's ear. "We need to talk." I believe that evening, after I was in bed, they talked and arrangements were planned.

My performance at Northolt had convinced them I could gain knowledge which could only come from the aircraft. The leaking undercarriage actuator was the final clincher, especially for the CO who, in a matter of seconds changed from condescending adult to believer. A similar change in perception had happened to Papa and my parents when I moved from a position of expensive responsibility to priceless asset.

I was still the only son of a loving family, but was aware of subtle changes in their attitude, the thoughtful glance and quick smile. However, my value to the government in the form of Papa had increased beyond measure.

After my latest chat with Papa, it was decided to attach me informally through him to British Intelligence. I was only eight and talking to Midge was not a particularly important part of life on Papa's estate, but he was interested and I was keen to tell him all her news. My father had flown him to an urgent meeting at Croydon and Midge was parked next to a sleek new passenger aircraft. Later at home she told me about her day and I passed on what she said to Papa the following weekend.

"Midge was talking to a strange aircraft Papa."

"Oh James, where?"

"At Croydon, she was parked next to it."

"Did she describe it to you? In what way was it strange?"

I had to think for a moment, to remember exactly what she said.

"She said it had black crosses on the wings and two tails with broken crosses on them. That's the Nazi sign isn't it Papa."

"Yes James, go on. What else did she say?"

"She said it had two engines, a long thin body and was very fast."

"How did she know it was very fast?"

"He told her."

"The aircraft told her. Did she say anything else about what he could do; anything strange or out of the ordinary?"

"She said he had places for passengers and mail, but also places where bombs could be fastened. That's strange isn't it?"

"It certainly is James. I think for the moment, we should keep this to ourselves. We don't want to worry anyone do we?"

So I thought no more about it, but later I would remember.

I wish I had valued my talent. It was so much part of life itself, I didn't think to keep it hidden like treasure of great price. I would chat to anyone who was interested. The more interest they showed, the more I would chatter on, prince or pauper, it made no difference. I didn't know any better. It was fortunate that most adults regarded it as imaginative ramblings, but there were some, only a few, who posed the question, 'what if?'

The first warm spring day has something special about it and I was desperate to finish breakfast and get out to play. That was my plan, but others had been made and they took preference.

"James."

"Yes Dad?"

"Papa has asked if you could talk to a bomber whose flying is a bit wobbly and no one knows why."

"Do I have to? There's somewhere I want to explore."

Dad gave one of his sighs.

"Please James, don't try my patience. It should only take half an hour to reach Duxford in Midge and if we ask her nicely I'm sure she'll have us back with lots of time to spare."

"Well, all right. What sort of plane is it?"

"It's a new Wellington bomber and if you can help her to fly properly, I'm sure her pilot will be very pleased."

It had been some time since we had flown anywhere in Midge and it was perfect flying weather. It could be fun. Breakfast was served in a room overlooking the terrace. I could see Midge being pushed from her hangar, her wings unfolded and her tanks topped up. As usual she was parked facing the lake.

"Dad, will Papa be at Duxford?"

"Yes James. He's travelling up from London by train. I expect he'll be flying back home with us."

It was always exciting preparing to fly and though I'd not forgotten my earlier plans, there should be time for them later. Before we reached Midge, my father turned to me.

"James, do you know what a secret is?"

"Yes Dad, it's a private thing isn't it"

"Yes James and private things have to be guarded and kept to ourselves, kept secret. I'm not explaining this very well am I?"

I must have looked as puzzled as I felt.

"When we meet Papa you'll get the chance to talk to some of the latest aircraft. They may tell you their secrets and because there are bad people who would be able to hurt our country if they knew about those secrets, you must tell no one what the planes say except Papa, your Mum and I. You will remember won't you?"

"Yes Dad, only tell you Mum and Papa what the planes say."

"Fine James, let's see if we can help this Wellington to fly better."

About half an hour later we touched down at Duxford and

checked in at the watch office. An airman was detailed to take us to the Wellington 'Q' for Queenie and act as guide to its controls and systems.

He led me through the strangely ribbed interior of the fuselage, making sure I didn't cause hurt to myself, or anyone else. If I was heard talking to the plane it didn't matter. I was regarded as an excited eight year old with a vivid imagination, pretending to be the gunner or the bomb aimer. It was fun too, until I sat in the pilot's seat and grasped the half wheel on the control column. Then it became serious.

The airman sensed something was wrong.

"Are you all right?"

"Could you please ask my father to come up?"

"Hang on a mo," and he scrambled down the access ladder. My father appeared immediately, almost missing his footing in his haste to reach me.

"Are you all right James?" putting his arm round my shoulders.

"Yes Dad, but Queenie is upset. You told me I shouldn't tell anyone else what the aircraft say."

My father relaxed and sat down in the co-pilot's seat.

"Quite right, quite right, what does she say?"

"Can I use her words?"

With memories of the old DH4, he was hesitant, but after a moment's thought, decided to risk it.

"All right, I hope it's not too rude."

Just to be on the safe side, I whispered.

"She says, 'some clown 'as left 'is bleedin' tools dancin' aroun' in me port elevator'."

My father smiled his relief and tried to find a more comfortable position on the small seat.

"Was that all right?"

"Yes James, that was indeed all right. Please tell Queenie we will investigate the problem and have it sorted out as soon as possible."

"Yes Dad. Is it lunch time yet? I'm hungry. When will Papa be here?"

"He's just arrived, so I'll have a word with him and see if we can find somewhere to eat."

I managed to convince Queenie that I understood what needed done, by which time the airman had returned to help me negotiate the steep access ladder. I could hear my father and grandfather laughing, before sending the airman off to find an airframe fitter.

While waiting for the fitter, they were able to decide on the best way of pointing towards the problem, without revealing the source of information. The story was, I had been running round the tail of the aircraft and bumped into the tailplane, which rattled.

My grandfather arrived for lunch after my father and sat down beside me.

"I've been speaking to the Commanding Officer and he's delighted. He says you've been a great help, so he wants to show you something special."

"What is it Papa?"

"Patience James, wait and see."

I wasn't good at being patient, aged eight, but I did my best. After a quicker than usual lunch, we were taken to a large closed hangar.

The CO asked us to wait while he ducked through a small door set into one of the larger doors. A few seconds later they started to roll back. On cue, the sun broke through the clouds, glinting on the metal surfaces of the most beautiful aircraft I had ever seen. Even the tan and olive camouflage couldn't hide her perfect lines.

The Spitfire sat glowing in the afternoon sun. I just stared. Great beauty can be intimidating as well as attractive. The CO was also looking with admiration at his latest aircraft.

"Isn't she a beauty?" he whispered, more to himself than anyone else. I think for the moment, he had forgotten I was there.

Eventually my voice returned.

"Sir?"

"Yes?"

"Can I sit in the pilot's seat?"

The CO raised his eyebrows and looked at my grandfather, who nodded.

"Certainly young man, let me help you onto the wing. I'll leave the door down, so you can see out. Oh and please don't touch anything."

"No Sir, I won't."

This was a totally different aircraft from Tommy Tailwind and though I could hear her talking, I felt shy about introducing myself. I say her, because as long as I can remember, I've heard aircraft talk with male or female voices.

Midge was the big sister I could always rely on to look after me and Tommy was like the big brother who played in the first fifteen. Queenie reminded me of our cook, a bit coarse round the edges, but an expert at her job.

However, the aircraft I now sat in, though undoubtedly female, was an absolute fire eater. She wasn't called Spitfire for nothing. I hovered on that fine line between excitement and fear. If I could only catch her attention, we could talk, but she did go on at such a rate.

"Why am in this dark hangar when I should be in the air? At least they've opened the doors. My wheels are too close together. How am I supposed to land on them? I must get back in the air again."

There was just enough of a pause to allow me to ask her.

"How do you manage to be so strong *and* so beautiful?"

The pause continued.

"That's a strange question. Most boys of your age want to know how fast I can go and how many guns I have. You would have to ask my designer for the answer, but he died last year, so we'll never know."

"I'm sorry he's dead. He must have been a great designer."

"This feels very odd. It's as if you can hear my thoughts, but that's impossible, isn't it?"

"Not impossible, just very unusual and I don't think your wheels are all that close together. My name is James. What can I call you?"

"This is amazing. You really can hear me. Let's see now, my call sign is 'S' for Sugar, but the CO calls me Sweetie, so there you are. Take your pick."

"I think Sweetie suits you. I wish I could fly you. Maybe I will, some day."

But of course, I never did. Sweetie was long gone before I was tall enough to reach her controls. We chatted on for several minutes more. She didn't seem so fearsome once I'd got to know her. I could have stayed longer, but there were places on the home farm I wanted to explore before dark.

The CO accompanied us back to Midge. He was talking to my father and grandfather about the deteriorating political situation, not that I understood. As we approached Midge he turned to me.

"Well young man, what do you think of her?"

I'm afraid without stopping to think, I said,

"I think Sweetie is perfect."

The CO looked as if he'd been struck and I realised I had blundered. It felt like an eternity, but could only have been a few seconds before my grandfather said,

"I believe the name is written very small on her side."

We were well on our way home when he leaned forward to speak in my ear.

"James."

"Yes Papa?"

"You must be more careful."

"Yes Papa, I'm sorry. It won't happen again."

My grandfather nodded. It was a valuable object lesson and as far as I'm aware, my last slip up. No one ever reminded me of the incident; as if it was something I'd ever forget.

The Boy Who Talked To Planes

From the confidential diary of Sir James Nettleton

Monday 3rd April 1939.

Now we know James can hear aircraft talk, I had to
warn him of the dangers of revealing his ability to
others. I felt bad about it. He's only eight and should
be out playing games and climbing trees instead of
being secretive and suspicious. I fear this war will
rob many a child of their childhood.

I've spoken to a Major, formerly of the Scots Guards,
who was invalided out with a bad leg wound. Splendid
chap; turned his house and estate into a boarding
school for boys. It's just the place for James and far
enough North to be safe from aerial bombardment. It
has its own airstrip which could prove useful. I'll
make arrangements for it to be brought up to modern
standards.

Anderson picked out an agent to look after James.
The Major has agreed to take him on as PE teacher
and House Master. He's a big Irish chap and a bit
dour. He belongs to some odd sect that forbids the
taking of life. I'm aware of his practical abilities, but
due to his Nationalist associations I've reservations,
possibly unfounded, regarding his allegiance to the
Crown. I shall arrange a small test.

I've written to Peter and Vicky and will introduce him
on James' birthday. I'll let them make the final
decision.

I've had a secure telephone line installed between
here and the house as I'm sure eavesdropping is rife.
I'm certain rumours have reached the dark embassy
with the broken cross. A double cross would be more
appropriate.

Chapter 4

Being the only one who could hear aircraft talk didn't feel all that wonderful now. I had pressures and responsibilities heaped on my young shoulders which were hard to bear. I thought everyone could hear aircraft and now I knew they couldn't, it wasn't fun any more. I wished I hadn't told anyone, but it was too late now. Now I was compelled by those who knew, not to tell anyone else. However, there were still times when I could forget my odd talent and happily be like the rest of humanity.

My ninth birthday was a grand occasion with a host of friends and family gathered at the big house. We had lots of games and a small film show, Laurel and Hardy if I remember right. It was fun and we had a great laugh. My tutor Mr Davies had been invited and joined in all the games even though he was older than Papa. He had a white beard, neatly trimmed and blue twinkley eyes, like the pictures of Father Christmas.

I liked Mr Davies. I knew he was here to teach me things, but he felt more like an old friend who was keen to tell me all the wonderful stories the world had to offer. I wanted to read and find out even more. Learning was fun, like a treasure hunt. He didn't teach in a classroom with a blackboard and stick. The classroom was the house and estate, the night sky a gateway to the stars, which he knew by name, friends and guides on our journey into the future.

My parents put on a brave face as they realised I would shortly be leaving home. However, I had a great time, not aware as they were that we would all be going our separate ways. It was possible we would never see each other again, though of course no mention was ever made of that likelihood.

I knew most of the guests, but towards the end of the evening, I noticed my grandfather with a tall athletic man who was introduced to me as Mr Wilson. I remember turning to look at

Mr Davies. He didn't look his usual cheerful self and at the time I wondered why. After the guests left, Mr Wilson stayed on.

The following morning I found him with my parents, when I joined them for what we called elevenses, the mid-morning break. We were in one of the smaller rooms in the East wing, chosen partly as it caught the morning sun, but chiefly for its single door, now closed with a guard stationed outside. I sat on a small couch with my mother. Father was in a chair to my left and Mr Wilson sat facing me across a low table that held the tea things and a plate stand full of cakes. To my right was a tall window that looked out on to trees and the small hangar that housed Midge, but we were not there to admire the view.

They were all looking at me and I was wondering if in some way, I had forgotten my manners.

"James."

"Yes Dad?"

"Do you remember Papa telling you about the very bad people who drop bombs on those who don't want to live as their slaves?"

"Yes Dad."

"Well James, we don't want to live as their slaves, so they may try to drop bombs on us."

"But Tommy Tailwind and Sweetie will stop them. They have lots of friends; and if the bad people drop bombs on us, then Queenie will drop bombs on them."

They paused at my childish outburst.

"Quite right James, but just to be on the safe side, we thought you would enjoy that super school in Scotland we told you about. You would be safer there, along with your unique gift, your talent."

I looked sharply at my father and Mr Wilson.

"It's all right James. Mr Wilson knows."

My mother had moved to the window. She stood gazing at our beautiful grounds, only just managing to hold back her tears. She turned to face us.

"Peter, is it not time you told James who Mr Wilson is and why he's here?"

"Yes Vicky dearest, I was working round to that."

I had been inadvertently staring at Mr Wilson. He raised his eyebrows and attempted a reassuring smile. Once again, it reminded me of the need to be careful. Like any child, I was summing him up, trying to decide if I could trust him. My parents and Papa obviously did, as they had told him about my special talent, so I felt I also must trust him.

"Perhaps Mr Wilson would like to tell us in his own words, with the assurance that what is said here will not be repeated outside this room."

Even allowing for the difference in perception, of a nine year old boy, he looked taller than average and very lean; not an ounce of fat anywhere. He had a long angular face; dark hair brushed straight back, and a largish nose between hooded eyes of a most piercing blue.

"Thank you yes, I'll try," said Mr Wilson, with just the trace of what I took to be an Irish accent.

"You must already know James that we are living in unusually dangerous times. You are very dear and precious to your parents, but you may not realise the value that the government places on you and your quite amazing talent."

I listened wide eyed.

"It is for this reason we feel you will be safer at school in Scotland, which is further away from where the bombs are likely to be dropped. Also it's a brilliant school and that's why I'm going there myself. I'll be teaching games, sports and gymnastics and I'll also be your house master. It'll be fun."

I looked at my father who smiled and nodded, but my mother had returned to my side and was now staring at the floor. Mr Wilson continued.

"That James is the easy, non secret part. I'm sure you'll make new friends and you can tell them we met here before going to school. What follows can only be talked of to myself, your parents and grandfather and certain special individuals that you may be introduced to by one of us. Is that clear?"

"Yes Sir, it is."

"Good. Perhaps it would help if I gave you all a brief résumé of how I came to be here."

My father nodded and my mother looked up.

"Yes, I would like that."

"I said brief," Mr Wilson continued, "so I'll try and make it just that.

I was born in a small fishing port in Antrim, Northern Ireland and my family still fish from there. I was hauling nets and lobster pots when I was not much older than you are now James."

His eyes had a hypnotic quality. I focussed on the cake stand, which was in line of sight and tried to concentrate. My mother was showing more interest.

"I worked hard at school and won a scholarship to a Scottish college of physical education with the intention of becoming a teacher. While there, a friend of Sir James your grandfather contacted me and asked if I would be interested in doing some specialised work for the government. It was made clear to me then, that though the training could be fitted into weekends and holidays, in the event of a national emergency, I would be needed full time.

About a year ago, the international situation was deemed bad enough for me to be called up for full time active service. Since then, I have been undergoing intensive training for my present role."

"Which is," said my father.

Mr Wilson looked directly at me with those eyes; most unnerving.

"To guard and protect you James, if necessary with my life."

"I believe you will, too," said my mother in barely a whisper.

My grandfather stepped in to the room, nodded to us all, sat in a chair with his back to the window and busied himself with the newspaper. He glanced at Mr Wilson, who turned to face him.

"Have you filled them in with all the details?" he said, nodding in our direction.

"Not entirely Sir. I was about to tell them when you came in."

"Fine fine, on you go."

Mr Wilson paused, collecting his thoughts before continuing.

"There is something else you should know about me. I must stress that Sir James has known of my convictions from the outset."

Convictions I thought, what sort of convictions?

"My family are members of a Christian Church that believes there can be no circumstances which can condone the taking of life, not even war. Therefore I will not carry a gun capable of killing another human, even an enemy of the state. If you feel this makes me incapable of defending James, I would understand. However you would be wrong. I mentioned intensive training and so it was. I can't go in to detail, but I'm confident I'm ready. Add to my armoury the shield of faith and the sword of the spirit and I believe James and I will be safe."

I sat mesmerised, unaware that my mother was in tears until my father hurried round the back of the couch to comfort her.

"It's all right Vicky, we can have him replaced before James goes to school."

Mr Wilson sat motionless as if afraid of what my mother would say. She dried her eyes and looked up at my father.

"Oh you silly sausage; don't you know tears of relief when you see them. I was terrified James would be guarded by some gung ho, armed to the teeth, secret agent."

She looked over at Mr Wilson whose smile of relief was all too genuine.

"I doubt if we could find anyone more suitable. The shield of faith, yes, I like that. From the epistles of Paul isn't it. Well, I believe we can have faith in you Mr Wilson, to look after James."

My grandfather had laid the newspaper on the arm of his chair and was looking enquiringly in our direction.

"Can I take it we're all happy with the arrangements?"

They smiled and nodded.

"Good then, if you'll excuse us, Mr Wilson and I have some preparatory work to do in Scotland."

Mr Wilson looked down at me.
"I'll see you in Scotland James; goodbye."
"Goodbye Sir,"
We sat down and mother set about pouring the tea.
"Can I have some cake now?"

Chapter 5

Preparations were immediately put in hand for my move north. A large cabin trunk was packed with everything I would need and was sent off by rail in plenty of time to be at the school for my arrival.

I don't remember much about the days between my birthday and going north, except an increasing amount of activity in and around the house. The only occurrence affecting me was the arrival of my school uniform, delivered by a tailor who stayed long enough to make sure it fitted, which it did. It was made of heavy tweedy material and quite unsuitable for the hot summer at the time. Later in cooler climes, I would be glad of its protection.

The day before our flight to Scotland passed in a barely controlled frenzy of preparation. Midge was thoroughly checked and fuelled, as we anticipated an early start. An emergency travelling case was prepared for me with night clothes and toiletries. In the morning I was encouraged to say my goodbyes to our various family members and senior staff, including cook, who I would for ever associate with Queenie the Wellington bomber. There was a similar comfortable roundness about their middle regions.

I took an apple to the pony as a goodbye gift. The dogs, especially the retriever, were aware of change afoot and restlessly sniffed the air.

In the afternoon we took tea in the room where Mr Wilson had introduced himself. I realise now that my parents had a great deal they wanted to say, but didn't know how to properly express their feelings. My father played safe by starting with the practical.

"We all need to get to bed early tonight, as I'd like to make a start first thing in the morning. Mr Wilson has telephoned to say that the airstrip at the school isn't ready and he'll meet us at Scone airfield with a car."

"Is Midge taking us?"

"Indeed she is; exciting isn't it?"

My mother found it difficult to hide her concern, but managed to remain outwardly cheerful. She poured the tea while they both decided what to say.

"James," my father began hesitantly. "There are some things we must make sure you understand before starting school in Scotland."

"Yes Dad?"

"I'm afraid the bad people that Papa told you about have not been listening to us. We will have to be strong in persuading them not to be such bullies and you know, bullies only behave properly when everyone stands up to them and says, 'that's enough'."

I sat listening. It all sounded very serious as my mother added.

"When your Dad says everyone, we mean every person in the country. We must all do our best in whatever way we can."

"Can I help?"

"You certainly can," said my father. "You're able to talk to Tommy Tailwind and his friends and tell them how important they are. They'll listen to you, because they know you'll listen to them and understand their needs."

"Yes Dad, but how will I manage when I'm at school?"

"In exactly the same way you met Tommy and Sweetie. We'll fly you wherever you need to go. That's why the airstrip at the school is being smoothed and lengthened. It will also let you miss as few lessons as possible. That's important."

"It sounds fun."

"Yes," said my father thoughtfully. "We'll certainly do our best to make it fun."

My parents were looking at each other, wondering who would be the one to broach the sensitive and possibly puzzling subject of security.

"James, you know how important it is to always tell the truth and not to lie."

"Yes Dad."

"Do you remember the film at your birthday party and how we all laughed?"

"Yes Dad?"

"You do realise that all the people in the film were actors and they weren't really hurting each other with the bats and bits of wood."

"Yes Dad."

"James, do you think they were lying?"

I remember being shocked by the question. I had to think for a moment before replying.

"I don't think so; it was just pretend acting, to make us laugh."

"Quite right James and it worked because we all laughed and had a great time."

My parents smiled and relaxed.

"Because it is absolutely essential that your ability to hear plane talk is kept secret, Mr Wilson may sometimes ask you to pretend. Do you think you could manage that?"

"Yes Dad. That could be fun too, a kind of secret."

"Exactly James and it's an important secret. You must understand that the fewer people who know your secret, the safer you will be and the easier will be Mr Wilson's task of protecting you from the bad people."

By now, I was sitting in wrapped attention, thinking, this could be a great adventure. Little did I suspect what a great adventure it would become. My father continued with what turned out to be my briefing before action.

"There will be about five other boys in the dormitory with you and I'm sure you will get to know them but, and I cannot emphasise this enough, you must never ever allow them to learn your secret, not even your best friend. This situation may change in time, but for the moment, the only person you can trust is Mr Wilson. You can trust him with everything."

This was the most serious I had ever known my parents. It was beginning to dawn on me that primary school was going to be different to the usual. We were, however, living in unusual times.

He looked at me and smiled.

"I'm sure you'll be fine and it will be fun. Now James, is there anything else you would like to ask?"

I thought for a moment.

"When will I be able to come home and see you?"

My mother answered.

"As soon as possible, but certainly at Christmas and there may be a half term holiday. You never know, we may try out your brand new airstrip as your Dad and I will be working for one of Papa's new groups, flying messages around the country, so we could drop in at any time."

I brightened at the thought.

"That would be brilliant. I could show Midge to the other boys."

"We'll see, but meantime, we should have our tea before it gets cold."

As we drank our tea and ate our cakes, my father was writing on a piece of paper which he handed to me. It was a series of numbers in red.

"James, this is an emergency telephone number, which you must keep with you at all times. It will put you straight through to one of Papa's offices at the Air Ministry. Only use it in the unlikely event of Mr Wilson," and he paused, thinking of the worst possible happening, "of Mr Wilson being hurt and unable to look after you.

If you want to speak to us, ask Mr Wilson and he will connect you to ourselves or Papa. He has all the numbers."

After the tea things were removed, we sat and chatted about the schools my parents had attended, but the world was changing. I excused myself and went to my room. I felt the need to remember it as it was then.

31

Chapter 6

The next morning I was wakened at first light. I dressed in my new uniform and went down to the room where breakfast was being served. My parents were already there.

"Tuck in James; it could be many hours before we get another chance to eat."

The room looked on to the terrace. I could see the top of Midge's wing, where she was parked in her usual place facing the lake.

My grandfather looked in briefly for a cup of coffee, but also to wish me well at school. He was about to leave the room when he turned to me, bent down and shook my hand.

"Take care James and do all you can to help Mr Wilson. If you help him, you will be helping me."

"I'll do my best Papa."

He looked at me with a more gentle expression than usual and ruffled my hair.

"I'm sure you will James."

We had no luggage apart from my small case, as my parents intended returning home the same day. My grandfather stood on the terrace to wave us on our way. I remember looking down at the solitary figure as we headed North over the house towards my new life in Scotland.

I talked to Midge during the flight. I was worried about things I couldn't talk to my parents about. They were both certain that Mr Wilson was completely trustworthy. I hoped he was as it was my first time away from home with its security and comforts. I would be in his care and would have to rely on him for everything. For the moment I could do little but trust him. I only wished he wasn't so cold and unfeeling. Midge hadn't been in contact with him, so she could only advise, but her advice stood me in good stead.

"See everything, hear everything, but say or do nothing until it's time to act. You'll know when the time comes."

As we droned north, I remembered my introduction to Mr Wilson and what struck me as odd. He only smiled with his mouth. His eyes had as much expression as a pair of blue marbles. There was a shutter between them and his mind. I decided then, I would have to judge him by his actions, rather than what he said.

After two hours flying, we were within sight of the North Sea. I would guess Yorkshire, or there about. It was the first time I had seen the tall wireless masts that were to play such an important part in the coming battle.

I also noticed far out to sea, the silver shape of an airship, carrying the unmistakable sign of the broken cross on its tail fins. Like the masts, its significance would only become apparent at a much later date. My father had also noticed the airship.

"I think it's time for a cup of tea. I'm sure there's an airfield round here somewhere. Ah there we are, over on the left."

The throttle was closed, Midge's nose dipped and soon we were turning into wind to settle on this small field. I'm now certain it had been part of his flight plan. Having parked near the flight hut, we climbed out to stretch our legs.

"Dad, did you see an airship over the sea?"

"Yes James, I did and it wasn't one of ours. I'm not sure why it was there."

My mother was pouring tea from a large flask into some tin mugs.

"I've only got some biscuits, but I dare say they will do for the moment."

Dad had spoken little while we were drinking our tea, but after we were ready to continue our journey, he said, as if thinking aloud.

"We'll stop off at Turnhouse near Edinburgh to top up the tanks and telephone Mr Wilson to let him know our arrival time."

The rest of the flight was without incident. We landed at

Turnhouse, our tanks were topped up and my father made his phone call from the terminal building. We arrived at Scone airfield to the North of Perth about midday.

Mr Wilson's large black car drove in some ten minutes later.

"Sorry I'm late. The traffic was heavier than anticipated."

I believe my parents wished to stay longer, but thought it better the discomfort of parting was made then, instead of later.

"Please look after him," my mother whispered to Mr Wilson.

"I will. Of that, you can be absolutely sure."

Mr Wilson picked up my small case and we walked over to the car. I climbed onto the running board and up to the seat. Sitting on the edge, I had a fine view along the bonnet to the mascot of a witch astride a broomstick. As we pulled away I waved to my parents. They looked so small beside Midge. Soon we were bowling along the road to Perth.

He drove carefully, lost in thought, then as if remembering he should make conversation said, "Good flight?"

"Yes Sir, thankyou Sir."

He grunted, but made no reply.

Soon we were threading our way through the streets of Perth and along the banks of the river Tay. Before long we turned on to a secondary road leading to the school. It was narrow; tree lined and would have been dark if the midday sun had not been shining along its length.

Suddenly he braked and switched off the engine.

"What's wrong Sir?"

He put a finger to his lips, wound the window open and signed that I should do the same.

"What do you hear?" he whispered.

"Nothing Sir."

He nodded slowly and grunted, "It's too quiet."

He gave all the appearance of a hunted animal, eyes narrowed and head turning one way then the other as if sniffing the air.

"There's something wrong, different. We're being watched."

He opened the door and stood on the running board, scanning

the road in both directions and the forest on either side. It was unnaturally quiet. He got back in and started the engine.

"Be ready to hide."

"What from Sir?"

He didn't answer, just shook his head and started moving the car forward. As we topped a summit in the main road, we could see a car causing a partial blockage. It looked as if it had broken down, as the driver was peering at the engine.

"I don't like the look of this. Get under the dashboard."

I curled up on the floor, as we pulled in behind the car. Mr Wilson called to the driver.

"Can we be of any assistance?"

I could hear the driver walking towards us. Mr Wilson had one foot on the running board when the other driver stopped a few yards away.

"OK, where's the boy? That's right. Get out. Keep your hands where I can see them."

Mr Wilson looked very frightened and started to whine.

"Oh no, oh no, please don't shoot. What boy would that be?"

Mr Wilson was stooped with his hands over his ears. He said be ready to hide, so I quietly opened the door and crept along the side of the bonnet; ready to dive for the cover of the undergrowth.

"Stop messing me about, I want him now."

He saw the movement and swung the gun round, pointing it straight at me. I was terrified.

"Hah, there you are, ye wee tyke."

Sunlight flickered on silver as the throwing knife sliced through artery and tendon below the hand holding the gun. The man screamed in pain and surprise, the sound cut off as a huge fist crashed into his jaw. The pistol clattered to the road with a loud report, the bullet whacking into a tree to my left.

I stood petrified, shocked speechless as Mr Wilson picked up the gunman, holding him round the waist with one hand and staunching the flow of blood with the other. He ran to the other car and pushed him into the driver's seat.

"James, get my knife. It's up the road somewhere."

Now his Irish accent was more pronounced. In my hurry I slipped on the blood spill, landing in the middle of the sticky mess and collecting a fair amount of road dirt.

"Get a shift on. We have to get out of here double quick."

I scrambled to my feet and ran up the road, searching either side.

"I'm being as quick as I can, Sir. I think I see it."

It was a long way past the other car, lying in the gravel verge. I picked it up carefully by its slim handle and hurried back to Mr Wilson, who was waiting by the driver's door of our own car, clearly in fear of something.

"Get in the back and stay down."

I handed him the knife, which he laid on the front passenger seat. The engine started.

"Let's get out of here."

Pushing the other car aside with the front bumper made enough room for us to squeeze past. He drove with the one thought of getting us away from the area as fast as possible. Trees and stone walls flashed past in a grey green blur. Eventually he slowed down, pulled into a passing place, secured the hand brake and turned off the engine. He turned round to look over his shoulder at me. Beads of sweat stood out on his forehead, soaking the dark brows above cold eyes.

"We should be safe now; you all right?"

"Yes Sir, thank you."

I tried to smile, but it was more a grimace.

"Scared?"

"Yes Sir, a bit."

"So you should be. He was trying to kidnap you. His accomplice was somewhere in the trees. I could feel his eyes. Why didn't he shoot? He must've seen what happened."

He opened the car door and stood, leaning against the mudguard.

"That was a close call. Get out and we'll try and get cleaned up."

I stepped down unsteadily from the running board while Mr Wilson rummaged through the door pockets for a rag which he wrapped round the radiator cap before gently unscrewing it. Steam hissed and water bubbled on to the rag.

"Let's see if we can get some of this muck off your good uniform."

The good uniform bought new, only a few days ago and carefully fitted by our family tailor. Mr Wilson sat down on the running board while I stood in front of him. His huge hands were surprisingly gentle as he wiped off the blood and dirt.

"I have a boy about your age, back in Ireland."

He looked me up and down, admiring his work.

"You'll do for the moment. It'll be a proper scrub once we reach the school. It's not far now."

He stood up and spent the next few minutes in an unhurried attempt to clean the worst of the blood spatter from his jacket, trousers and shirt cuffs. He finished by cleaning his hands and with great care, his throwing knife, which he returned to its sheath below his jacket collar.

"Say nothing about the gunman, the incident, you understand?"

"Yes Sir, but what if they ask about the mess on our clothes?"

He flung me a frustrated look.

"If anyone asks, and only then, tell them we came across a road accident and stopped to help one of the injured, all right, got that?"

"Yes Sir."

Father did say I may have to pretend, like the actors in the film, but we all knew they were pretending, so it wasn't lying. If I was asked to say something that wasn't true, would that not be lying? The edges between reality and Papa's grey world were beginning to blur, confusing for a nine year old. Best to say nothing like Midge advised.

"I'll phone your grandfather. He knows people who will arrange everything, including the press."

We drove the rest of the way in silence. I had been brought up to always tell the truth, so what would I do if asked to explain the state of my new uniform. I would have to say something which would satisfy my own conscience and Mr Wilson, who could be kind one minute and the next, scary. Yet he was supposed to be my protector and trusted friend.

Protector yes, he had already proved that, trusted, I had no choice, but friend, I wanted him to be, but oh those eyes, so cold and humourless.

We stopped at the gatehouse to the school estate and Mr Wilson stepped down to talk to the janitor. He was asking for cans of water and a stiff broom to be ready for him in five minutes. Once more I had to pretend I hadn't heard.

Article in the Perth Advertiser
dated Saturday August 12th 1939

The body of a young man was found in a car at the side of the Pitmeddan road yesterday evening by a passing motorist. The police were called to the scene, but our reporter was told there was no evidence of foul play. The man had clearly taken his own life by slashing his wrist with a stiletto flick-knife found next to his body. He carried no means of identification and the car had been stolen from a garage near the ferry port of Stranraer. The police are not pursuing any further enquiries.

Chapter 7

Once we reached the main school building, Mr Wilson rang the bell, handed me my case and waited until the Headmaster appeared.

"Headmaster, this is James, your new pupil. We were involved in an incident on the way here and I'm afraid we're not looking our best. I must go back to see if I can help. I'll explain later."

"Later will do," said the Headmaster. "James, welcome to my school. This is Matron. She'll help you get cleaned up and something to eat. Would you like that?"

"Yes Sir, I am rather hungry."

"Good then, off you go."

Mr Wilson turned the car and drove off as Matron guided me through the main doors into the central hall. It wasn't at all what I expected after our encounter with the gunman.

The hall was a calming symphony of browns. Walls and ceiling glowed in a rich variety of woods and sunlight cast bright gems of colour picked from a stained glass window. Old weapons were arranged in patterns on the walls and in show cases. The Headmaster's ancestors looked down with kindly gaze from numerous portraits. It felt familiar, like many of our rooms at home.

Matron wisely gave me time to stand and take in the atmosphere of the place. She stood looking at me, her head tilted to one side.

"Well James, do you like it?

"Yes Matron I do. It feels good."

"That's because it is good, like the Headmaster. He was a Major in the last war, decorated by the King," she added proudly. "This is his house, as well as the school. Now I think we should try and wash off the dirt from this morning. If only we could wash away the memories too."

She took my hand and led me through doors and corridors to a room with a bath. It didn't have the splendid décor of the hall, but it was bright, warm and had the smell of cleanliness. She ran warm water and took a new bar of pink carbolic soap from a small cupboard.

"Your trunk is upstairs by your dormitory. I'll fetch some clean clothes for you while you get undressed and washed. There's a stool to help you in and out of the bath. You'll be all right?"

"Yes Matron, I'll manage."

"I'm sure you will. I won't be long."

My heavy uniform had protected me from the worst of the blood and dirt, but my legs and feet needed a good clean up. The warmth of the water was pleasantly relaxing, soothing away the stresses of the morning. Apart from the odd abrasion I was fine. At that age one tended to collect bruises on a daily basis, so I wasn't aware of the colourful patches on my back. I was clambering out of the bath when Matron returned.

"Oh ma wee lamb, look at your poor back. What on earth have you been doing?"

I looked up at her kind face, remembering what I'd been told to say by Mr Wilson, but the lie stuck in my throat. I couldn't speak. She wrapped a warm towel round me to comfort and dry. The sound of car wheels on gravel brought the morning terror flooding back and I wept uncontrollably.

"There there ma wee bairn, I won't ask again. When you feel ready, you can tell me. I fear your young eyes have seen sights today they should've been spared."

She held me, wrapped in the large towel, rocking back and forth, stroking my hair and crooning softly. Mr Wilson looked in, stared at me with those piercing blue eyes, shook his head, sighed and walked out; not the action of a caring friend. I vowed then I would never again shed tears in his presence. Gradually my sobs subsided to the occasional sniff. She gently dried my tears and combed my hair. I was beginning to feel I'd let myself down.

"Please don't tell anyone," I pleaded, "about that."

She looked at me kindly.

"Young man, you have nothing to be ashamed of, nothing whatsoever, so take no heed of what others may think. However, your secret's safe with me. Now, would you like something nice to eat? I've got some broth on the stove."

I'd never had broth before and had no idea what it was. It could have been the food of the Gods, wonderful, tasty and just what I needed at the time.

"Now get yourself dressed and I'll see if there are any other tasty bites I can tempt you with."

For some reason I was absolutely ravenous and thoroughly enjoyed everything that was put in front of me.

In the afternoon Matron showed me the top floor dormitory I would be sharing with five other new boys. This was also their first year at the school, so the Headmaster had decided to put us all together in the same dorm. My bed, wardrobe and chest of drawers lay between two windows, with three other beds on the opposite wall and two to my right. The door to the landing was in the opposite corner and next to that, a door led to toilets and wash basins. Mr Wilson's room was across the landing.

We ate our evening meal in the small room next to the kitchens where I had sampled Matron's broth. Matron served us then left us alone, believing we would want to talk in private. I had no choice in the matter, but had given it some thought and decided that the safest way would be to trust Mr Wilson, but keep other feelings in reserve. When I sat down I got another of his stares.

"All right?"

"Yes Sir, I'm sorry about my earlier lapse. It won't happen again."

"Forget it, you did fine."

Nothing else was said until we finished eating.

"It shouldn't have happened. I went back, but the gunman was dead. There were footprints in the road that didn't belong to us, but no sign of anyone. I can always tell if someone is watching, even if I can't see them."

I didn't interrupt, just sat, watched and listened. He shook his head.

"It's wrong to kill. I phoned your grandfather and he's arranged discreet protection, so we'll be safe in the school's estate. He'll clear it with the newspapers too."

Maybe he is a trusted protector, I thought. I want to believe he is.

"Sir, can we confide in anyone else in the school?"

He read my mind.

"You mean like Matron? I think not. She's a good sort, but it wouldn't be fair to burden her with such trust. I'll sleep on it and phone your Papa in the morning for his advice. He'll know what to do."

That night I slept well, except for a strange dream in which I was sending a message in Morse code, at least I think it was a dream.

The Boy Who Talked To Planes

From the confidential diary of Sir James Nettleton

Wednesday 16th August 1939

This morning I received a report concerning the attempt to kidnap James on the road to the school. Road blocks and snipers were in place to allow for all eventualities, but I'm sure Mr Wilson sensed their presence, even though they were expertly camouflaged. The outcome was not as I wished. The gunman died through blood loss before he could be saved for interrogation; most unfortunate. I had hoped to gain useful information but no matter, James' safety is my main consideration.

According to the report from our trusted mole, he coped well for one so young. I would have liked to reduce the danger further, but all conflict carries risk.

Explaining the throwing knife to Vicky will require all my tact and diplomacy. I must give it some thought as she's nobody's fool. They both have enough worries, without me burdening them with my doubts about the protector of their only son.

Whatever else I may suspect; we're forced to accept Mr Wilson saved James from a kidnap attempt. The press willingly co-operated and reported the incident as the suicide of a young man of unbalanced mind.

Chapter 8

Having washed and dressed I made the long descent to the ground floor and the small room next to the kitchen. Matron was already there, working her magic with smells various and appetising.

"Good morning James. Did you sleep well?"

"Yes thank you Matron."

I was about to mention the dream, but decided it could wait.

"Would you like some porridge James? It's made the Scottish way with salt and oatmeal. You never know, you could get to like it."

"It sounds interesting Matron. Our cook makes it with sugar, but I'd like to taste a small helping."

"One small helping, James and I hope it meets with your approval. You can always cheat and put some sugar on it. Don't forget the cream, makes all the difference."

I was about to start when the Headmaster walked in, supported by a shooting stick and carrying a shot gun.

"Ah James, I see you've found Matron's porridge, famous throughout the county, eh what; some for me too, if you please."

Matron turned to face him.

"Any luck Headmaster?"

"Afraid not, blighters keep moving."

He propped the gun and shooting stick in a corner, before sitting down beside me.

"I hope you slept well last night after your excitement down the road. You never did tell us what happened."

Matron scowled at him and shook her head. I had my mouth open to make some excuse when Mr Wilson walked in and sat down opposite me.

"Matron, could you join us. There's something I have to tell you about yesterday's incident."

Matron sat across from the Headmaster and we all waited for

Mr Wilson to begin. I wondered what lies would come and how I would manage to get round them, but to my relief he told it exactly as it happened. He looked first at me.

"I was in touch with Sir James, your grandfather and told him what happened as accurately as memory would allow. It was all so quick. He advised, as you suggested yesterday James that we should confide in you." He said, shifting his gaze, "Headmaster, Matron and enlist your help in keeping James safe."

"Of course, we'll help in any way we can, once we know what the score is, eh Matron."

"Certainly Headmaster."

Mr Wilson continued.

"On the road through the forest, an attempt was made to kidnap James. We were stopped by a gunman, who I suspect was in the pay of a foreign power. I thought he was going to shoot James, so I tried to disarm him with a throwing knife, but I missed the gun and hit his wrist. He bled to death, a terrible mistake, but what else could I do? I went back, but it was too late."

Plausible, I thought, but it doesn't fit. Why waste time at the side of the road getting cleaned up, when you want to hurry back to save him. No, for some reason, you wanted him dead.

"For myself," said the Headmaster. "I say jolly well done, you've nothing to reproach yourself for."

"Thank you Headmaster, but his death will always be on my conscience."

Mr Wilson gave me a quick glance before turning back to the Headmaster and Matron.

"You may be wondering why a foreign power would want to kidnap James."

"The question had crossed my mind," said the Headmaster.

"Before answering, I have to ask a couple of questions."

"Fire away."

"Apart from ourselves sitting at the table and the boarders who still have to arrive, will there be others living full time in this building?"

"No, no one else."

"Good, one more question. Are you aware of having your background checked from the point of view of security?"

"I don't know about you Matron," said the Headmaster, "but I certainly got the message. When a couple of muscle bound types from Special Branch knock at the door to check if you have a school capable of looking after what they called a valuable and gifted pupil, I take notice; Matron?"

"No, but they would have asked up at the farm, not here. Can we assume that James is the valuable and gifted pupil?"

Mr Wilson looked at me.

"Correct. Some time in the near future you will both be invited to sign the Official Secrets Act, but for now, Sir James will accept your solemn promise, not to repeat anything discussed between the four of us."

"Mr Wilson, I'm an officer and a gentleman. You have my word, and my word is my bond, Matron?"

"You also have my word and it would be an insult to my family's honour, if it were questioned."

Mr Wilson looked up and almost smiled.

"Good, that's all I need to know. You'll have gathered that what I'm about to say is top secret."

It's funny how odd things flit through the mind. All we need now, I thought, is a fanfare of trumpets and a roll of drums.

"James and I are part of British Intelligence."

I could guess the reaction. Matron, in one movement, looked at Mr Wilson down her nose, raised her eyebrows and tilted her head back and to the side. The Headmaster laughed.

"Oh, I'm sorry, you're serious."

He turned to look at me for confirmation.

"James?"

"Yes Sir, it's true. My grandfather is Sir James Nettleton at the Air Ministry. I think he advises someone. We're both attached to Intelligence, but I'm more, sort of unofficial."

The headmaster sat back in his chair and looked at Mr Wilson.

"Sorry, shouldn't have laughed, shock you know. I need hardly add that you will have our full co-operation. James is now a pupil of my school and if anyone should have the temerity to threaten him, they will have me to answer to. Yes by Jove they will."

Matron had been listening quietly and now spoke the still unanswered question.

"Mr Wilson, you still haven't told us why a foreign power would be interested in kidnapping James."

"Yes of course Matron. I shouldn't go in to detail, but James has a talent; a power which we believe is unique. Our potential enemies would like to have it, and if that means kidnapping James, they will."

Matron nodded sagely.

"I've come across strange powers, we understand. His secret is safe, agreed Headmaster?"

"Absolutely safe, and so is James. If they try anything else, we'll be ready. If they turn out to be who I think, I can't wait to get a crack at them. They've made a big mistake threatening one of our pupils."

"Headmaster," continued Mr Wilson. "Can I leave the security of the school and its grounds in your hands, while I concentrate on keeping James here out of trouble?"

"You certainly can. The way the world is, we can never have security too tight. Leave it with me. I'll make this estate as secure as possible with the means at our disposal."

"I believe you were a Major in the last War," said Mr Wilson.

"I certainly was."

Matron looked on, brows knitted.

"And where do I fit in?"

"In a most important job," said Mr Wilson, "if we are to carry off our deception effectively. Let me explain. When war starts, James's services may be urgently required in various parts of the country. That is the real reason for the airstrip being renovated, so ambulance planes can land and take off."

"Ambulance planes?"

"Correct. The cover story for James's absences is that he suffers from a rare condition, unspecified as yet, which requires treatment in a specialised clinic. Perhaps I could leave the choice of medical condition to you Matron. Your nursing experience may suggest something of a suitably obscure nature."

"I'll do my best Mr Wilson," she said, looking at me. "I hope you're not tempting providence. He looks the picture of health."

"I trust that under the circumstances, a kind providence will understand."

Mr Wilson looked at us in turn.

"Now we all know how the land lies, are there any other questions?"

Matron rose to her feet.

"Yes, could I possibly persuade you all to have some breakfast?"

There were smiles and nods all round.

"Fine, I'll re-heat the porridge."

Chapter 9

We all dutifully ate our breakfast. Oddly enough, it was the Headmaster that Matron had to encourage most, as she said, 'to keep his strength up'. He couldn't wait to resume his post as Major in command. He was soon making his way to the door, his bad leg adding a nautical roll to his gait, determined to check every inch of the perimeter to his estate. He stopped, turned and picked up his shot gun from the corner.

"I might get lucky; have to remind the blighters who the boss is round here."

By nightfall he had established the weak spots and worked out how they could be strengthened.

Matron was busy looking through her medical dictionaries and text books, trying to decide which of the more obscure conditions could be convincingly replicated.

Mr Wilson took me aside to explain my task for the day.

"James, I want you to make a thorough exploration of the house, especially the hall, stairs and landings. Find all the creaky floor boards, doors and steps. Get to know the different sounds they make. Can you do that?"

"Yes Sir, but why?"

"You're a great one for asking questions James." He sighed.

"With a little practice and your exceptional hearing, you'll be able to tell exactly where everyone is in the house. I bet you can already tell the difference between the Headmaster and Matron, just by the sound of their tread, when walking across the floor."

"Yes Sir, I can."

"Good, so if a stranger were to enter the house, you would know wouldn't you?"

"Yes Sir, I think I would. Can I start now?"

"Yes and I'm off to find out why the airstrip isn't finished. I'll be much happier when we can fly in and out without being seen."

I followed Mr Wilson to the top of the small flight of steps, leading from the covered porch. He was heading for a foot bridge which crossed a small tributary of the Tay as it flowed between the cliffs of a narrow gorge. The path beyond led to a walled garden and eventually the airstrip.

I had my work to do, observing, listening and remembering, so I started straight away. The stone floor had an unusual ring to it, due to the porch spanning a dry moat. There was a loose metal grating which rattled, followed by the main door which didn't creak but juddered as it rubbed on a raised tile in the marble floor.

I continued up the main staircase, lots of creaks there, to the main landing of wooden planking covered with a large carpet. From there a few small steps led to a half landing, then a door to a spiral stair within one of the towers. This gave access to the top floor and my dormitory.

My exploration of the house took all day, walking backwards and forwards, opening and closing doors and generally setting to memory all the sounds an old house makes. It was exciting, in a nice way, unlike our earlier experience. Like any small boy, I had thoughts of secret passages and hiding places, but so far the house was keeping such things well hidden.

Having thoroughly inspected the inside, I decided to have a good look at the outside. The building was about the same size as my own at home, but that was the only similarity. Whereas my family house was designed by one architect and built some hundred years previous, the one I was looking at had its beginnings at least four hundred years ago as a fortified keep. Over the years parts had been added to satisfy the whims of various owners, the latest, including the main entrance, during the reign of Queen Victoria.

All buildings have a history, but on this day in 1939, I was simply looking at a large house, not nearly as pretty as my own, but a great deal more intriguing and mysterious.

I walked towards the river, but the oldest part was perched next to a sheer drop. I could go no further, as the edge of the gorge was protected by a sturdy stone balustrade. Walking back past the entrance to the east side, the ground dropped away to the level of the dry moat, giving access to a basement area belonging to the most recent addition. A short way round the north side of the house, my way was once more barred by a fence and another steep drop to where the river fell amid curtains of spray to a deep pool far below.

Looking up, I could see the windows of my dormitory. Its location had been well chosen. I decided to have another look inside the house. Matron was standing in the hall.

"Have you had any lunch yet?"

"No Matron; is it lunchtime?"

"It's nearer afternoon tea. You must be famished. Come on into the kitchen and I'll get you something to keep you going."

I sat at the table where we had eaten breakfast, while Matron made up some sandwiches for us both. She returned, carrying a tray with a pot of tea for herself and a glass of milk for me.

"We won't be able to do this once the other boarders arrive and school begins. It'll be up in the morning early and down to lessons."

She paused, looking at me; "a penny for them James?"

"Matron?"

"Yes James, I'm listening."

"Do you know if there's a secret passage in the house? It's very old."

"Oh, that's what the puzzle is, all those creaky floors and wooden panelling. Well, I'm sure I don't know at all and if I did, it wouldn't be secret, would it. Mind you, I do know a house not far from here that has a small secret room, more like a cupboard. When it was discovered, it was full of old swords and pistols."

"Mr Wilson says he doesn't like guns."

"I know, but the Headmaster does. In fact he has quite a collection."

In all innocence I gave voice to my thoughts.

"Perhaps he keeps them in a secret cupboard."

Matron gave a veritable explosion of laughter and patted me on the back.

"Oh well done James; perhaps he does. Now off you go to your dorm and finish unpacking your things. I'll give you a hand later, but it's something you must learn to do yourself. Come down for tea when you hear the clock in the hall strike six."

"Yes Matron," and off I went to sort out my belongings.

It was a sharp reminder that I could no longer rely on parents or servants to do these things for me. Suddenly I felt alone and homesick. I had to remind myself that I had important work to do and the small figure walking back from the airstrip was not only my house master, but my defender against those who would cause me harm.

Chapter 10

A short time later I heard the main door open and close as Mr Wilson entered the house. Standing at the window, I could see part of the airstrip, with the workmen busy applying the finishing touches. If I put my nose to the glass, I could look almost straight down to where the river fell over a rocky sill to a deeper part of the gorge.

My trunk was empty, but there were still a few things on the bed, waiting for a suitable resting place.

The clock in the hall struck six, so I made my way downstairs.

The Headmaster and Mr Wilson were already seated. Matron was busy bringing through plates of food and with a silent nod, indicated where I should sit. It was noticeable that the Headmaster was now sitting at the head of the table.

"Food first, then progress reports."

Apart from the odd pleasantry connected with manners at table, we ate in silence. Once finished, Matron cleared the plates and cutlery from the table, before placing a medical dictionary at her own place and a folded map before the Headmaster. The map was a large scale contour map of the estate, with all the main features clearly marked.

I had to kneel on my chair to see it properly. The Headmaster started without any preamble, running his hand over the map and pointing out the relevant parts.

"I've been round the whole perimeter, several miles and these are the weak points where someone could gain access. I've contacted the local Territorials and they've agreed to provide a presence at weekends. Permanent solutions can be constructed at a later date. In any case, once school starts in two days time, there will be more eyes ready to spot any intruders. Mr Wilson, how is the airstrip coming along?"

"It's almost finished Headmaster. The foreman insisted on

giving me a tour of inspection. They've done a thorough job, which is probably why it's taken them so long. He was a sergeant in the REME during the last lot and really knows his stuff."

"Excellent, now Matron, have you found anything suitably nasty in that book of yours?"

Matron carefully opened the book at a marked page. She then attempted to read out a word which appeared to use the entire alphabet more than once. It started with 'H' and that is honestly all I can remember. I think the Headmaster said,

"Pardon!"

"Well Headmaster, you did ask for something obscure."

"Would it be possible Matron, to describe it in layman's terms?"

"Put simply, it's a random acute malfunction of the kidneys, requiring immediate treatment which can last up to two days. Does that fit the bill?"

The Headmaster looked enquiringly at Mr Wilson.

"Yes, that sounds exactly what's needed. We only need to convince the rest of the school and between us, we should be able to manage."

The Headmaster turned to me.

"Now James, if you're feeling well enough after Matron's description of what you hopefully haven't got, could you tell us what you discovered?"

Now they were all looking at me in good natured expectation. I managed to fight off a sudden attack of shyness, coughed nervously and made a start.

"Yes Sir. The house makes lots of noises, all slightly different, depending on where they're coming from."

"Can you tell where someone is in the house, solely by the sounds their feet make?"

"Yes Sir, I think I can. Once the other boarders arrive, I'll have more practice."

The Headmaster looked thoughtful.

"That could be very useful. Now James, there's something else you may be able to help with."

He rubbed his chin and turned to look at me.

"Matron tells me that you were asking if the house has any secret rooms or passages."

Oh dear, I thought. Have I caused offence by being too inquisitive? He obviously noticed my worried look as he smiled and continued.

"Don't worry James, there's nothing wrong with a good healthy curiosity. That's how we learn; why we have schools, indeed why we're all here. Matron, do we have a plan of the house?"

"Yes Headmaster. It's with the map of the estate. I had a feeling you would need it."

"Thank you Matron. Secret rooms and passages, I wonder. I remember as a small boy being shown a dungeon with a magic well and told all sorts of scary stories, so the short answer is I don't know, but I'd like to. For years I've suspected there may be a passage leading to the outside, but its existence was of no great importance, that is, until now."

We listened attentively.

"Secret passages are of use only if we have the secret and the enemy don't. The passage, if it exists, may have originally been an escape route, but it could also be a way in for unwanted and possibly dangerous intruders. You see what I'm getting at. If it exists, we should know about it, agreed?"

We all nodded in earnest agreement.

"Right James, come and have a look at the house plan."

I swapped seats with Matron and knelt on the chair. I had never seen a house plan before, but recognised it as being like a map, only of a smaller area. The Headmaster was ready to explain.

"This is the ground floor. Imagine if we could slice off the rest of the house and look straight down on the floor and walls. You see how thick they are here at this square bit. That's the oldest part of the house and where the passage is most likely to be, possibly inside the thickness of the walls."

I looked on, absolutely fascinated.

"Sir, what are the round bits in the corners?"

"The round bits, ah yes, spiral stairs, but they've been blocked off for ages. In any case they don't lead outside."

He had another look at the plan.

"They're in the corners of the original keep, where we hold morning assembly. The main hall also doubles as a gymnasium where no doubt Mr Wilson will put you through your paces. However James, what is of paramount importance is your safety, so I don't want you crawling along narrow passageways on your own and try as he may, Mr Wilson can't be with you all the time; understood?"

"Yes Sir."

"Good, now, there will be five other new boys with you in your dorm, all carefully vetted Mr Wilson?"

"Yes Headmaster."

"Decide which one you can trust most and enlist his help. Take your time over your choice, remember, the fewer people who know a secret, the more easily is it kept."

"Yes Sir, I'll be careful."

The Headmaster sat back in his chair. "Good, I think that about covers everything for the moment. Matron will show you where everything goes in your dorm, then you can show the others when they arrive tomorrow."

We all stood up to go our various ways. As the Headmaster reached the door he turned to Matron.

"I think we can safely say, let battle commence."

"Do you mean the stushie in Europe Headmaster, or the beginning of term?"

With a distinct twinkle in his eye, he said, "Both Matron, both."

Chapter 11

Matron followed me up to my dorm. I found the stairs in the turret particularly steep, but that was due to my small size. Matron however, had similar difficulties with the climb, but more to do with developing arthritis caused by her wartime years in nursing. She sat down on the bed opposite my own.

"Give me a moment to get my breath back James, then we'll get everything in its place. The Headmaster likes things neat and tidy."

I stood by my bed, waiting to make a start. Matron was looking at the other beds.

"James, I've had a thought."

"Yes Matron?"

"The head of the dorm usually sleeps in the bed next to the light switch, which would probably be that one."

She pointed to the one next to the washroom at the other end of my row.

"Would you like to be head of dorm?"

It hadn't occurred to me there would be such a thing as 'head of dorm', so I had to think for a moment.

I'm an only child, so this was my first experience of living as part of a group on a daily basis. Following the custom of the time, every group had to have a leader. I'd never thought of myself as a leader, or indeed a follower, so this was a new concept with which I would have to come to terms.

"If I'm likely to be called away with that illness you read out to us, it may be better leaving head of dorm to someone else."

Matron had another glace round the room.

"Yes James, quite right. I'm sure someone will want to be head of dorm. Let's see how you've managed putting your things away. You seem to have some left over."

I hadn't appreciated the compact design of the locker and drawers where every inch of space was utilised. Once Matron had my clothes in the places designed for them, it all made sense. It became a thing of beauty.

"It looks neat and tidy. Thank you Matron."

"You're welcome James. Now get yourself ready for bed. Remember what your parents told you about washing your face and brushing your teeth."

"Yes Matron, goodnight."

"Goodnight James."

I could hear her heavy tread on the turret steps and couldn't help but wonder how many times she had to do the same journey in the course of her work.

That night I had a recurrence of the dream involving a message in Morse, except this time I was certain it was real and had wakened me. By the time I was fully awake it had stopped. I lay listening, but all was quiet. The next day I was too busy with other chores to give it much thought.

In the morning both domestic and teaching staff arrived for a day of preparation. Some made their own way to the school, but most came in a small hire coach from Perth. During the rest of the day, the boarders arrived, singly and in groups according to their mode of transport.

The first of the five sharing my dorm arrived just after lunch in a large chauffeur driven car. He was introduced to me as Allan and I was instructed to show him the dorm. He was taller by about half a head, but of slender build. His dark hair tended to fall across his face and he had a habit of tilting his head back to look at folk down his long thin nose, not difficult in my case.

On reaching the dorm, he threw his small case down on the end bed and plonked himself beside it, facing away from me.

"I thought I would be here first," he mumbled, "how did you get here so quick?"

"Oh, I flew in earlier. By the way, I'm James."

He half turned to look at me, but didn't answer, so I continued.

"The end bed is usually for the head of dorm."

"So?"

"So would you like to be head of dorm?"

"Of course."

Well, that's a relief I thought, while wondering how I was going to explain to him his duties, as I understood them.

"The Headmaster was an army Major and likes things to be kept neat," I said and before he could interrupt I rattled on.

"With everything in its proper place and Matron has shown me where it all goes and if you like I can show you so you can make sure the other boarders do things correctly, like this."

I opened my locker to reveal a fairly good example of military precision. He looked from me to the locker.

"Are we expected to do all this by ourselves? Are there no servants here?"

"No servants, it's all up to us."

He looked round wildly. His eyes glittered as he fought back tears.

"Come on," I said as I walked out to the landing where the boarder's trunks were lined up.

"I'll give you a hand with your kit and show you where it all goes. Then it will be up to you to show the others, as they arrive."

Once he had his task and a few folk to boss around he was back to his own supercilious self.

I can't say I ever took to him, but we managed to rub along without too much friction. He was never high on my list of 'the boy I can most trust'. It wasn't until the last boarder arrived that I felt this could be someone whose sharp mind felt in tune with my own. His name helped too. He was called Peter.

Ministry of Information, LONDON.
To agent 5, sector 13.

GCHQ report a short coded message originating in your area. When decoded it reads as follows.
'landing area ready – target in position.'
Investigate soonest.

M.

Chapter 12

.rted, it wasn't long before we all got used to the weekly ᵢ◡_   e. Our classroom was a large south facing room on the ground floor, airy and light.

A blackboard stood on an easel and the walls had various charts pertaining to words and numbers. There was a large map of the world with the countries of the British Empire coloured in red. A cardboard clock with moveable hands had the numbers in different colours. Oddly enough, I still associate the number four with pale green and five with orange, strange how the mind works.

Our teacher in Primary five was a tall angular lady with grey hair brushed straight back and tied in a bun shape. Her slight stoop and long flapping black cloak gave rise to her nickname of 'old crow'.

Rather unkind, I thought, as her firm discipline was tempered by an obvious concern for the welfare of the children in her care. In class, I sat next to Peter.

At first I thought he was shy, as he was so quiet, but that was his nature. He watched, observed and remembered. He wasn't boastful about his family, as some were, though he had every right to be.

Before confiding in him my thoughts on secret passages, I decided to ask the Headmaster. We had about half an hour after lunch before resuming lessons, so I knocked on the door of his study.

"Enter, ah, hello James."

"Sir, can I ask you something?"

"Of course, how can I help? Sit down."

I climbed onto the seat facing his desk.

"I was thinking about what you said about choosing a boy I could trust, to help find the secret passage."

"Yes, do you think you've found one you can trust?"

"I think so Sir. It's Peter, Peter Anderson. He's in my dorm, but I wondered if there was anything else I should know."

"You mean about Peter?"

"Yes Sir."

"First of all, tell me why you think you can trust Peter."

There was a pause as I tried to find the right words. He looked at me across his large desk.

"It's only a feeling."

"Go on," the Headmaster encouraged.

"He's quiet, but he listens and watches, thinks before he does anything. We help each other in class. I like him.

"It sounds as if you've made your choice already and no, I don't think there's anything else you need to know. You've summed him up well. I've met his father. He's a good sort."

"Thank you Sir, I'll speak to him."

"James, for the present, think carefully about how much you tell him, you understand?"

"Yes Sir. I understand and thank you."

"Off you go then."

I hopped down from the seat and carefully closed the door behind me, then crossed the hall with its old armour and older portraits, through the main door and down the steps. I found Peter outside, standing at the stone balustrade. He was deep in thought, watching the river as it tumbled between the rocky walls of the gorge.

"Peter." He turned and smiled as I walked towards him.

"Can you keep a secret?"

"Yes, what sort of secret?"

We now had our backs to the balustrade so we would have ample warning if anyone approached.

"The Headmaster thinks there could be a secret passage from the old part of the school to the outside and he's asked me to find it, but I need someone to help."

Peter's eyes widened and his mouth opened in a whispered,

"Wow! That's some secret and you want me? Oh wow, that's brilliant."

He looked past me to the solid walls of the old keep.

"And you reckon it's in there," he said, nodding towards the featureless walls. "I was wondering why none of the windows lined up. I bet it's in there."

"But Peter, if we find it we must keep it secret. The only other people we can tell are Matron and Mr Wilson."

Peter became serious.

"The Headmaster must trust you if he wants it kept secret and now you want to know if you can trust me."

The Headmaster had followed me to the door and was now watching us. I held my breath, wondering if I'd done the right thing. Peter was obviously giving the idea much thought and I was glad of that as it was vital we both trust each other.

"Dad says your word should be your bond and a promise once given can never be broken."

He held out his hand.

"You have my word James."

I smiled took his hand and that was that, the pact was sealed and I started to breath again.

"We can make a proper start on Sunday after church, but meanwhile I'll ask Matron if we can have a look at the house plans, so we can decide where to explore first."

"Good idea," agreed Peter.

However, things took an unexpected turn. The Sunday church service was held in a small chapel attached to the school and was only for boarders, as the day pupils would be with their families. At the end of the service the Headmaster stood up and asked us to remain seated. He had been handed a note by the janitor.

"I'm afraid I have the gravest of news."

He paused and let his eyes scan the small congregation.

"The Prime Minister has been speaking to the nation on the wireless and has informed us, this country is now at war."

There was a shocked silence.

"I would like to see the seniors in my study, the rest are dismissed for the day."

Peter and I looked at each other. Secret passages didn't feel so important now, but in that we were wrong. They would take their place, alongside the other secrets in our forthcoming battle with the enemy.

Part 2

At War and School

Chapter 13

The Headmaster was busy with the seniors, so we asked Mr Wilson for advice concerning the search for the secret passage. As usual, we didn't have far to look. He was standing near the door to the chapel, looking at the hills to the south. It was fitting, as a few moments ago, we had been singing, 'I to the hills will lift mine eyes.'

"Sir?"

He sighed. "What is it now James?"

"Peter and I were going to look for the secret passage today, but now with the war, we're not sure if we should, if it's important."

He looked at us for a few moments.

"Let's go back inside and have a seat."

There was a bench in the entrance porch where we could talk without being overheard.

"I can only tell you how I see things. I believe this will be a war fought not by armies, but nations, where every man woman and child will be involved.

The Headmaster has given you both the task of finding the secret passage, assuming it exists. I think he believes it could have an important use.

What I'm trying to say is this. We have no way of knowing how important even a small task may be, so it's better to carry it out to the best of our abilities. Does that make sense?"

We both nodded.

"Yes Sir, it does."

"The good book says, 'seek and ye shall find', so off you go and seek."

"Yes Sir."

"One more thing, if you do find any hidden passages, you come and tell me first, understand?"

"Yes Sir."

I was aware of those gimlet eyes boring into our backs as we wandered off towards the school.

Without conscious thought, our feet took us to the balustrade guarding the steep drop to the river. We stood mesmerised by the water as it curled round time worn boulders.

"I had hoped for some practical help Peter, but it looks as if we're on our own, so what do we do next?"

"We could have a look at the walls of the oldest part. There may be a door that hasn't been used for some time."

We strolled over to the fence that protected the dry moat.

"That would be the most obvious place for a passage to exit, but I don't see any openings apart from the arrow slits, it all looks pretty solid."

"How about the stone flags at the bottom of the moat," said Peter.

"Possible. Let's cross the bridge and have a look at the other two sides. There may be some clue there."

We crossed the bridge and walked along the path towards the walled garden and the airstrip. The walls of the keep were rooted firmly in the solid rock on both the side next to the river and the other one facing north. Grass and moss clung to the lower parts, but the only gaps were the odd arrow slit and they were far too narrow to afford a way in or out.

"This is a waste of time. Let's go back to the dorm until lunchtime."

"Right Peter, we may get some ideas on the way."

Through the main hall and up the stairs, looking round to make sure no one was watching and tapping the odd panel to see if it sounded hollow. It all felt as solid as the rock the house was built on. We were the only folk in the dorm, so we both lay on our respective beds gazing at the ceiling. Peter spoke first.

"Do you see what I see?"

I looked up, following his gaze.

"Yes, definitely worth exploring."

Directly above Peter's bed was a square hatch leading to a roof space. If this house was anything like my own and I'd no reason to believe otherwise, the roof space would cover all the rooms on the top floor, a secret highway for small spies. Peter stood on his bed, but couldn't reach it.

"I've an idea Peter."

I ran through to the toilet area, fetched the long handled brush used for sweeping the floor and handed it up to him.

"Try that."

"Great, that should shift it."

Using the brush end he pushed the hatch up and to the side.

"What do you see?"

"Rafters and there's a bit of wood going across the way. If I put the brush across the corner, I could climb up the handle."

"Will it take your weight?"

"Of course, I'm not that heavy."

Peter grasped the brush handle, heaved himself up and promptly fell back on the bed still holding the brush handle, leaving the brush head across the corner of the hatch.

"Correction, I *am* that heavy."

The gong sounded downstairs for lunch.

"We'll need to get it all back before anyone sees it."

"It's all right. I can jiggle it back in place with the handle."

It felt like an age, but it was only seconds before the brush head was down, the handle jammed back on and the hatch replaced. Instead of returning to the dorm after lunch, we walked out to our meeting place by the balustrade next to the bridge. The sound of the river flowing through the gorge had a soothing effect on the mind. It allowed ideas to develop.

"We need a ladder" said Peter.

"Right."

"Small enough to be stored in the loft space."

"How do we smuggle it into the dorm, assuming we find one?"

"That could be difficult, but if it was a rope ladder, that would make it easier. I bet there are bits of rope lying about at the airstrip from packages and crates."

"Good idea Peter, let's find out."

We scampered over the bridge and along the path past the walled garden, leading to the airstrip. Sure enough, there were plenty of short lengths discarded at various places beside the runway. We would be tying knots in it anyway, so that was no problem.

We collected every bit we could find, with the idea of hiding any spare rope in the loft above the dorm. It was smuggled in wrapped round our bodies under our jackets. If anyone did notice, which I doubt, they probably put our extra bulk down to a hefty lunch.

There was still no one else in the dorm, so we dumped the bits of rope on the floor, collected the brush and pushed back the hatch cover.

"Peter, we still have to get into the loft space before we can tie the rope ladder to that bit of wood above the hatch. How do we do that?"

"Let me think. I'm sure there's an answer."

We sat on the bed gazing at the open hatch with the roof truss in exactly the right place for attaching a rope, if only we could reach it. Peter was leaning on the handle of the brush which we had used to move the hatch cover. He smiled.

"I've an idea. It could work. We need some string, even strong thread or cord would do and a weight, something small and heavy."

"I've an alarm clock with a handle on the top. It's quite heavy. How much string do we need?"

"About twice the length of the brush handle and the clock should be heavy enough."

"I had a package from home and I never throw string away. It may be long enough."

"Let's see. Yes, that should do. We tie one end to the clock and the other to the longest piece of rope. I'm good at knots, learned all about them in the Cubs."

I had to admire Peter's ingenuity. Holding the brush bristle up, he passed the string over the brush head with the clock one side and the string the other, which he held against the brush handle. Carefully manoeuvring the brush above the roof truss until the clock was hanging the opposite side from the string he paid out the string until he could reach the clock. He handed the brush back to me and I propped it against the wall. Pulling the string with rope attached, the rope was soon looped round the roof truss, the two ends dangling against the bed.

"Peter, that's brilliant. I am most impressed."

"Thanks, I'm quite pleased myself. It's great when an idea works."

He untied the string from the alarm clock and the rope, which he then tied in a reef knot as high as he could reach. Tying the ends together in similar fashion created a simple two rung rope ladder. It would serve the purpose. Peter's ready smile was now broader than ever.

"Peter, I have no doubts about your ability with knots, so yours is the honour of first ascent."

The ropes creaked as they stretched, but easily held. Peter was soon standing on the joists, leaning against the roof truss. I hauled myself up to the second rung where I could see the full size of the roof space.

"This is going to take time to explore. We should prepare for a full day next Saturday."

"I agree and I think we should knot the rest of the rope into a decent length in case we need it."

It was getting near tea time, so we tied the rest of the pieces together using neat reef knots and stored it in the loft next to the hatch. We were standing beside Peter's bed admiring our work when I heard Allan's short quick steps on the middle landing.

"Let's see how quickly we can hide everything."

"Will do."

Peter looped the rope ladder over the brush and pushed it through the hatch. I could hear footsteps on the turret stairs. They reached the landing as Peter manoeuvred the hatch into place. As Allan came through the door, I was putting the alarm clock back in my locker and Peter was kneeling to brush under his bed.

"Glad to see you're doing some work for a change," said Allan.

"Just finished," said Peter cheerfully, as he took the brush back to the toilets.

Chapter 14

We planned a day of exploration for the following Saturday. As previously arrange, Matron made up some sandwiches and a small thermos flask of hot chocolate. They were placed in one of the Headmaster's old haversacks, the strap suitably shortened for our small frames.

"I'm not going to embarrass you by asking where you intend going, but if it should have anything to do with secret passages, please please be careful."

She bent down and hugged us both.

"Mind and be back by tea time."

"Yes Matron."

We climbed back to the dorm and changed into our oldest play clothes. Along with the haversack, we had the coil of rope waiting above the ceiling and a torch each.

Allan had gone home for the weekend and the other boys had taken the bus into Perth for the day. We had no idea of Mr Wilson's whereabouts, so I kept my ears alert to any warning sounds.

We hooked the ladder down and put the brush back in its proper place. Peter climbed up first. I handed our gear up to him and quickly followed. Once in the roof space with the ladder hauled up and the hatch back in place, we took stock. I looked across beyond the domed glass above the landing.

"That's where Mr Wilson's room is. Do you want to have a look while we have the chance? I don't think he's there."

"Yes, I think we should. Dad says 'knowledge is power'. The more information we can gather, the more we have to work with."

We walked balanced on the joists, supported where possible by roof trusses. They creaked as we passed the stained glass dome, which made us stop and hold our breath. A hatch like our own was set in the ceiling above Mr Wilson's room and above the hatch an arrangement of copper wire.

"Don't touch that, it could be live. Maybe he has a wireless."

I remembered the sound of the Morse transmitter I had heard at night. Could there be a connection?

"Yes, maybe he has. James, you look as if you've just remembered something."

"I thought I heard a Morse transmitter during the night, but it only lasted a few seconds."

"Do you think it was something to do with the copper wire? Should we tell the Headmaster?"

"I'm not sure. Anyway, let's explore the roof space first."

We were moving across the joists at right angles to their length. The ridge of the roof was above our heads in the darkness which deepened as we moved slowly into unknown parts. It felt like ages, stepping carefully from joist to joist, until the darkness was relieved by a small window casting light on a grey wall which blocked off half the width of the roof space. The wall formed part of the square tower built against the original fortified keep. In the feeble light from our torches we could make out the ancient stones of half a gable end.

"It looks as if we've come to the end of the roof space." A shuttered window in the gable promised access to the loft above the old keep.

"Let's try the skylight first," said Peter. "If we open it we'll get an idea of the roof shape."

Wooden steps had been fastened below the skylight, so it was a simple matter of opening it and putting our heads out to take our bearings.

"There's a ladder fastened to the roof and it goes all the way up to the top of the tower."

"Yes," said Peter, "and if you slip off the ladder, the fresh air at the edge of the roof goes all the way down to the river."

"True, so we put that down as only to be used in cases of extreme emergency."

"Exactly."

We closed the skylight, sat on the bottom step, drank some hot chocolate and waited for inspiration.

"Before we go back, let's have a closer look at the window in the gable end."

The old shutter had never been fastened. With a creak of rusty hinges and an odorous blast of pigeon droppings, we entered the loft above the old keep. There was no obvious exit and we were about to retreat to the comparatively fresh air of the newer roof space when we discovered near the gable wall, a hatch cover set into the ceiling of the room below.

We looked through the hatch into a small room. Below the hatch a large table was set against the wall. A window gave light and a view of the river Tay. Peter wriggled through the hatch, hanging on to its edge to find he was standing on the table.

"The table is much closer than I thought. There'll be no trouble getting back out if we need to."

He dropped to the floor and I followed. Opposite the window was a door, locked from the other side. Near the window was a smaller door which led to a spiral staircase.

"I remember the round bits on the plan of the school the Headmaster showed me. He said they were stairs and could lead to the dungeon with the magic well."

"That's more like it. Let's go," said Peter and down we went. No need for torches now as there was an arrow slit at each turn. A long way below us we glimpsed a narrow view of the river, as it dropped towards the Tay. With every spiral we drew closer to its level, eventually entering an enormous shadowed area unlike anything either of us had ever seen.

"Wow," whispered Peter. "Where are we?"

"I'm not sure. The Headmaster mentioned a dungeon and a magic well. Let's think. The spiral stair would be in the corner of the old keep, so we must be under the main hall. Maybe this is the dungeon."

We stood on the bare rock where the oldest part had been first built many hundreds of years ago. Thick pillars sprouted huge pointed arches at regular intervals which met in vaults over our heads like the crypt of a cathedral. It was scary and intimidating at first sight, but it also had a grandeur which was strangely uplifting.

"If there's a way to the outside it must come from here."

"Agreed, but where?"

"Mr Wilson said 'seek and ye shall find'. I think that means explore, so let's explore, which way Peter?"

"That's the side next to the river and over there is the dry moat, which would be the most likely, so let's try there."

"Great."

We moved along the wall next to the newer part of the school and found another opening to a spiral stair in the corner, which we decided to leave until a later date. Part way across the wall next to the moat we found a pipe which allowed water to drain. It was too small for an adult, but Peter wanted to have a look. He tied the rope round his waist and wriggled up the short distance to the slab he had pointed out the previous week. He was right. It was a way in for water and small people, but not much use as an escape route for the adult size. I pulled him back down into the dungeon area.

"It's a drain for water, that's all. We could get out, but it would take two of us to lift the slab."

"Peter, could I ask a rather obvious question. The water drains from the moat, but where does the water drain to?"

"True, it must go somewhere, or we'd be up to our armpits."

In the past a channel had been cut in the rock leading to a well in a natural hollow near the centre of the pillared area, the Headmaster's magic well. It was easy to miss, hidden in the darkest part farthest away from what little light filtered through the arrow slits.

The well had an iron ladder fastened to its inside. It could have been used for raising water, but why, with a crystal clear river running only a few yards away.

We stood looking into the well, the light from our torches reflected by a water surface a long way beneath us.

"What do you think Peter."

"I think it's time for another drink of hot chocolate."

We sat with our backs to the well's surrounding wall, allowing the hot liquid to impart some warmth. I was cold. I needed some of the heat and light slanting in through the arrow slits.

"You said the Headmaster called it a magic well," said Peter. "So what's magic about it? I know. It never rises to the level of the river, so it must drain somewhere. That's it, there must be an outlet."

"One of us will have to go down and have a look, or we'll always wonder if there's a passage to the outside from the well. Do you want to toss a coin Peter?"

"No need, I'll go. I trust you to hold the rope and I trust myself to tie a proper bowline."

"Point taken, you must show me how some time."

So Peter started on the long way down with the rope securely tied under his arms. He checked every rung and occasionally the well sides for any sign of a gap.

"The rungs are slippery and the sides are dripping with something green and disgusting."

After a few more grunts from Peter and rattles from the iron ladder, he called up.

"James, there's a narrow gap in the side of the well. Wait a minute."

I could hear him going down several more rungs.

"The gap definitely gets wider. Oh wow, yes, this is it. We could get through here. The water from the well is trickling into the opening, so it must go somewhere."

"I'm coming down."

"James, pull the rope up and get into the loop at this end, then loop the rope over the top rung. It's all slippery green slimy stuff, horrible."

I was soon down beside him in the opening, a natural fissure that had been widened at the bottom. A stream of water flowed from the well to some lower area.

"I bet this comes out in the side of the gorge," said Peter, as he hurried on ahead. Suddenly he lost his footing on the slippery rock and came down with a splash.

"Are you all right Peter?"

"Oh just dandy, I was only cold, now I'm cold and wet."

"Well don't just lie there. You're creating a small dam."

He eased himself on to his feet.

"Oh yugh, I feel as if I've wet myself."

"And you have, most efficiently."

He gave me that sideways look, that many were to learn was a warning not to push the situation any further. He turned back to the passage.

"I can see light up ahead. Put your torch out. See, reflecting off a large pool, we'll have to wade."

I was about to make another comment, but stopped myself in time. The passage was twisting and widening as the roof came ever lower until we had to crouch to splash through the pool. We had no need for our torches now as light filtered through a small opening, our exit from the nether regions. The stream ran out to join a curtain of falling water, the waterfall we could see from our dorm.

"Peter, another small snag, I can't swim."

Peter splashed forward and squeezed through the gap in the rocks. He turned round.

"You may not have to. In fact we needn't get wet, or should I say wetter. Come and see."

He disappeared to the left. I pushed the haversack through and followed Peter. To the left, a narrow walkway had been cut in the rock, allowing access to the side of the gorge, where another sloping path took us up and away from the river. We found a flat rock and sat as small rivulets dribbled from our clothes and pooled on the warm stone.

"Time to sample Matron's goodies," said Peter. "Any hot chocolate left?"

I shook the flask.

"A couple of mouthfuls I should think."

We sat munching and sipping while the afternoon sun dried and gave warmth.

"Now I'll show you how to tie a bowline knot," said Peter and I doubt if I'll ever forget how to tie Peter's bowline knot.

"I don't know about you Peter, but I've had enough of crawling about in the dark and wet for one day."

"I'm with you there. It'll take from now to teatime to get ourselves cleaned up. Oh no, do you see what I see?"

The unmistakeable figure of Mr Wilson was standing on the bridge, looking our way.

"Do you think he saw us come up from the falls?"

"Let's assume he did," I said, "how much do we tell him?"

He was walking towards us.

"Let's go and meet him James, as if we're pleased to see him, but only tell him about the cave beneath the falls. I've a feeling we should keep the roof space to ourselves for the moment. If we find another way into the dungeon, then we can tell him about the well. Smile, look happy, it never fails to confuse."

We met about half way to the bridge.

"Sir," said Peter, "you'll never guess what we found."

"Would I be right in assuming it's something to do with water?"

"Yes Sir, there's a cave behind the waterfall with a stream running through it."

"Which you fell in to, am I right?"

"Yes Sir."

He nodded, as he walked off towards the airstrip.

"See you both at teatime, clean and presentable, right?"

"Right Sir."

Chapter 15

It was as well we had our oldest clothes on. We were disgracefully filthy, as Mr Wilson had noted. We asked Matron if she could help and she did. She also remarked later that if the success of our day should be judged by the tidemark round the bath, we obviously had a whale of a time.

After our evening meal, we told the Headmaster about the cave behind the waterfall and asked if we could have another look at the house plans to check on possible access to the area below the main hall. We looked again at the spiral staircases on the corners of the keep where the new building had been attached.

"Sir, could there be any access to the spiral stairs?"

"If there is," said the Headmaster, "it's more years than I care to remember since it was used."

He looked over our heads as we peered at the plans and pointed to the one we had used earlier in the day.

"I had this one blocked off for safety reasons, but the other one. Let me think. There should be an entrance in the corner of the main hall."

"Can we have a look Sir?"

"Yes, of course, off you go. Let me know if you find anything."

"Yes Sir,"

We closed his study door and walked away as quickly as possible without breaking into a run. Mr Wilson had gone to his room and the boarders were returning from their day in Perth, meeting in dorm or common room, so at this time on a Saturday evening, the main hall was deserted.

The door was surprisingly obvious when you knew where to look. It was partially hidden by a heavy wardrobe and looked more like a cupboard than a secret passage. It was also locked. We returned to the Headmaster's study with the news.

"Locked, you say."

"Yes Sir."

"Tell you what. It'll take me at least a week to find the key, as I have only a rough idea where it may be, so let's say next Saturday and we'll have a look and see what we can find. How does that suit?"

"Great Sir, that would be brilliant."

"Fine, now run along and get yourselves ready for bed. I'll see you in church tomorrow. Goodnight."

"Goodnight Sir."

The main hall wasn't a through route as in many schools, and was only used for gymnastics or the morning assembly. When Peter and I looked in on the following Saturday, the only clue to it being occupied was the jingle of keys. The Headmaster, shielded from view by the wardrobe, was patiently trying the keys, one after the other, in the door to the staircase. As we walked forward, we heard a satisfying click.

"Eureka," said the Headmaster. "We have the key."

He turned to greet us.

"Well timed boys. I've only just found it and I've remembered why it was locked."

"Why was it locked Sir?"

"It was locked to prevent small boys of a mischievous and curious nature from getting into even more trouble."

He looked at our troubled expressions and laughed.

"I should explain. I was one of the small boys. Don't look so surprised, I *was* small once, a long time ago."

We looked at each other wondering how much we should tell him and hating ourselves for withholding information from such an open and honest man. I looked at Peter.

"I see you have something else to tell me," said the Headmaster.

"Yes Sir," said Peter. "We have a confession to make. We know what's down there in the dungeon with the columns and the pointed arches and of course, the well."

"Ah yes, the well," said the Headmaster, "the magic well that never fills, even though it's below the level of the river; the well with a ladder."

"Yes Sir. The well feeds a stream that runs through a crack in the rock and comes out in a cave behind the waterfall. We explored the cave last weekend and told you, but we weren't sure of the connection with the school. We're sure now that this door is the connection."

"You could be right. Let's find out."

He leant against the door and after a little persuasion it opened with a creak of hinges long rusted. It was a low door and after stooping to get through we all stood on a small landing with stairs going up to the left and a wooden floor to the right.

"There should be a trapdoor. Ah here we are."

He pulled it up and propped it open with his stick.

"After you, I'll wait here. Straight back as soon as you've had a look round."

"Yes Sir."

After one complete turn of the spiral stair we came out through the opening we had noted a week previous. It only needed a quick look round to establish our whereabouts and make our way back up to the Headmaster.

"All right," he asked.

"Yes Sir, it comes out in a corner of the dungeon next to the dry moat."

"Yes, I thought it would. So that's the secret passage."

He closed the trapdoor and we trooped out through the small door to the stairs. He locked the door and looked at the key.

"Only one key, so I'll need to get another one cut. If you have to use the key in an emergency, you must lock the door from the other side, so I'll need an extra one. Now we have to hide this one, but where?"

"There's a ledge above the door Sir, or on top of the wardrobe."

"Too obvious, come on Peter, use that brain of yours."

I could almost see the light go on above Peter's head.

"Sir, I've got it. Leave it in a lock, not the door lock, but the wardrobe; it's never locked so no one would notice.

"Excellent," the Headmaster beamed and put th
wardrobe lock.

"Something in full view is invariably overlooked."

It was a lesson I would remember and use to advant ᵒᵉ.

The Headmaster returned to his study and we walked out to our thinking area by the river.

"Peter, why didn't you tell the Headmaster about the roof space and the other spiral stair?"

"Because I don't think we should tell the Headmaster any information that we wouldn't want Mr Wilson to know. The Headmaster has no secrets, but Mr Wilson does."

"Why do you think that Peter?"

"I don't know. It's just a feeling."

It reminded me that I had the same feelings of unanswered questions about the death of the gunman. However, the answers could wait as better things beckoned.

Chapter 16

The half term school holiday was getting near and I expected to be collected by my parents and Midge, but now no petrol was available for private flying. I was upset until I found other arrangements had been made. The Headmaster was able to explain and put my mind at rest.

"James, I know you're disappointed at not getting home, but I've arranged with your grandfather and Peter's parents for you to spend the October break with them at their house in the Scottish borders."

"Oh that's brilliant Sir. Does Peter know?"

"I expect he will know by now. Would you like to speak to your parents by telephone?"

"Yes Sir, I'd like that."

"Remember it's not a secure line, so anyone could be listening. Your parents know where you're going, so there's no need to say anything about your travel movements."

"I'll be careful Sir."

So I told them about the school and the teachers, our own in particular. I asked how everyone was at home, especially Midge, who I missed. This must have been the longest time I'd spent, without talking to an aircraft. They said I'd definitely be home for Christmas, so that was something to look forward to.

However, the question of security bothered me, so I asked Mr Wilson.

"Sir, will you be coming with us, in case anything happens?"

"No James, I have to see my parents in Ireland. Peter's Dad will look after you and make sure you're safe. You could say we're in the same line of work."

"Oh, I see, thank you Sir."

Mr Wilson drove Peter and I to Perth railway station where I was introduced to Peter's parents. Mr Wilson spent some time talking to Peter's Dad, with the occasional glance in our direction; no doubt, putting him in the picture. He planned on getting the next train to Stranraer for the ferry to Ireland.

I remember standing on the station platform with my small case and noticing every other passenger was, like myself, carrying a gas mask. The containers varied from cardboard to canvas and the tailor made, but quite unmistakable, due to their shape and size. Fortunately, they were never required.

We didn't have long to wait for our train. It may seem strange, but I had never travelled by rail, as Midge had always managed to get us within taxi distance of where we wanted to go. It was therefore a new and exciting experience, travelling through countryside that, up until then, I had only gazed on from several thousand feet.

On our way south we crossed the river Forth, the track slung between a lattice of enormous girders. Several warships were moored nearby; their long grey shapes a reminder of how the war had drained the colour from our lives. I was given a penny to throw from the bridge and make a wish, but I can't remember what my wish was, or whether it came true.

The journey took much longer than Midge would have taken to fly to my home in the south. We stopped at countless stations with strange names and I remember changing to a different train at one point. Eventually we arrived at our destination and found an ancient taxi to take us to the house on the outskirts of the town. It was late evening and I was tired out.

After a good night's rest, we were ready to enjoy several days of active fun. I now realise it was part of our preparation for the expected invasion.

Peter's Dad gave us lessons in unarmed combat, showing us how, as a team of two, we could take on much larger opponents. He also showed us how to handle an air rifle and pistol in various positions from standing to prone. I found I was rather good, with a better than average score.

"You're doing well. I see a natural ability there," said Peter's Dad.

"Mr Wilson says he doesn't like guns." I said, remembering his religious convictions

"In a way he's right. One should never rely on them completely. The bully boys we're up against think all they have to do is wave a gun around and we'll do what they tell us but you know better James, don't you."

I looked up sharply.

"Did Mr Wilson tell you about the attempt to kidnap me on the way to the school?"

"He did James, but don't worry, we're all part of the same group, trying to do the best for our country."

Peter was looking at the two of us, suddenly aware the world had changed from what he knew to what he suspected and strangely, it was making more sense.

"Sir, can I tell you and Peter what happened. There's a lot that doesn't add up and I need to get it sorted out."

"Why not, you have the makings of a good team, so perhaps a simple explanation would be appropriate. Let's have a seat. There's no one within earshot out here."

"Trouble is, I don't know if there is a simple explanation."

I knew I could trust Peter and had reason to believe he had been well trained by his Dad, which followed that he could also be trusted. That was my thinking anyway. I had been told I could trust Mr Wilson with everything, but had to admit, I didn't. I took a deep breath and made a start.

"I have an ability, a talent you could say, on which the government puts great value. For this reason I have been attached unofficially to British Intelligence through my grandfather Sir James Nettleton, whom Sir, you may know."

"Yes James, I certainly do, though not personally."

"Mr Wilson is also from Intelligence and has been appointed my minder or bodyguard. The reason he got my mother's full approval was his belonging to a Christian Church which forbids the taking of life, so he wouldn't carry a gun, even in a war situation."

"I wasn't aware of that," said Peter's Dad.

"So when we were held up at gun point, I felt defenceless, but I was wrong. A short way in to Pitmeddan Forest, Mr Wilson stopped the car, switched off the engine and wound down the window. He could feel enemy eyes watching us, so when we encountered the gunman, it didn't come as a surprise.

I was trying to hide when the gun was pointed straight at me. I was terrified."

I hesitated for a moment as the memories flooded back.

"What happened then," said Peter's Dad.

"I saw the flash of the throwing knife and blood. I'd never seen so much blood. Mr Wilson knocked him out and in one movement, caught him and bundled him in to the other car. I found his knife in the grass verge and brought it back to him, while he scanned the forest on both sides of the road, clearly expecting a bullet at any second. He told me to lie down on the back seat, started the car, rammed the other one out of the way and drove like mad to the school and this is the part I don't understand."

"Yes, go on."

"Before reaching the school, he stopped the car in a passing place. He asked if I was scared and I said 'yes'. I must say, if he was afraid, his fear was well hidden. We must have stayed there a good half hour while he used the hot radiator water to clean off the worst of the blood and dirt. Last of all, he cleaned his throwing knife and returned it to its sheath, which he kept here," and I pointed to my back between the shoulder blades.

"Wow," whispered Peter.

"After leaving me at the school, he collected cans of water and a stiff brush to tidy up, but the gunman was dead. Why waste time at the side of the road, if he wanted to save the gunman? It doesn't make sense."

Peter's Dad had been listening intently, trying to imagine himself in Mr Wilson's position.

"There are a few contradictions in his actions, but let's see if we can make some sense of them; any thoughts Peter?"

Peter paused for a moment, mentally arranging the facts.

"If he's a member of this church which forbids killing, why was he carrying a throwing knife?"

"Good point Peter," said his Dad, "hardly a suitable knife for sharpening pencils."

"Another unanswered would be, where's the gun?"

"That's right," I said. "It hit the ground and went off. I don't remember seeing it after that. I thought the police had it. Do you think Mr Wilson picked it up?"

"It's possible."

"The stiff brush and cans of water would be to wash the blood from the road," I said. "Do you think he was trying to make it look like a suicide?"

"It was reported in the local press as a suicide," said Peter's Dad, "with a word of encouragement from Intelligence no doubt. There's a couple of folk I'd like to talk to, then I think I'll sleep on it. We'll talk again in the morning."

It was near lunchtime the following day before we had a chance to talk to Peter's Dad. Leaving the house by the back door, he walked towards the lawn where we had been practising some of the combat moves taught earlier.

"Let's talk."

We found a garden seat and sat either side of Mr Anderson.

"Mr Wilson was correct in his belief you were being watched, though the watchers were more concerned with your safety James, than your kidnap. Mr Wilson had no prior knowledge of the kidnap attempt, which was in fact genuine, the gunman following orders and working alone. The kidnap wasn't staged, but one could use the term, engineered. It's amazing how the course of events can be influenced by the odd word overheard, a crossed line or a misplaced letter."

"Papa," I whispered.

"Who," said Peter?

"My grandfather," I said.

"You know your grandfather better than I do James, but I

think we can only guess at his involvement. I've thought about the half hour you both spent at the roadside getting cleaned up, but without access to Mr Wilson's mind, we can only guess. However, considering the known facts, these are my thoughts.

Mr Wilson was brought up in a household that believed it is wrong to kill, yet he agreed to be trained by Intelligence to do just that, no doubt in a variety of interesting ways."

"Hence the throwing knife," said Peter.

"Exactly, so having killed his first man, accidentally I believe, his mind would be in an emotional turmoil of guilt and fear. He needed the half hour to calm down, regain his self-control and decide what to do next. Getting you both cleaned up was a good excuse. I believe the gunman was already dead and Mr Wilson knew it. Cleaning the blood off the road was to help Intelligence, the rest, window dressing and an attempt to quieten his conscience. How does that sound?"

I was impressed. His lawyer's mind had taken the known facts, slotted them in to place and the completed picture made sense.

"It sounds right," I said. "Everything fits."

Peter's Dad smiled and gave us both a hug.

"I think that's as close to the truth, we're going to get, except for one other item James, which is something you must decide yourself."

"I know; my special talent. Mr Wilson knows, so I don't see why you shouldn't, especially as I trust you a great deal more than I trust him. You're not going to believe this, but it's true. I talk to aircraft and I can hear them talk to me."

A series of expressions flickered over their faces, but they said nothing.

"Difficult to believe, but it's been tested and verified at the highest government level, so you see why I have to be protected. Everyone, including the enemy, wants me to help them."

Peter and his Dad looked at each other and nodded.

"Yes, we believe you. It makes sense of the whole sorry business. Does the Headmaster know?"

"No Sir, he doesn't and I'd rather this knowledge went no further."

"What knowledge would that be," said Peter's Dad with a smile and Peter made a zip movement across his lips.

"Thank you both. Being different isn't all it's cracked up to be. I wouldn't wish it on anyone."

"When this sad war is over, I hope you'll be able to tell us the whole story, but until then your secret is safe with us. One final request, I'm not a Sir, or ever likely to be, just plain Mr Anderson."

"Yes Sir, Mr Anderson."

Chapter 17

Mr Anderson, Peter's Dad, escorted us north. As arranged, we were met at Perth railway station by Mr Wilson. We returned to the school to find that several changes had taken place, while we were away. A new lifting barrier by the janitor's gatehouse was guarded by an armed RAF station policeman, who carefully examined our identity cards and noted the car's registration number.

A similar arrangement had been put in place at the gate on the north side of the estate, which gave access to the airstrip and walled garden. More RAF personnel were camped nearby. They were busy erecting a hangar for the glider which would be arriving shortly to give flying experience to the growing group of Air Training Corps cadets. They also hoped to complete a couple of Nissen huts to protect them before the worst of the northern winter arrived. Part of the walled garden had been turned into a twenty-five yard shooting range to give the seniors an introduction to weapon handling. The rest was being prepared to grow vegetables.

The Headmaster had clearly been busy. He had also given some thought to the secret passage and decided, due to its obvious dangers; it should only be used in cases of dire emergency.

Our formal education continued along smooth and established lines. Peter was usually near the top of the class. I admired his ability to absorb knowledge and grasp new ideas. I, in contrast, pottered about the middle, flying neither high nor low, a comfortable position which didn't attract attention.

I had hoped that Peter would come home with me for Christmas, but I could understand why, in these troubled times, his parents would want him with them at this time of year.

About a week before the end of term, Mr Wilson called me into his room.

"James, you'll be flying home for Christmas."

"That's great Sir. Have they got some petrol for Midge?"

"No, the RAF is sending a transport aircraft for you, so it's my guess you'll be asked to talk to one of your winged friends on the way home."

"Sounds interesting Sir, I wonder what kind it is. Will you be coming too Sir?"

"I don't know. My orders have yet to arrive. We'll have to wait and see."

I took the opportunity to give his room a quick scan, but could see nothing out of the ordinary, apart from a combined wireless and gramophone, with a wire leading to the hatch in the ceiling. The rest looked neat and tidy, if like him, cold and austere.

In the event, his orders arrived late, as no secure phone line was available. A message was delivered to the school office, asking Mr Wilson if he would like to spend the holidays with Papa Christmas in the south. This was something akin to a royal command, as my security was a priority and the location of enemy agents still based largely on rumour and guess work.

The De Havilland Rapide landed towards nightfall, two days into the holidays, when the rest of the staff and pupils had left. We took off early the next morning, making full use of what little winter light there was and landed at Duxford almost three hours later.

I was excited and eager to find out what my task would be, but had no inkling of the nasty shock waiting for me in the same hangar where I had talked to Sweetie.

I was greeted by a high ranking officer who took Mr Wilson and I first to a private room. I was given a long serious stare before he spoke.

"James, your grandfather, Sir James Nettleton has been in touch and tells me you may be able to help."

He looked at the floor, then at Mr Wilson.

"He claims that you have a unique ability to discover

information about aircraft. He also told me that if I divulged knowledge of this to anyone else, it would result in instant court martial, or worse."

I was beginning to get worried. This sounded serious, so I listened carefully as he continued.

"Whatever you can tell us about this aircraft could be of immense importance in the coming battle. The French captured it last month. It's an enemy fighter, a Messerschmitt 109."

I sat for several moments in silence, trying to take in the enormity of my task. Was it possible to talk to an aircraft which was so utterly alien, foreign and unfriendly?

"Sir," I stammered. "I have only err, examined, our own aircraft and I'm not sure if…"

At this point Mr Wilson interrupted, obviously afraid that I would let slip more than I should.

"James, I'll come with you and help translate the instruments," and he turned to the officer, "if that's OK with you Sir."

"Yes, that's fine. I'll show you where it is then you can have a look and come back here if you find out anything."

He sounded as if he thought finding out anything was to be more hoped for than expected. As we walked towards the hangar I asked.

"Could I talk to the pilot who flew the aircraft here?"

"Afraid not, he's no longer on the station."

"I was wondering," I continued, "if he said anything about the aircraft after he landed."

The officer stopped and I almost bumped into him. He looked at me, then at Mr Wilson.

"Yes, he did, but I'm not in the habit of repeating that sort of language."

Mr Wilson suppressed a smile.

"Oh," I said.

We entered the hangar by the side door and there it was, smaller than I had imagined, but dark and ugly with an air of brooding menace. It was the first aircraft I had met, that I disliked on sight. Even the RAF roundels and camouflage made little improvement.

The officer switched on the overhead lights.

"Best of luck, let me know how you get on before you leave."

We were now alone. Mr Wilson was standing to one side, waiting to see what I would do, as this was a new situation for him as well. I decided to walk round the 109 without touching it, as if I feared contamination, silly really. I was only delaying the inevitable when I had to climb into the cockpit.

I was concentrating so much on avoiding the enemy fighter that I bumped into a propeller blade belonging to another aircraft.

"Hello James." The words burst into my consciousness. "I hoped you would come back to see me. How do you like my new propeller?"

"Sweetie, is that you?"

Mr Wilson must have been surprised.

"James, who are you speaking to?"

"Sir, it's all right, she's a Spitfire called Sweetie. We've met before and it's given me an idea. Could you help me into her pilot's seat?"

"One moment James."

Mr Wilson climbed on to her left wing, slid back the canopy and let down the small entrance door. I climbed in and settled myself in her seat, resting my hands on her control column.

"Sweetie, we need your help."

"Yes James, I'll help if I can."

"I've been asked to talk to the Me 109 sitting next to you and find out its strengths and weaknesses, so we can use the right tactics in battle. I wondered if you've learned anything from him during his time here."

"Now James, let me think. He doesn't say much, but I gather his name is Emil. He was bragging about being able to do something that I can't."

"What's that Sweetie?"

"Fly upside down. If I try that my engine coughs and bangs

and loses power, but his doesn't. He says it's due to his superior engineering."

"Well, I suppose that's a strength. Do you think he has any weaknesses?"

"I'm not sure if it's relevant James, but he's lost more friends in training accidents than in battle. I don't think he's as strong as he likes to make out, and look at his wheels. I thought mine were too close together, but his are even worse."

"You're right Sweetie. They don't look very strong. I better talk to him. Oh, before I forget. You're new propeller looks very good. It suits you."

"Thank you James. Come back soon."

Mr Wilson helped me down from Sweetie and on to the wing of the 109. It was a struggle getting into the cramped cockpit. It must have been even worse for a tall pilot. As soon as I touched him, I could hear him grumbling away.

"Now they're sending me children. What sort of people are they? They don't deserve to win."

I suddenly felt very cold. I'm not sure why, but I decided not to indicate that I could hear his thoughts, so I listened. I could also feel sensations in my own body, as I had when meeting Tommy Tailwind the Hurricane, for the first time.

I ran my hands over the various controls and dials, not that I understood the latter, as they were calibrated in a strange way. All seemed normal until I touched the gun sight and my thumbs itched, how odd. I took hold of the control column and pulled it back towards me. Without warning the whole hangar whirled round and I felt very sick.

"Stupid child," I heard him say.

I waved to Mr Wilson and he climbed up and helped me out. I was exhausted.

"You're shivering James. Let's get you into the office so you can warm up."

The pilot of the De Havilland Rapide was already there talking to the officer. He turned as we entered.

"There's snow forecast. I'd like to get you all delivered before it arrives, but it looks as if Bicester will be the closest I can get you to home."

"Can I use your telephone Sir," said Mr Wilson.

"Certainly, go ahead."

I heard him talking to Papa, asking if he could arrange transport from Bicester, which I was sure he could. Once the pilot had left to get the Rapide warmed up, we were able to talk. It involved a similar charade to that used with Tommy, though I think this one was a great deal more important.

I said the 109 could fly upside down, without losing power, unlike the Spitfire and Hurricane. I also told him about the training accidents and the possible connection to the narrow track of the undercarriage. I think he may have had prior knowledge of this, as from then on, he took me seriously, just as well for the understanding of my next move. I stood with my arms straight out like wings.

"Sir, if I was an Me 109, what would be at my thumbs?"

"Your thumbs James, let me see, you mean in the position you have them now."

"Yes Sir."

"Thumbs, right, that would be the leading edge of the wingtips. What does the 109 have there? Let me think, slats, that's it slats; delays the stall."

"Sir, is there any connection with the gun sight?"

"No, no connection, they're automatic, but you think there is some connection."

He was talking to himself now.

"Think man think, what happens when the slats deploy?"

He was pacing about, now deeply involved in the excitement of the problem. Suddenly he thumped the desk making the phone jangle.

"I've got it, I've got it. When the slats deploy, the nose drops and spoils their aim. That's the connection with the gun sight. Well done James, well done. Is there anything else?"

"Well Sir, I don't know if it's important, but when I pulled the stick back, I felt very dizzy. I thought it was just the cold."

"Important, I'll say it's important. That clinches it. The little beast has a vicious stall and they've tried to cure it with the slats, but they work against them when they're trying to hold an aim in a tight turn. Brilliant James, absolutely brilliant; we've got them nailed."

"Thank you Sir. I'm glad I've been of some help."

"You certainly have James. Now you and Mr Wilson can cut along and not keep the pilot waiting. I'll write up a report with my own conclusions and send it on to Sir James, your grandfather. Have a great Christmas; you've certainly earned it."

I don't remember much of the rest of the journey, as I'm told I slept all the way wrapt in a blanket to keep me warm. Mr Wilson even carried me from the aircraft at Bicester to the waiting car.

I wakened as we stopped outside our house. Snowflakes were beginning to fall and it looked as if the first Christmas of the war would be a white one. Many hoped it would prove a good omen.

Chapter 18

Most of the house had been converted to a hospital for burn victims, but our family still had plenty of room in the East wing. Papa had an office on the ground floor with adjoining rooms where he was in constant contact with the Air Ministry through secure phone and teleprinter.

Whenever possible, Mr Wilson joined my parents in helping out in the hospital. They were still waiting for notice to join the Air Transport Auxiliary. Midge also, sat in her hangar waiting to join the same organisation. I was eager to tell her all my news, but first, I had to tell Papa about the enemy fighter at Duxford.

I joined my parents, Mr Wilson and Papa for elevenses and to confer. It was the same small room where we had first met after my ninth birthday but on this occasion the atmosphere felt more relaxed. I think we were all more aware of our roles and relationships. Also the expected aerial assault hadn't materialised.

"I've heard from Duxford," said Papa "and I believe your visit met with some success. I've still to receive the officer's report, but well done both of you. Tell me James, what you thought of the Messerschmitt 109; any impressions?"

"I didn't like it Papa."

"In what way James, because it was an enemy fighter, or were there other things you didn't like."

I struggled to turn my thoughts and feelings into words.

"It didn't feel safe Papa, not like Sweetie and Tommy. It didn't feel as strong, though it had bigger guns. It was very small and cold, not nice."

While I was talking about it, I was slowly pulling my arms and legs in, trying to make myself as small as possible. My mother was getting worried and put her arms round me. They were looking at me with some concern.

"That's all right. Don't worry about it," said Papa. "We can wait until the full report arrives."

"Come on," said my mother, "we have much nicer things to think about. It's nearly Christmas and cook has been baking. Look at the fine spread we have here."

She started pouring tea and Dad handed round the plates. I was beginning to relax again.

It's strange how an aircraft should have such an effect, but since then I have never set foot in another Me 109. Even the sight of one gives me a feeling of dread in the pit of my stomach.

The snow was still falling, but I wanted to see Midge, so dressed for the cold, I made my way to the hangar where she sat waiting for her call to the ATA. I climbed into her cabin which felt only marginally warmer.

"Hello James. How is school, interesting I hope?"

It was a relief to be with Midge where I didn't have to think about what I said, so the words all tumbled out in a rush.

"School's great Midge and on the way there a man tried to shoot us and Mr Wilson stopped him and Mr Wilson says he doesn't like guns but the Headmaster does and he has lots of them and he asked me to find the secret passage and my friend Peter and I found it and it comes out under a waterfall and I went on a train with Peter to his house and his Dad showed us all about ju something so we can stop bad people with just our hands and feet and now it's Christmas. What have you been doing Midge?"

"Well I did ask. I'm afraid I've been doing nothing as exciting, as there's no petrol available."

"Oh never mind Midge, once the war is over, we'll all get back in the air again."

I didn't tell her anything about the enemy fighter, odd that. I think I wanted to avoid associating Midge, even in my mind, with its dark memories.

Back at the house there was talk of a great naval victory in the South Atlantic. It was good to be able to celebrate some success, as elsewhere the news was at best ominous. Papa may have had some influence on the outcome of the battle, though as usual in an advisory capacity.

Apart from the lack of petrol, the war was having little effect on our lives. Certain imported foods were in short supply, but we had our extensive garden and the home farm, so at present, life in the house was much as before. It was only transport that was affected, but the harsh winter was making travel well nigh impossible anyway.

I remember Christmas 1939 as different in so many ways. Cook did amazing work in organising the Christmas dinner and everyone in the house received a present, our family, the servants, doctors, nurses and every patient.

My parents had been preparing for weeks before hand, to make sure that there were enough items to go round. For me it was memorable not so much for what I received, but for the presents I was allowed to give. I spent a large part of Christmas Day walking through the wards carrying small parcels. I was told by the nursing sister how I should address each patient before presenting their gift. It was a duty I accepted and in time, learned to cherish.

1939 changed to 1940 in the quiet of a snow covered land. The road to the house was cleared quickly, to allow ambulances access. Fortunately at this time there were few patients, a situation which would change dramatically during the coming year.

Before I returned to school, Papa called me into his office.

"Sit down James. I have the officer's report here and I want you to know your unpleasant experience at Duxford may prove the saving of some of your friends like Tommy and Sweetie, so well done."

He ruffled my hair and looked thoughtful before continuing.

"I wouldn't want to put you through that again James, so you must tell me if you feel it's going to be too much for you."

"It's all right Papa. Aircraft are like people, there are good ones and bad ones and he was bad, very bad. I'll be fine the next time."

And the next time I did manage with little difficulty.

The weather was still making travel hazardous, so even with Papa's best efforts, it was a week into the New Year before we flew back north in the same Rapide. The RAF cadets had done sterling work in clearing the snow from the airstrip in time for our arrival. The winter weather had delayed the return of some boarders, but most, including Peter had managed the journey.

However, at that age snow was fun and we made the most of the opportunities it afforded.

From the confidential diary of Sir James Nettleton

Monday 29th January 1940

The trains are still running so I managed to reach the office before lunchtime. This is the harshest winter I can remember. I managed to get James back to school in a flight from Bicester. He discovered some useful information from our captured Messerschmitt. I'm worried about the effect it had on him, though he assures me, all aircraft are different. However, I mustn't ask too much. He's a valuable resource and must be conserved.

Our navy put up a fine show in the South Atlantic, but we're still losing ships at a terrible rate. The rationing system will need to be extended to give a fair share to all.

The hospital part of the house is settling into an efficient routine. I have great admiration for the work Peter and Vicky have put in to make Christmas a pleasantly memorable time for all. They found small presents for all the staff and patients, though I've no idea how. My guess is we have a few less family heirlooms than before. No matter, it's in a good cause. With the help of the ward sisters, James delivered the presents to every patient. I was impressed by his sympathetic manner, quite remarkable for one so young. Perhaps I'm biased. Mr Wilson has been helping in the hospital part of the house. He's a good listener. Something many a patient needs. He's still an odd one. I can't decide if he's for us or against us. I hope all will be resolved eventually, in our favour.

Chapter 19

It was March before winter lessened its grip and a brief spring paved the way to a warm summer.

Though the fighting part of the war was hundreds of miles from the school, there were still many visual reminders that it could arrive with little warning.

The Headmaster had made sure that every window in the school was effectively blacked out at night with shutters or heavy dark curtains. Every window pane was treated, to prevent splinters of glass from flying about, should a bomb explode nearby. Matron organised that by having old lace curtains cut and stuck on the glass with wallpaper paste.

Car lights were fitted with metal hoods and bumpers, running boards and the edges of mudguards were painted white, to be more easily seen in the blackout.

The Square tower we had seen while exploring the roof space was chosen as an ideal site for an observer post. It was one of a chain with secure communication lines to the local fighter control centre. It also doubled as a control tower for the airstrip.

Spare time in the evening was limited, but I enjoyed listening to the wireless. We were allowed, even encouraged, to listen to certain BBC programmes. The one that made the greatest impression was called 'Into Battle'. It consisted of the National Anthems of the countries that had been invaded and conquered by the Nazis. It became noticeably longer as the weeks passed.

Arrangements had been made for Peter and Mr Wilson to spend Easter with me at our house in the South. We were expecting a long uncomfortable train journey, but a day before we were due to leave, a message was sent from Papa, via the observer post on the roof. It said, 'Be at Scone no later than 7am tomorrow'.

By 7am the next morning, we were standing in front of the

control tower at Scone airfield. Mr Wilson's car was tucked round the back to await our return. His haversack had a large thermos flask poking out from the top. Matron had made sure we all had a good breakfast and were carrying enough sandwiches to last us all day.

"You never know when you'll eat next. I don't trust those flying machines. I know what they were like in the last lot. You could end up anywhere."

Ten minutes after seven, we thought we'd been forgotten. I heard the aircraft first, but it was Peter who saw it, to the North of the airfield. The Anson landed and taxied up to the control tower, the engines left ticking over.

The single occupant, a lady pilot, opened the access door and waved us over. She would be about the same age as my mother, maybe younger.

"Come on chaps. I've got to get this old crate to White Waltham and I'm not cleared to fly at night."

We all scrambled through the narrow door.

"I'm Wilson and this is James and Peter. It's Peter's first flight. We're very grateful for the lift."

"That's OK. Peter, you come up here and sit beside me. Wilson, you can show your gratitude by winding up the undercarriage, once we're safely in the air."

Mr Wilson nodded to the pilot, as he helped Peter to get strapped in. We were bumping over the grass at the edge of the field towards the downwind side. I was already in the navigator's seat, not that I was required to navigate.

The pilot turned round in her seat, partly to look at us, but also to check that our takeoff run was clear.

"By the way, I'm Jill. We're a few minutes late, because I couldn't get the gear raised, on my tod, so couldn't wind the handle," pointing to a handle below her seat, "and fly the old kite at the same time."

We turned into wind and after getting the green light from the tower, were soon in the air and turning towards the south.

Once we were safely trimmed and on course, Mr Wilson made his way forward.

"May I?" he said, pointing to the handle.

"Please."

Even shouting to each other, it was difficult to make ourselves heard above the noise of the engines, so we had to use sign language.

After countless turns of the handle a red light on the instrument panel winked out. Jill tapped Mr Wilson on the shoulder and with a 'thumbs up', he returned to his seat.

Peter was fascinated by everything that was happening, the controls, the instruments and the country we were flying over. Jill handed him a map and pointed to a spot showing a river, then pointed outside. There, a long way below was the unmistakeable shape of the Forth Bridge. Peter waved to me to come and look, which of course I did. It was great to see him enjoying himself so much. He had this happy knack of enjoying and in turn, bringing enjoyment, to everything, especially the new and exciting.

I had hoped to have a chat with the Anson, but mindful of the need for secrecy, I only listened. I gathered she was being moved from Coastal Command at Lossiemouth, to White Waltham and the Air Transport Auxiliary. She was naturally apprehensive about leaving her old friends.

We reached cruising height and the engines took on a more restful beat. Mr Wilson made his way forward with some tea in the cup of the thermos and handed it to Jill. She looked up and smiled.

"Cheers."

An hour later, we arrived over Bicester, much earlier than expected.

"Made good time, bit of a tail wind," said Jill as Mr Wilson busily wound the wheels down. Tailwind, I thought and wondered how Tommy was fairing.

After landing, we made our hurried goodbyes to allow Jill to take off and resume her journey back to her base at White Waltham.

Papa had managed to persuade someone with an RAF staff car

to give us a lift back to our home in time for lunch. However, Matron's fine sandwiches didn't go to waste. They were much appreciated, as she insisted on the best of ingredients.

Peter and I had a great time running about the estate. I enjoyed showing him round and introducing him to my parents and Papa. We looked in on Cook, who dropped the pan she was carrying and ran to me, bent down and gave me a hug. I think there were tears in her eyes, but she said it was the onions.

Mr Wilson's help in the hospital was most welcome as there were noticeably more patients from the fighting in Norway. He could be really bad tempered as a teacher, yet was willing to spend hours listening to the wounded when they wanted to talk about their grumbles and fears.

I tend to keep the good things until later, to experience the pleasure of anticipation, so it was afternoon before I introduced Peter to Midge in her small hangar. We entered by the side door. She looked enormous in the small space. Peter stood there admiring her gleaming white fuselage.

"Now I know what you've been going on about. She's beautiful, absolutely brilliant. Can I sit inside?"

"Of course, that's why we're here."

I opened the door and could hear Midge as soon as I touched the handle.

"Is this Peter? Well, you can tell him I think he looks beautiful too."

"Midge, you're embarrassing me straight off. I can't tell him that."

"You can't tell me what?"

I looked at the floor, blushed and muttered.

"She says you look beautiful too. Now get in the front seat before she shows me up any further."

Peter laughed and climbed in, while I crept into the seat behind him. He was immediately taken up with the instruments and controls.

"Is this the joystick? The Anson had a half wheel on the top.

Why's that? The pedals, they're for the rudder aren't they and the levers, throttle isn't it?"

"Peter, give me a moment and I'll take you through everything and explain. Midge says she has control locks attached to prevent damage while being moved."

"Sorry James, I'm prattling on, but it's all just so wow, look at the wood on the dashboard. It's like a Rolls Royce and the mascot, it's all so, so wonderful. I meant what I said and I didn't mean to embarrass you, or Midge. Sorry, you were going to explain the controls."

"James," said Midge." Will you tell him about the controls before he takes off through the hangar doors?"

"All right Midge, if you could please keep quiet. This two way conversation is giving me a headache."

I leant over Peter's shoulder to point out the levers and dials.

"The stick is forward down, backwards up and the side to side is the same as the Anson's half wheel. The two levers on the left are throttle, the big one and mixture."

How about this one on the right, that's where the throttles were on the Anson."

"No, that's the air brakes and she doesn't have any wheel brakes."

"Is that the Speedometer?" said Peter pointing to the one in the middle.

"No, that shows engine speed. The one on the left is air speed and the one like a clock is the altimeter. It tells you how high you are."

"It's wonderful," said Peter. He moved his hands over the dials and levers, lightly touching them with his fingers, setting them all to memory.

"Can I talk to Midge?"

"Yes Peter. She hears everything."

"Some day, I shall be a pilot. I wish I could hear you talk."

He gently opened the cabin door and climbed out. I followed him, while listening to Midge.

"Yes Midge, I'll tell him."

I closed the cabin door, then the small door in the hangar. I'd never known Peter so quiet. We were some way towards the house before he spoke.

"James, is it all right to tell me what she said?"

"Yes, of course. She likes you, says you have the touch and she's never wrong. You'll make a good pilot. She also said and I've no idea how she knows, that some day you will be her pilot and she will talk to you in her own way and you'll understand."

We had wandered on to the terrace overlooking the avenue of trees and the lake. He walked slowly to the stone balustrade where he rested his hands. He stood there for several minutes without moving. I felt unwilling to interrupt. The silence was broken by the swelling sound of a flight of Spitfires as they approached from the right in a sweeping turn to the south. His gaze lifted to follow them as they flew low down the course of the river. He lifted his arms, stretched, turned and smiled as he walked back towards me, wiping his nose with a hankie.

"I think I'm starting a cold. Let's see what Cook's making for Afternoon Tea."

Chapter 20

The day before we were due to head back to school was spent gathering together the various items needed for the journey. Peter was sitting absorbed in reading, would you believe, the Pilot's Notes for a Puss Moth, when my father beckoned me to follow him to the next room.

"James, before you go back to school, I wanted to let you know what's happening with the war and how it could affect you."

"Yes Dad?"

He obviously didn't want to worry me, but at the same time, to prepare me for the worst that could happen.

"It's more than likely that the enemy will turn their attention in our direction. They may try to invade our country and should they succeed."

He was visibly upset at the thought.

"Should they succeed, you must stay with Mr Wilson and help him in any way you can."

"Yes Dad."

This sounded serious.

"What will happen to you and Mum?"

"Oh we'll be all right. They won't attack a hospital. They're not barbarians. In any case, they still have to get past your winged friends, so it may never happen, but if it should."

He hesitated, looking at me.

"You know what to do."

"Yes Dad, we'll be all right."

Papa had once again managed to arrange a lift for us in an aircraft flying north to Lossiemouth. I remember it as a Wellington like Queenie.

Mr Wilson's car was waiting for us in the same place behind the control tower and the sentry at the gate house still checked our identity cards, even though by then he must have known who we were. If anything, security was tighter now than at any time before, with rumours abounding of spies, fifth columnists and Quislings.

I know the Headmaster was armed at all times and I suspect Mr Wilson was too, though in no obvious way. I don't remember feeling afraid of the enemy. The idea that we could be beaten never occurred to me. We had right on our side, so without doubt we would win.

That's not to say I hadn't known fear. When the gunman pointed his gun at me, I was terrified, but it was only momentary before the situation dramatically changed in our favour. When I met the enemy fighter, the Me109, I felt a different kind of fear, a dread, akin to that now felt by our parents and teachers.

A few weeks into the summer term, there were a series of events that, on the face of it, should have made us feel much worse and yet, they didn't. It's difficult to describe, but I'll try.

It was generally accepted that the enemy army and air force were the best equipped in the world. They were invincible, sweeping all before them, completely unstoppable. Now, they were coming our way, at a frightening speed. It only seemed a matter of time, before they would invade and conquer our country, like all the others they had attacked.

Tommy and his friends had been sent to France to try and stop them, but the enemy were too strong and numerous. By the end of the summer term they were looking at us from across the channel. Things looked bad and yet there was a new feeling in the air, a stiffening of resolve, of unity.

We had a new Prime Minister who made it clear that we would never surrender. Our Royal family, the King and Queen and their two daughters would also, against all advice, be staying here and not moving to the safety of Canada. With a lead like that we had little choice but to fight and win. Defeat was unthinkable.

A part time volunteer army was formed, later known as the Home Guard, so now the Headmaster was a Major once more. The entire school staff, without exception, volunteered their services towards the war effort.

Typical of the support given to the armed services by civilians, was the armada of small coastal craft, manned by peace time sailors. They helped to bring back hundreds of thousands of soldiers from the beaches of Dunkirk, soldiers of every nationality that had suffered under the common oppressor. Mr Wilson had been proved right in saying it would be a people's war.

However, I still don't understand the details. All I know is there had been a shift of attitude. Surrender was no longer an option.

It may not be far from the truth to say as a nation, we suffered a form of collective delusional madness. It was obvious to the rest of the world that we were in most respects defenceless and open to invasion. So why didn't they invade? The answer to that must lie with the historians, or maybe the psychologists.

I only had one way of helping and about the middle of the summer term I was asked to chat with Tommy Tailwind, the Hurricane fighter, who somehow, against all the odds, had managed to survive the air battles over Europe.

This was the first time it was felt necessary to use the deceptive cover of my unpronounceable illness. Looking dreadfully ill, thanks to some expertly applied make-up; I was stretchered across to the airstrip and the waiting Rapide.

After takeoff, instead of turning south we headed east to RAF Leuchars where we transferred to a Blenheim bomber. Two hours later we were flying over London to land at Croydon.

I was looking forward to meeting Tommy again, but was ill prepared for the battle scarred sight parked at a dispersal point on the perimeter of the airfield. Mr Wilson was walking a few steps behind me when I turned to him.

"Sir, are you sure this is Tommy?"

"Let's see. There's a big 'T' on his side, but I better check the serial number."

He pulled a piece of paper from his inside pocket.

"Let's have a look, yes, it's Tommy. I expect he was a lot cleaner when you last saw him."

That was certainly true. I'm not sure how long I stood looking, taking in the changes, good and bad. He had a three bladed metal propeller, replacing the original wooden one and a new fairing had been added under his tail. Those were the good changes.

On the other hand, he looked tired; his paint work dull and weathered. There were scrapes and chips where wing panels had been hastily replaced while reloading his eight guns. Cleaner areas showed where fabric patches had been applied to cover bullet holes. One aileron didn't match the rest of the wing and great areas of burnt on oil stretched back from his exhaust stubs.

It was one of those occasions when I felt emotionally pulled in different directions. I wanted to help. Indeed that was why I was there, but at the same time, I didn't want to intrude.

I looked at Mr Wilson, straightened myself, walked over and gently laid my hand on the trailing edge of his left wing. All was quiet.

"Tommy?"

I felt a stirring of consciousness.

"Tommy, it's James."

"James?"

"Yes, it's James. We met at Northolt about a year ago, not long after your famous flight from Scotland."

"James, yes, I remember and you've come back. You've come back to see me."

"I said I'd try."

"Oh James; I'm so glad. Sorry if I'm a bit slow. I'm just so desperately tired. Climb up and have a seat, then we can talk easier."

I swung myself onto the wing and Mr Wilson handed me the cushion which had become one of the essentials.

"Don't touch anything James. I expect my guns are loaded and primed."

I sat with my hands resting on the spade grip of his joystick, carefully avoiding the firing button, which should have been on safety, but I couldn't be sure.

"Tommy, no one has told me why I'm here, but it must be urgent as we were flown down in a Blenheim bomber."

"Can't help there James. Those of us who survived, are absolutely exhausted. You can have no idea what it was like, so many, like an aerial tide."

"It sounds bad."

I could feel the weight of memory flooding over Tommy; his words whispered with many a pause.

"We tried to keep them from the beaches where the soldiers waited. We tried, but there were so many, so many. I'm told we managed to save thousands, but at the cost of many friends. Sweetie bought it, well inland from Dunkirk, her and many more."

It was like a physical blow. I didn't say anything, though I may have gasped. Tears coursed slowly down my face, dripping onto the control rods and dusty floor below the seat. It was only a few months ago that we had talked, barely feet from an aircraft similar to her killer.

I couldn't speak, but resolved then to do everything in my power to bring about our enemy's downfall. Tommy was all too aware of my discomfort.

"James, I'm sorry. I thought you already knew."

I gave a slight shake of the head.

"Now listen James. I want you to remember this. If you and Sweetie hadn't managed to winkle such vitally important information from that diabolic heap of evil, which I refuse to grace with the title aircraft, many many more of your friends would have perished. So please, will you remember that and remember Sweetie for the hero she will always be?"

I nodded.

"I think you're all heroes," I whispered.

"I'm not sure, but if we are, I believe our heroism is about to be tested even further."

I looked up and wiped my eyes with the back of my hand. This was no way to win a war and win I was determined we should.

"Sorry about that Tommy. How can I help?"

"Well for one thing, you're here and listening. That's something we've never had before and it's important to all of us."

He didn't sound so tired now.

"We need to solve the problem of flying upside down. When we come up behind a 109, they try to escape by pushing their nose down and diving away. If we do that our engine coughs and bangs and we've lost them. My pilot's wise to this and does a falling barrel roll and we're on their tail in no time, but it's not the complete answer."

I sat listening.

"You'll have noticed the mirror screwed to the top of my windscreen. It's from an old car and it gives my pilot an idea of what's happening behind. That's important and I think they should be fitted as standard at the factory.

Now, let me think, what else, yes, guns. We need bigger guns. These are fine if we get in close, but some of their bombers can absorb a deal of lead and still keep flying."

I listened while Tommy listed the necessary design changes but couldn't help feeling this was not why I'd been sent. Papa could learn all this from the pilots.

"Tommy, can you think of any problem that only you know the answer to?"

"Good question James, I see what you mean. Not much point in telling your Papa problems he's already half way to finding a cure for. Give me a moment to think."

I was aware of Mr Wilson standing on the wing.

"James, your Grandfather's car has arrived from the Air Ministry. He'll want to have a word with you."

I stood up and Mr Wilson helped me out. I climbed down from the wing and patted the side of Tommy's fuselage."

"I'll be back in a moment Tommy."

Chapter 21

Papa looked tired, as if he hadn't been allowed a decent night's sleep for some time.

"Hello James, Mr Wilson. Let's have some lunch. We can talk while we eat."

I took his hand as we walked towards the aerodrome's restaurant, with Mr Wilson, ever watchful, a few paces behind.

I told Papa about the various changes that Tommy had suggested. He nodded, but made no comment until I had finished.

With the rest and nourishment, Papa was getting some colour back in his cheeks. He smiled at me.

"That's very good James. Rolls Royce are looking into the problems that negative 'G' has on the Merlin engine, but I like the solution Tommy's pilot has come up with," and he made a swirling motion with his fingers, "very elegant. I'll send a note to the other squadrons, though I imagine their more experienced pilots will have thought along similar lines.

I'd heard that some pilots were fitting car mirrors. We should've thought of that, very remiss. I'll get orders to the factories today. Heavier armament could pose more of a problem. I've had a word with the designers and they all agree that we need cannon fitted, but that could take time."

He was looking into the far distance.

"Time however, is something we have very little of, but you can tell Tommy that Hawker have come up with an interim solution."

His eyes twinkled.

"Ask him how he likes the idea of twelve machine guns, instead of eight. It would mean carrying more weight, but it would pack quite a punch at close range."

I looked up and smiled.

"Yes, I think Tommy would like that. He *would* pack a much heavier punch."

Papa was looking more serious again, gazing into the grey blue of distant skies.

"I wish I could get another crack at them."

He shrugged and sighed. Took out a hankie and held it to his nose.

"Papa, is there anything else you would like me to ask Tommy?"

He looked at me, bringing his mind back to the present and more pressing problems.

"Yes James, there is. We have a navigational problem, especially with Hurricanes. It could be worth asking Tommy if he has any ideas on the matter. We have nothing to lose by asking him and a great deal to gain if he can provide an answer."

He was lost in thought for a few moments, trying to decide how to explain a fairly complex problem to a nine year old who was still in his fifth year at primary school. Eventually he looked at me.

"James, do you know what a compass is?"

"Yes Papa, it's like a clock with one hand which always points to the north."

"Yes James, that's a good description. Perhaps you know that the hand points north and south because it's a magnet, just like the one that your mother has for finding pins that have dropped on the floor when she's sewing. Now the compass hand finds bits of metal attractive too, so as well as pointing north, it also wants to point at anything made of metal, like Tommy's engine and guns."

This all sounded terribly complicated.

"Papa, how does it know it's pointing north and not at Tommy's engine?"

"It's quite difficult James, but our clever mechanics are able to cancel out the other attractions, so the compass hand always points north, no matter what way the aircraft is pointing. But they can only do this on the ground. The trouble is, once in the air, the compass becomes unreliable. The less experienced pilots thought it was their fault and didn't report it, but when experienced pilots and qualified navigators found their compass needle wandering about, we realised something was wrong, but we still don't know what."

"I think I understand Papa. The compass works on the ground, but not in the air. Is that right?"

"In a nutshell James and if you can find out why, then it will give back confidence to many a young pilot. A lack of confidence can be deadly."

I left Papa resting in an easy chair, while Mr Wilson and I walked back to Tommy. I had much to think about, but at least I now knew why I'd been sent for. With Mr Wilson's help I was soon back in Tommy's seat.

"Hello Tommy, I'm back."

"Did you see your Papa? Is there any news?"

"Yes Tommy, good news, it's all in hand. How do you fancy another four machine guns?"

"It's worth a try James. Now, are there any more clues as to why you were sent here?"

"Yes Tommy, it's your compass. It works fine on the ground, but doesn't point the right way when you're in the air."

"Of course James, the compass, should've thought, but I've been so tired, haven't been thinking properly."

"I know, but have you any idea why it doesn't work in the air?"

"Oh yes, I know why it doesn't work. Dead simple really, but I'm not sure what the cure is."

"Well, don't keep me in suspense; tell me why the compass doesn't work."

"Right James, lean forward and tell me what you see."

"The compass."

"And underneath the compass are two holes. Do you see them?"

"Yes?"

"And what do you see through the holes?"

"Nothing, just the ground."

"So what do you think fills those holes when I'm in the air?"

I had to think for a minute before it dawned on me.

"Your wheels Tommy."

"Right James and they're made of..?"

I quickly finished the sentence.

"a metal that attracts the compass hand. Wow! We've got it! We've got it!"

I fairly bounced out of the cockpit, punching the air in my excitement.

"Sir, we know what's wrong, but I'll need to let Papa see for himself. Can you fetch him?"

"Yes James, I'll be back as soon as I can. Stay in the cockpit where you can't be seen."

In no time at all Mr Wilson was back and helping me out on to the wing. Papa was following on, at a slower pace. I slid down off the wing and ran to take his hand.

"It's the wheels Papa, the wheels. Come and see."

I was standing under Tommy's nose and pointing to the wheel wells. Papa stooped and peered up into the space.

"If you look through the holes Papa, you can see the compass."

"So you can James. I do believe you've found the cause. Well done James and well done Tommy."

He was standing beside Tommy patting his side, much happier and more relaxed now that a solution to the problem was in sight.

I was leaning against Tommy's air intake.

"Thanks Tommy."

"Only too glad to help James. Try and come back to see me soon."

"I'll try Tommy, take care."

Papa was keen to get us back to school as soon as possible.

"It'll save too many questions being asked."

After several phone calls he located a De Havilland Rapide, or Dominie, as the RAF now called it. It was about to leave Northolt with a couple of ferry pilots, but would wait for us provided we were quick.

We travelled through London in the Air Ministry car, while Papa once again reminded us of the need for secrecy.

"Remember James, if anyone asks, you've no idea where you've been, except it was a big white building and everyone was very nice to you."

"Yes Papa. We had lunch in a big white building and everyone was very nice, so that's true."

Papa laughed.

"Quite right James, always tell the truth, but not necessarily the whole truth."

Three hours later the Dominie was flying over the walled estate that surrounded the school. From the air, I could appreciate the good defensive position of the original building as it stood on its rocky outcrop with the river flowing round two sides and the waterfall hiding the exit from the secret passage.

A green light flashed from the observer post on the tower and moments later we touched down on the school's airstrip. The Dominie taxied to the downwind end of the airstrip and our identity cards were once more checked by an RAF policeman, who was kind enough to ask how I was feeling.

We walked past the walled garden as the Dominie flew over our heads, answering our wave with a gentle waggle of wings. Matron was at the door of the school, waiting to greet us.

"It's good to have you both back safely; and you, young man, are looking a great deal better than when you left this morning," she said with a broad wink.

"The Headmaster and boarders are in the dining room. We've kept places for you both."

"Thanks Matron, I'm starving."

"I could do with a bite to eat too," said Mr Wilson. "It's been a long day, but a fruitful one. James certainly earned his keep. I was impressed."

As we entered the dining room, there was a swivelling of heads and a few seconds of silence as everyone looked in our direction; not the entrance I would have wished. I sat next to Peter.

"Are you all right James?"

"Yes, fine," I whispered. "I'll tell you later."

Mr Wilson sat next to the Headmaster. They exchanged a few words with the odd glance in our direction. The meal was eaten mostly in silence. Alan looked down his nose at us, as usual, in mute disapproval and we, as usual, ignored him. I believe he sensed, feared and respected our growing strength.

After we were allowed to leave the dining room, we met at our favourite spot near the gorge.

"Peter, it's another secret."

"Yes James?"

"I wasn't ill this morning."

"You *did* look ill."

"I know, but it was all makeup and pretence, so the rest of the school wouldn't ask questions. Did I ever tell you about Tommy Tailwind?"

"Tommy Tailwind, who's that?"

"He's a Hawker Hurricane fighter, just back from Dunkirk. His compass didn't work properly and he knew why, but no one else did, so they asked me to ask him."

"And did he tell you?"

"Oh yes, it's all being sorted."

"That's brilliant. I wish I could be of more help."

"You can have no idea how much help you are already. Having someone I can trust, to talk to and know it won't go any further is great. I think I'd explode otherwise."

I looked at him for a few moments.

"There's something else Peter. We may have to use the moves your Dad taught us, at any time and without warning. I'll need your help then."

"You mean there's still a risk of another gunman trying to kill or kidnap you."

"I'm afraid so. We must always be ready for a surprise attack or ambush."

Peter was probably the smallest boy in the class, yet his level gaze and confident bearing spoke volumes. The 'would be bullies' invariably backed down. I recognised the look, which was now directed at a distant enemy, as yet unseen, but anticipated.

"We'll be ready."

Chapter 22

The rest of the summer term passed without incident, or the expected invasion. Peter and I returned to our homes and families for the summer holidays. As usual Mr Wilson came with me. He took his duties very seriously, as the perceived state of danger remained unchanged. I hoped that Peter would be able to come down for my birthday in August, after which, we could travel back to school together.

A few days before my birthday, Papa asked if I would talk to an enemy aircraft which had been captured intact. Our scientists had examined it in detail, but so far had failed to uncover its secrets.

"James, are you quite sure you can manage this? It's an enemy bomber, quite different to the fighter and brand new."

"I'll be fine Papa."

We flew to Duxford in a Dominie which collected us from the lawn below the terrace. Papa came with us to lend authority and speed of action to my hoped for discoveries. As we circled Duxford prior to landing, I noticed many more unfamiliar aircraft, some still with their foreign markings.

We were shown into a private office where two scientists attempted an explanation of what they were looking for, but couldn't find; difficult when I was still trying to master long division. However, even at that age, I had good spatial awareness and could easily imagine things in three dimensions.

Papa realised this and did his best to translate the information I needed to uncover the aircrafts secrets.

"James, do you remember when you were in the dungeon under the school and you had to find your way with a torch?"

"Yes Papa."

"If Peter was holding his torch and yours went out, do you think you would be able to find him?

"Yes Papa; I would walk towards his torch."

"That's right James. Now imagine you were an aircraft trying to land on a runway in the dark. If there was a searchlight shining down the runway, you would be able to land by flying down the brightest part of the beam."

"Yes Papa, but wouldn't the light be shining in my eyes?"

"It certainly would James, but if the light was invisible, like a wireless signal and you had an instrument which could see it, that would work, wouldn't it."

"Yes Papa, I think so."

"James, we think the aircraft we want you to look at uses an invisible beam to find its targets like airfields or factories, but we haven't been able to find the instrument that sees the beam and we need to find it so we can stop them."

"We've looked everywhere," said one of the scientists.

I could feel the urgency and frustration.

"I'll do my best Papa."

"Yes James, I know you will. The aircraft is called a Junkers 88 and we think it was over here testing the device. They would be relying on it to guide them home, but as you can see, they still managed to get lost. So James, if you're ready to have a look, it's in one of the hangars."

"Yes Papa, I'm ready."

I tried to put on a brave face, but with dark memories of the Me 109, I was a little apprehensive.

The hangar doors were rolled back and the three of us were left on our own.

"Well James, there it is, our own brand new Ju88. So what do you think?"

I tried to analyse my first impressions. It was big. Behind the large tapered wings stretched a long slim fuselage, ending in a large single fin. The crew compartment and two enormous engines stuck out in front, giving rise to its nick name, 'three fingers'. It had large wheels and the sunlight reflected spots of light from the facetted Perspex nose.

I would never think of it as beautiful, but it bore itself with a handsome practicality. All I could think of saying was,

"It's nice."

Papa smiled.

"I've just had an idea. We could use it in films. If you think it would help, ask it if it would like to be a film star."

"Yes Papa."

Mr Wilson, ever watchful, was checking it for anything which could cause harm. I walked towards the tail and gently ran my hand along its body. I'm not sure what I expected, but it certainly wasn't the voice of a small girl.

"I'm lost."

I drew my hand away in surprise and turned to Papa who was watching. He raised his eyebrows and put his head to one side in a questioning gesture.

"It's all right Papa," and we both smiled.

This time I placed both hands on the fuselage near the tail. Again I could hear the voice of a small frightened girl some years my junior.

"I'm lost. I can't find my way home."

"It's all right, you're safe here. I'm James, what's your name?"

"My name? I have no name, only a number."

"My Papa has a rock that sits on his desk. It looks just like your front window. He calls it a crystal. Can I call you Crystal?"

"Crystal? I like that name, Crystal. Yes James, you can call me Crystal. James, are you my friend?"

"We're all your friends Crystal, but we need your help. Can I sit in your pilot's seat?"

"Yes James, come and sit."

I pointed at the ladder which gave access to her crew compartment. Mr Wilson walked over to hold it while I climbed the widely spaced rungs. I struggled up into the airy crew space, full of windows and machine guns, which poked out in all directions. He noticed my worried look.

"It's all right James, they've been unloaded."

It still smelled of paint, with just a hint of something else which at the time I couldn't place. There was a splendid view from the pilot's seat through the front window, but I was there to discover, not to admire.

"Crystal, how did you get lost?"

"We turned the wrong way and lost the path."

"What was the path like Crystal?"

"Like a big road, in the sky, but we lost it. We listened, couldn't find. James, please help."

This wasn't going as easily as I'd hoped. The sun was heating up the inside of the aircraft and I was feeling very uncomfortable.

"Crystal, you said you listened. Was it a sound path?"

"Yes James, a sound, different sounds."

"Crystal, how do you hear the path?"

"Ilse hears it."

I looked at Mr Wilson who was sitting on the floor near the entrance hatch. Of course, he was only able to hear my side of the conversation, but could still get a rough idea of the flow.

"Sir, she says Ilse hears it. Does that make sense?"

"If Ilse is spelt ILS, it could stand for Instrument Landing System, possibly the same, or a similar device."

I had to think carefully before I asked my next question.

"Crystal, does Ilse help you land when you can't see the runway?"

"Yes James."

I looked down and nodded at Mr Wilson who replied with a raised thumb. I ran my hands over the panel of instruments; stopping at what I guessed was the position indicator.

"Crystal, is this Ilse?"

"No James," she said with laughter in her voice. "That only tells my pilot what she's doing. She's behind you, in the radio."

I turned round to look at the radio. It was a stack of grey metal boxes with unmarked knobs and dials. I scrambled round to sit in the radio operators seat.

"You're getting warmer," she giggled, enjoying the game. I

joined in, pointing to one box after another while Crystal shrieked with laughter, telling me I was warm or cold or freezing. I noticed one of the boxes differed from the rest by having a diagonal yellow line painted on it. I left it until last. As I slowly moved my hand towards it, she was shouting,

"Warm, hot, hotter, burning, you've found it James, you've found Ilse. That was a good game."

"Yes it was. Thank you Crystal, I enjoyed that game.

I turned to Mr Wilson.

"Sir, have you got a pencil?"

"Should have James," and he rummaged through his pockets until he found a small one, which he handed up to me. I carefully pencilled a cross on the box.

"Sir, I need some air."

I was dripping with perspiration and beginning to feel groggy.

"We've found what we came for so let's go. I'll guide your feet on the ladder."

Papa was sitting in a folding canvas chair, shaded by the hangar wall. He stood up as we emerged from the aircraft.

"We've found it Papa. I marked it with an 'X'."

"Oh well done James, well done."

He waved to the two scientists who were waiting outside. Mr Wilson, prepared as ever for all eventualities, handed me a small towel to dry my face.

"We both need a long cool drink, but we better brief the scientists first."

Papa smiled and brought the scientists forward.

"I believe James has something to tell you."

"We've found the box that hears the beam. It has a yellow line and I've marked it with a cross in pencil."

The scientists looked puzzled.

"We found that box," said the senior one.

"It's their instrument landing system."

"It still is," said Mr Wilson. "But my guess is it's been modified to fulfil the added function of identifying the target beam."

"Well, I don't know," said the scientist. "If you're right, that cross marks the spot where treasure has been buried of immeasurable value to this country. We must dig deeper, so to speak."

Their digging achieved spectacular results, results which altered the whole course of the war in our favour.

Mr Wilson and I managed to get something long and cool, though being wartime; it was a welcome glass of simple tap water.

Before leaving, I returned to the hangar to have a quick word with Crystal.

"Crystal, my Papa is so pleased with our little game, he asks if you would like to help in making a film. You could be a film star."

"Yes James. That will be fun. Do I have to drop bombs? I don't like bombs."

"Don't worry Crystal, it's all pretend. Goodbye and perhaps I'll see you at the cinema."

Two years later, the whole country saw her on screen.

We returned in the waiting Dominie, stopping off at Northolt so Papa could visit the Air Ministry and set in train all that would be required to exploit our recently acquired knowledge. The lawn in front of our terrace was still dry and firm, so we landed in the same place from where we had taken off earlier in the day.

Neither of us had eaten since breakfast, but cook managed to work her magic, even supplying some home made lemonade. I can remember the clink of the beads holding the protective net in place against the glass jug.

I also remember my father gently pointing out that even though my visit to Duxford had been markedly successful, joining our civilised company for the evening meal would be much enhanced by a wash and change of clothes.

It was while washing that I remembered what the faint and until now unidentified smell had been in the Ju88. It was the pink carbolic soap we used at the school, the soap I had used to wash off the gunman's blood.

Chapter 23

Midge had flown off to join the Air Transport Auxiliary. It was upsetting not being able to say goodbye and perhaps because of this, my birthday turned out to be a more subdued affair than the one a year ago. I had hoped Peter would be with me too, but all non-essential travel was discouraged.

There were many more patients in the hospital, mostly suffering from burns of various degrees. I was allowed to speak to them and do small tasks, under the supervision of the ward sister. One patient I remember in particular was the pilot of an enemy bomber, another Ju88. I suspect our meeting was arranged by Papa, but I can't be sure. The pilot spoke very good English, having been educated here.

"I have a son about your age. You look very like him."

He showed me a photo of a fair haired boy in shirt and shorts, standing smiling at the camera, his eyes screwed up against the bright sunlight. Behind him was a dense forest, the tops of the trees cut off by the edge of the photo. He looked like the brother I didn't have. I smiled and nodded, but couldn't think of anything to say. Before I left him he stretched out his hand, which I held.

"Please don't think too unkindly of us. We're not all Nazis. We only want this silly war over, so we can go back to our families."

His last words to me were indeed strange. His eyes glistened as he looked round, almost furtively before whispering.

"Keep up your good work."

I told Papa, though it felt like a betrayal. He told me it wasn't important and I shouldn't let it worry me. Later events proved this pilot more friend than enemy. We would meet again.

My father had been given a date to report to the ATA and my mother would be following a short time later. Papa was spending more time at the Air Ministry, so now there were more people I knew at school than at home. I was glad to be heading north, not a situation I had anticipated.

An RAF Dominie was dropping off an urgent case at the lawn below the terrace, so a lift north was arranged for myself and Mr Wilson. The school had become my second home.

It was good to see Peter again. Even Alan gave a condescending sniff. We were now moving to the sixth class and were no longer new boys, but we had a new teacher. She looked little older than the senior pupils, very kind but in constant fear of 'old crow' and the Headmaster. In time, she proved an excellent teacher, building on the educational foundations laid in previous years.

The Ju88 pilot's words, 'keep up your good work' kept running through my mind, so eventually I spoke to Peter at our usual meeting place and asked him what he thought they meant.

"Do you think he meant your ability to talk to aircraft?"

"That's what I'm afraid of."

"Let's think. You were working in the hospital, so at best; he could've been referring to that. At worst, he meant your special ability to hear the innermost secrets of aircraft and that opens a whole new can of worms."

"I know and I don't want to think about it."

"But we should James. Suppose the enemy does know and is still intent on your kidnap. Dad says 'prepare for the worst and hope for the best', so let's do that. We're getting better at the jujitsu, you know, the unarmed combat. If we stick together we can take on anyone."

"I hope you're right Peter."

The following Saturday, bombs dropped on London. It looked like a navigational error, but was directly related to what I had discovered in the enemy bomber at Duxford. The scientists had worked quickly. It provided the excuse needed to mount a reprisal raid on the enemy's capital.

Weeks turned to months. The threat of invasion receded and I managed to relax a little. Peter and I spent even more time practising our unarmed combat, our improvement confirmed, as no one else was willing to join in. It settled into the weekly routine of lessons, sports and leisure. It was this same routine, or rather the breaking of it, that first alerted us to trouble, big trouble.

Squads of the Home Guard provided round the clock armed protection as part of the general security of the school and grounds. Their shifts changed at midnight, eight in the morning and four in the afternoon. The afternoon squad comprising eight soldiers would arrive in one of the buses sent from Perth to collect the day pupils, but on a certain Wednesday in mid November, they arrived an hour early and on foot. The RAF policeman at the main gate checked their papers and, as usual, phoned the school office to say that they'd arrived.

It was standard procedure to report anything out of the ordinary, no matter how trivial. Later I was told about the call, which was to the effect that an unfamiliar squad of Home Guard had arrived, earlier than usual, marching smartly and looking remarkably young.

I was first aware of something amiss when, with a brief knock at the door, a smiling Matron entered our classroom.

"Good afternoon Miss. I wonder if I could borrow James and Peter."

"Certainly, James, Peter, off you go with Matron."

"Yes Miss," we chorused, as we made our way to the door.

As soon as we were out of the classroom, Matron's whole demeanour changed. I could feel her fear and concern.

"There's a squad of enemy soldiers near the school. They're disguised as Home Guard. We have to get you away James and we'll need your help Peter."

"I'll help all I can."

"Good, now do you trust Mr Wilson?"

Peter and I stood still, looking at each other.

"Your silence speaks volumes. Is there another way into the secret passage?"

"Yes Matron, we can get there from the dorm."

"Then off you go, quick as you can. Keep hidden, or it can find a way out of the school grounds then even better. We manage here somehow."

"Yes Matron."

We scampered up the main staircase to the first landing and the short flight to the turret. I could hear the main door opening with its characteristic judder, then a man's voice in cultured English.

"Good afternoon Matron. I'm looking for one of your pupils, James Edwards. I'm his uncle, just wanted to say hello."

"Oh now, James will be in class. Come away through to the kitchen, both of you. The kettle's on for a nice warming cuppa. You can have a seat while I find him."

That's all we heard as we shot up the turret stairs and into the dorm. Peter ran through to the toilets for the brush while I grabbed a torch from my locker. In a matter of seconds, the hatch was moved and the rope hooked down.

"Up you go James; I'll put the brush back."

I scrambled up into the loft space, closely followed by Peter. Once the rope was hauled up and the hatch back in place, we paused to take stock. Daylight was fading fast, so we had to be doubly careful not to fall, or in any way make our presence known.

"Let's check our pockets for anything useful. What've you got Peter?"

"One hankie, used, a penknife, a gobstopper and a catapult."

"A catapult? They're armed with rifles and bayonets."

"I might get lucky."

"You mean like David and Goliath?"

"Exactly."

I rummaged through my own pockets. I had another hankie, a conker on a piece of string, the torch, a small pencil and tuppence for the phone. The phone, of course, the emergency number and I patted my top pocket which crackled. The piece of paper was still there.

gave me a phone number so I could contact Papa's
lergency. If we can reach the observer post, they
support to lift us out."

can safely call this an emergency," said Peter with
statement.

We moved towards the other end of the roof space, urgency
tempered by the realisation that there was now no room for error,
feeling the joists with our feet before each step and supporting
ourselves on the sloping rafters to our right. Light filtered through
the skylight, from the after glow of sunset.

Peter was tying the rope in a bowline below his arms.

"If you give me the paper James, I'll take it up to the
observation post."

"Thanks for the offer Peter, but I have to do this myself."

"At least take the rope."

"No, there's no time. I'll be all right."

I felt for the metal ladder and eased myself from the skylight.
I was shaking with fear and cold. A slate came loose, skittering
down the roof and disappearing. A long time later I heard it break
on the rocks far below. There are times one can have too much
imagination. I eased myself up a rung at a time until my head
cleared the parapet of the tower. A powerful torch shone in my
face.

"Who the hell are you?"

"I'm James Edwards and I need your help."

"Come on then James, I'll help you over the wall."

"No, I have to go back. Please listen. There's a piece of paper
in my top pocket. Please take it. I can't let go. There's a phone
number on it."

He lifted it out and shone his torch on it.

"I see it."

"Please phone the number and tell my grandfather, Sir James
Nettleton, that the school is under attack from enemy soldiers.
They're trying to kidnap me."

"Are you sure?"

"Please just phone. Tell him we need lifting out and I'm making for the airstrip with a trusted friend. I'll signal the aircraft by waving a torch in a circle. Hurry, we don't have much time."

I started making my way back down the ladder as a shot rang out, followed by two more.

"Good grief, I'll get on to it straight away. Good luck."

If anything, going down was worse than climbing up, feeling for each rung until Peter grabbed my arm.

"It's all right, I've got you."

"Thanks Peter, let me get my leg through. That's me, fine."

"Are they phoning up for an aircraft? I hope it's an Anson."

"I don't care what it is as long as it's got RAF roundels. Let's go."

Peter had taken off the rope and coiled it over his shoulder. It was an unspoken statement. Calculated risks must be taken to save time. We made our way into the loft of the keep, dropped into the small room and down the spiral stair. Neither of us spoke until we were in the dungeon area below the hall.

Peter looked up at the pointed arches.

"I wonder what's happening. Do you think the other soldiers will be outside looking for us?"

"Yes, I do. Come on let's find the well, better not use the torch. The light could be seen through the arrow slits."

Peter found it first and without hesitation climbed onto the ladder and started his way down. I let him get a reasonable way down then followed. It was pitch black, but now we knew what to expect, we could feel our way using our memory and sense of touch. We had to wade the last part and the water was freezing cold. No need for words now. We could hear the waterfall before seeing the slightly lighter shape of the gap in the rock. Peter was feeling around in the stream.

"What are you doing," I whispered.

"Ammunition," he whispered back.

We squeezed through the gap and made our way along the walkway under the falls. Our senses were on full alert as we moved towards the path to the airstrip, using bushes and undergrowth to hide from predatory eyes. An aircraft was approaching from the east. We quickened our pace. The western sky was still light, but the land was in darkness. The aircraft passed overhead and the runway lights were switched on, leaving us easily seen in silhouette by anyone behind us.

A shout in a foreign tongue needed no translation. The light from a powerful torch glinted off a rifle and fixed bayonet. We stood for fractions of a second like rabbits in headlights before taking off as fast as our legs would go towards the runway lights and the approaching aircraft.

We had no chance when it came to speed. Despair and rising panic threatened to overwhelm me as thundering boots drew ever closer.

Chapter 24

Running like mad, I turned to look at Peter whose white teeth were gleaming in the dark. He was smiling.

"Move three!" he shouted and in one fluid movement, turned, lifted and fired his catapult. The missile clanged on metal.

"Bull's eye."

"What's move," but by that time he'd vanished. I looked round, trying to find him and remembering what move three entailed. The pattern of running footfalls changed to skids and scrapes as a foreign oath exploded from the darkness. I tried to position myself to catch the enemy soldier under the ribs as he fell, stupidly forgetting the rifle and bayonet. A huge shadow blocked out the light as something hard clattered the side of my face, knocking me over as the body of the falling soldier pinned me to the ground.

Peter was dragging me free by the legs and pulling me upright.

"Come on, come on, we've got to get away before the others get here."

He was urging me along. Blood was running down my face. I was dazed and could only see with one eye. The aircraft, a twin engined Anson, had landed and was halfway down the runway. We could hear the sound of running feet behind us.

"The torch," yelled Peter.

I fumbled in my pocket, dragged it out, switched it on and frantically waved it in a circle as Peter turned and loosed off another missile. The Anson immediately veered towards us. Rifles cracked in the darkness, a bullet whining uncomfortably close. We ducked under the right wingtip and ran to the already open door where eager hands hauled us aboard. We scrambled up the sloping floor as the access door slammed shut.

"Keep down and hang on," shouted the pilot before swinging the aircraft round and opening the throttles to take off in the opposite direction. From my position on the floor, I could see the crew member who had helped us aboard, wriggle up into the turret. A rattle of fire from the Lewis gun sent muzzle flashes flickering light through the cabin, as we gathered speed, banking to the right over the river Tay and into the enveloping darkness.

At last, we could relax a little, find a seat and strap ourselves in. The pilot's face shone ghostly green from the instrument lights. He turned round, smiled and raised a thumb.

About ten minutes later, we landed at Leuchars and taxied up to the main complex. The pilot and gunner helped us to the watch office where, for the first time since entering the roof space, we were able to see each other. I was shocked and so were the office staff. Several seconds of stunned silence followed as Peter and I turned to each other.

"I've dropped the rope somewhere," said Peter.

If I look like Peter, I thought, no wonder they're staring in shock. He was covered in blood and green algae. He put out a hand to touch my arm. My jacket sleeve was missing.

"Are you all right James?"

"Think so."

The senior officer was the first to react.

"I want blankets and something hot and sweet for these two."

One of the airmen dashed off to fetch the items. The officer put his arms round us.

"Come and sit down. I can't begin to imagine what a ghastly time you've both had."

The airman returned carrying blankets which were quickly wrapt round our shoulders. He was closely followed by a WAAF nurse from sick quarters. She stood for a shocked moment, her hand to her mouth, before recovering her poise.

"It's all right Sir. I'll take over now."

I looked up with my good eye and tried to smile. We were both much wetter than I had thought and small puddles of gory water were forming on the polished floor. She carefully examined our heads, one at a time.

"Wherever the blood is coming from, it's not from head wounds. We'll have a better idea once we've cleaned you up."

Cups of sweet milky tea appeared magically in front of us.

"That'll get some warmth back in your bones," she said and sat watching us. Work in the office had come to a halt. I was aware of someone sobbing quietly. We must look bad.

"Let's get you both to sick bay and a warm bath. Can you walk?" We nodded.

"Oh no you don't," said the senior officer. "You've both had quite enough action for one day."

So saying, he picked me up in his arms with scant thought for what my state was doing to his beautiful uniform.

"Airman, get the other one."

"Sir!"

We were cleaned, cosseted and our wounds such as they were, eased with lotions and sympathy.

The nurse put us to bed in one of the wards and, I believe we drifted off to sleep as soon as our heads touched the pillows. We must have slept round the clock, as it was broad daylight when we woke.

I felt my face to find my right eye bandaged. I could see Peter who was still asleep. His cheek was bruised and a fair sized lump stood out on his forehead. His eyes opened, looking at me.

"You look terrible," He mumbled through swollen lips.

"Look who's talking," I replied with half my mouth. He smiled crookedly and sat up.

"Oh, that's sore."

A nurse stood up.

"Back in a moment."

She returned with a doctor, who pulled up a chair so he was facing us both. He smiled.

"I'm glad to tell you that the blood you were so liberally covered with, belonged to neither of you so, any ideas?"

We looked at each other, but it was Peter who spoke.

"It was dark."

"Fair enough," said the doctor. "The good news is, apart from scratches bruises and abrasions, you're OK but," and he held up his hand, "you've both taken quite a beating. In fact, it would be no exaggeration to say you both look as if a giant has been using you as a football."

He looked at us in turn, a questioning eyebrow raised. We said nothing, but we knew the giant.

"I'll get something made up to ease your pain and help you to sleep. I'd like to keep you here for a few days before you go back to school, which, incidentally has been informed of your rude health, along with your parents." He looked at me, "and of course, your Papa. He says 'well done'."

I turned away to hide my tears, perhaps from tiredness, or relief or maybe because Papa was pleased with what we'd done. Who knows how the mind works?

On Saturday Matron visited the sick bay with the station Medical Officer. She looked as if she had been weeping and it was only through force of will that she didn't start again on seeing us.

"Wounded in action I see. Are the nurses looking after you both?"

"Yes Matron," said Peter. "It all looks worse than it is, just bruises and scrapes."

"Don't minimise it," said the MO. "You've had a traumatic experience and will need to rest up for a few days."

"I'm afraid there's worse to come," said Matron. "The doctor says you're better learning sooner rather than later, so you can come to terms with all that's happened. I've told him everything, so you can safely fill in any gaps."

She sounded so tired, as if the laughter and energy had been beaten out of her. We looked at each other, suspecting the worst.

"I'll tell them if you like Matron," said the MO gently, "though I think it's better coming from you, if you can manage."

Matron nodded and sat up straight, once more in command.

"James, Peter, there's no easy way of saying this, so best get on with it. The Headmaster is dead. He died as he would have wished, a good soldier, facing the enemy, defending the country and people he loved."

She was overcome momentarily with the emotion of the situation, but quickly recovered, dabbed her eyes with her lace hankie and continued as the MO looked on, his face a picture of concern.

"Mr Wilson is in hospital with a leg wound. He lost a lot of blood, but should make a good recovery."

"What happened to the enemy soldiers," said a subdued Peter.

"They're all dead, except for the two you heard entering the front door and they soon will be. I disarmed them and let the SPs deal with them, none too gently, I would imagine. They will no doubt be tried, sentenced and executed."

Peter and I looked at each other trying to imagine our gentle Matron disarming two Nazi storm troopers. It was something else that, for the moment, didn't add up. My mouth was so swollen; I had difficulty speaking, so I left it to Peter.

"What happened to the soldier we bumped in to?"

Matron looked at us, trying to decide how much we should be told. In the end she settled on the unvarnished truth.

"He got tangled up with a coil of rope, dropped his rifle and the bayonet caught the side of his neck, cutting through to the vertebrae. That's why you were covered in so much blood."

Peter looked at his hands, remembering the heavy boot knocking him aside. Sorrow vied with anger and anger won.

"So that's where the rope went. I'm glad he's dead."

Article in a local Berwick-on-Tweed newspaper dated Friday 15th November 1940

Luck ran out for a Dornier reconnaissance aircraft when it was shot down in the early evening of Wednesday the 13th by a local coastal battery. Speculation surrounds the disappearance of part of the crew of four, as only two bodies were found in the wreckage.

Chapter 25

Sunday passed in a dream state, thanks to the Medical Officer's medication. The CO and MO looked in after church parade.

"We'll be sending you back to school tomorrow," said the CO, "where Matron will take care of you. The swellings have gone down and doc's knock out drops should have worn off by then."

The MO smiled and patted my shoulder.

"You've both made a good recovery. You're a couple of tough wee lads right enough."

Our clothes had been taken away and we were wearing borrowed shirts as night wear. Early Monday morning, our clothes were brought back to us, well, most of them. Our jackets had been beyond redemption, but everything else had been cleaned and pressed in the camp laundry.

After a mostly liquid breakfast, we were taken back to the office. It was full of station personnel, all smiling and asking how we were. We had no idea what it was all about, until the CO arrived with the pilot and gunner who had rescued us.

He bent down to speak to us.

"How are you both?"

"Fine Sir," I said.

"Just a bit stiff Sir," said Peter.

"Well, you look a great deal better than when I first saw you. Now I want you to meet the rest of the staff."

He brought us to the front of his desk, I on his right and Peter his left. The chatter died away and everyone looked in our direction.

"I'd like to introduce you to two remarkable young men. This is James and this is Peter. I say young men and I mean precisely that. They may have gone to school that morning as boys, but when we rescued them from a force of Nazi thugs, they were men, bloodied in every sense of the word, as my office staff will be quick to assure you. What none of you know and what the are too modest to tell you, is this. In the darkness of last Wednesday evening, they were attacked by an armed Nazi thug, one of a squad of eight masquerading as members of the Home Guard. Did they turn and run? Certainly not, they turned and fought. What's more, they won. The blood they were covered in was not theirs," and he wagged his finger, "but was shed by their vanquished foe. In a way, I wish we could send back their attacker, to tell those bent on enslaving our nation, that if you tweak the lion's tail, even the cubs will turn and bite."

There was some applause before the CO continued.

"You will have noticed they didn't emerge unscathed, but these are honourable scars to be worn with pride. In time of war, many brave acts go unreported and for security reasons this whole incident must be kept under wraps. However," and he patted our shoulders, "we feel your bravery is an example to us all and we would like to show our admiration by making you both honorary members of RAF Leuchars."

We looked up and smiled, wincing slightly from the painful bruising. The WAAF nurse came forward amid more applause and presented us each with an RAF jersey. They must have been made for the smallest of WAAFs as they were almost small enough to fit. What made them special was the miniature pair of RAF wings sewn on the left breast. It is now treasured and kept for special occasions.

Our possessions were in two piles on the COs desk. While we were stuffing them into our trouser pockets, Peter turned to the CO.

"Sir, my gobstopper is missing. Oh, it's all right, I must've used it as ammunition."

"Oh, well done Peter," said the CO. "Did you all hear that? Peter downed the Nazi with a gobstopper."

I turned to Peter.

"You said you might get lucky and you did."

There was much laughter in the office. Now clad in our new

uniforms with the sleeves rolled up clear of our hands, the CO made his closing remarks.

"Now we have to get the two of you back to school and we," he said looking at the crowd of airmen and airwomen, "have to get on with the war."

He then turned back to us.

"Your pilot and gunner insist that as they snatched you away from school by air, it's only right that they should return you in the same manner."

He stooped to shake our hands.

"I'm proud to have met you both. Come back and see us again."

"Thank you Sir," we replied. "We'd like that."

We flew back in the same Anson, this time in daylight. We noticed two figures as we approached to land on the school airstrip. They were standing at the end of the path leading to the school. I recognised Matron, but not the other.

We taxied back along the strip, turned in to wind and stopped opposite them. It was only yards from the spot where we had been hauled aboard five days ago. Matron was dressed in black, a grim reminder of how the school and our lives had changed.

The pilot and gunner stood by the left wing tip, the Anson's engines ticking over noisily behind them. There followed an awkward pause, as everyone waited to be introduced. Matron wasn't about to stand on ceremony, came forward, bent down, hugged us both and kissed our bruised cheeks. She was the only constant in our changing world. It was the pilot who spoke first.

"We dragged the pair of them off last Wednesday, so we felt it only fair that we bring them back the same way."

The man with Matron spoke to the airmen in a voice easily heard in the next county.

"We're very grateful for your help. Jolly good show I say."

He pointed at the Anson, then himself.

"RAF in the last lot, fighters."

"Please excuse us," said the pilot. "We'll need to get back. It's been an honour meeting you all, especially these two," pointing at us.

"Jolly good, keep up the good work," boomed the newcomer in the loudest voice I'd ever heard.

"We'll look after them now, thanks again."

The Anson took off and circled to the left low over the school. It dipped a wing and the pilot and gunner waved. We all waved back, watching it get smaller as it returned to Leuchars and the war.

"This is Mr MacAlpine," said Matron. "He will be our new Headmaster and your protector James while Mr Wilson is in hospital."

"I'm pleased to meet you both. Now we should get back to the protection of the school before the pair of you freeze to death. We have much to discuss," he boomed with only a slight reduction in volume.

He walked smartly ahead. We followed in his wake, on either side of Matron, firmly holding her hands. She told us of the changes that would affect us as we walked back to the school.

"The school has been closed temporarily, as a mark of respect to the Major and everyone has been sent home. I've made up beds for you downstairs, so I can keep and eye on you both. You need to rest and recuperate."

"We're feeling fine Matron, honest," said Peter.

"I'm sure you are, but you've been through worse than you realise, physically and mentally, so you'll do as I say, please.

"Yes Matron."

"No more thoughts on secret passages for the moment. Mr MacAlpine is on your side," she whispered, "and you want to keep it that way. He's not a man to cross, believe me."

He wasn't as tall as Mr Wilson, yet he emanated a feeling of height and physical strength. Peter wasn't one to be cowed by anyone, yet even he gazed on the broad shoulders and straight back with something akin to awe.

My feelings on entering the school were in sharp contrast to my first impressions over a year ago. Now it felt cold and dark. The happiness had gone with the Major's passing.

Mr MacAlpine entered the Headmaster's study and closed the door. It felt symbolic, the closed door, yet the situation would prove more complex. We followed Matron to the small room next to the kitchen.

"Come away in. There's some broth on the stove. That's a cure for most things. James will tell you that Peter. Sit yourselves down and I'll get a couple of bowls with not too many bits in. I see the RAF looked after you well then?"

"Yes Matron, they were very kind."

Lunch was extended, as our mouths were still rather tender and we were inclined to dribble; most embarrassing. Mr MacAlpine looked in as we were clearing up. I don't know where he had lunch, or indeed if he had any at all.

"Three o'clock in my office, you too Matron; I want to acquaint these two with the latest information and you can help with that."

He closed the door without waiting for a reply. We looked at Matron for an explanation.

"He doesn't make requests, he gives orders and woe betide anyone who questions them, or fails to carry them out to the letter. I fear many tears will be shed before the school adjusts to his ways."

Peter and I looked at each other. I said nothing but thought 'no Peter, don't even think that. We need him'.

At three o'clock to the second, Matron knocked on his office door.

"Come,"

I could've sworn the door shook. We trooped in and sat as indicated, in chairs opposite the desk. It was our first chance to look at the face that would be running the school. It was dominated by a nose that had come in fast contact with something hard, like a gun sight or fist. Ginger hair, greying at the sides connected to a beard, neatly trimmed to a point. Bushy eyebrows met in a vertical groove above green eyes; green? Is that possible? But green they were.

"Not a pretty sight is it James, but it's the only one you'll see. Lord knows I have many faults, but two faced is not one of them."

"I'm sorry Sir, I didn't mean to stare."

"To be good agents, you must be able to observe, without making it obvious."

We all sat up and took notice.

"That's better, cards on table, let's talk."

Chapter 26

He sat back in his chair, looked through the window at the view towards the Tay and ran a forefinger along a scar on his left cheek. We waited for him to speak. In his presence, one only spoke when spoken to.

"I have been talking to several people on the telephone. The Commanding Officer at Leuchars is singing your praises. He tells me that you Peter, downed a Bosch storm trooper with a catapult and a gobstopper. Well, did you?" he roared.

"It was dark Sir. I hit something metal."

"You did indeed," said Mr MacAlpine in a quieter tone.

"With this?"

He smiled; a rarely used expression and with a conjurer's sleight of hand, produced the missing gobstopper. Peter's face lit up in surprise and admiration.

"Yes Sir," and was about to reach for it when Mr MacAlpine raised an admonishing palm.

"Exhibit 'A' I believe," and placed the gobstopper on his desk.

"Exhibit 'B', if I'm not mistaken, is in your pocket. Hand it over."

"Yes Sir," said Peter, hastily dragging the catapult from his trouser pocket and laying it on the desk.

Mr MacAlpine examined it with the eye of the connoisseur, turning and checking the strength of the elastic, adapted from an old inner tube.

"A fine weapon, crafted by a true artist. Who made it?"

"My father Sir."

"Ah, of course. Normally I would confiscate this and you would be soundly thrashed for owning and using it, that is, in times of peace, but we are at war. So I say damn fine show. Now here's what we do."

He leant down behind his desk and picked up a sheet of brown paper and some string. He put the catapult and the gobstopper on the brown paper, wrapping it in a parcel and tying it securely.

"When you return to your dorm, you put this in your trunk, where it will be safe and out of sight. Take it home with you at the Christmas holidays and give it to your father for safe keeping. From now on it's one of your most treasured possessions. In years to come, you can tell your children how you downed a Nazi with it, a Nazi who was trying to kill you and your friend."

He handed it to Peter who carefully cradled it on his lap.

"If I see it again you're in big trouble, understand?"

"Yes Sir and thank you."

Mr MacAlpine consulted notes on his desk and looked directly at me. He was the most terrifying man I had ever met.

"I have been speaking to your grandfather who has charged me with your protection and how the blazes," he bellowed, "am I supposed to do that with you taking nocturnal perambulations on a sloping roof a hundred feet above the nearest bit of terra firma, eh?"

The windows shook and so did I.

"However, I realise it was a tricky situation and risks had to be taken, but never again, right?"

"Right Sir," I mumbled. "Sorry I can't talk properly, my mouth Sir."

"Of course, of course, your battle scars, well done both of you. Now I bet you're wondering what else happened last Wednesday, when you were shinning up ropes, along roofs and through secret passages and you needn't look so surprised. We're not fools."

He looked at his notes.

"Let's see, you pair were making your way up to the dorm, while Matron was enticing two of the soldiers in to her lair, where she trussed them up, before handing them over to the station police," looking sideways at Matron, "and she won't tell us how."

Matron sat up straight and returned Mr MacAlpine's stare.

"A lady has her secrets."

He almost smiled, before turning his attention back to us.

"You climbed into the roof space and made your way towards the old keep, right?"

"Yes Sir."

"Now boys, I don't want to labour the point, but I could get most upset if I suspected you of withholding potentially useful information. I said 'cards on the table', so let there be no doubt of our relationship. I am the Headmaster, here at the instigation of Sir James Nettleton, your grandfather. I belong to the same organisation, like Peter's father and of course the pair of you in an honorary capacity. There are others similarly employed for your safety James, with me so far?"

"Yes Sir."

"Then answer me truthfully. Had you previously explored the roof space and the secret passage and if so when?"

I let Peter answer.

"Yes Sir, about a year ago, not long after we arrived at the school. It was at the Headmaster's request."

"Does Mr Wilson know?"

We had to think for a moment before Peter answered.

"Sir, we told him about the cave behind the waterfall and he may know about the secret passage, but we've said nothing about the roof space."

"Good, good, now did you notice anything unusual in the roof space, for example, above the room that he uses?"

Peter looked at me and I nodded.

"There was a hatch in the ceiling, similar to the one above my bed."

"Anything else?"

"Yes Sir. Above the hatch, copper wires were stretched between rafters and roof trusses."

"Excellent," and he added something to his notes.

"Then you made your way to the skylight, climbed up the ladder and alerted the observers on the tower, giving them a piece of paper with a telephone number on it. Is this it?"

"Yes Sir."

He handed it back to me.

"You must still keep it with you at all times in the top pocket of your uniform jacket. Matron, replacement jackets are organised?"

"Yes Sir," said Matron.

Again Mr MacAlpine paused, consulted his notes and read the following.

"The observer on the tower phoned your grandfather, Leuchars was alerted and the Anson dispatched. The observer also contacted the main gate and the Nissen hut on the airstrip, warning the real Home Guard to stay out of sight, as they could be mistaken for the enemy and get shot.

I'm told shots were heard coming from the other side of the river. Is that correct?"

"Yes Sir, one shot, then two close together."

He made another note and turned to Matron.

"Shots close together would suggest a pistol, but the Home Guard use bolt action rifles. Who would have a pistol?"

"The Major had several pistols," said Matron. "There was one beside him when, when we found him."

She fell silent, gazing at the floor. Mr MacAlpine pretended not to notice and continued piecing together the activities of that evening of carnage.

"I'm told Mr Wilson belongs to a Christian sect that forbids the taking of life, so won't carry a gun," adding sarcastically. "I suppose that's because he manages quite well with a throwing knife."

I got the impression that what Mr MacAlpine knew of Mr Wilson was not to his liking.

"However, is it possible that Mr Wilson was carrying a pistol, even though no firearms were in his possession when found, so any thoughts on the matter?"

I only hesitated for a moment as I realised I was being tested to see if I would volunteer information Mr MacAlpine no doubt already possessed, so I told him about the first kidnap attempt and the gunman's vanishing pistol. He nodded.

"So he may well have been carrying a pistol, now most likely in the river. I shall take a turn round to the hospital, once he's well enough to talk. It should be interesting to hear his version of events, though I doubt if it will be the truth."

He cast a sly glance in Matron's direction.

"Perhaps we could slip him a shot of sodium pentothal. That would do the trick, eh Matron?"

I'd no idea what he meant, but Matron looked at him as if he'd said something rude. He nodded.

"Maybe not."

He lifted a larger piece of paper.

"I've made a diagram of where the bodies were found and following the trail of blood, where Mr Wilson was most likely shot. Give him his due, he's a tough resourceful character, found a handy piece of rope," he looked pointedly at Peter, "made a tourniquet to slow the bleeding enough to crawl to the Nissen hut and get help. By that time he was the only one left alive outside."

We couldn't bring ourselves to look at the diagram with its bodies pencilled in, not today.

"Sir," said Matron. "I should get these two a bite to eat and ready for bed. They've had a long day."

"Quite right, quite right, enough for one day, I've plenty here to be going on with. Don't go spoiling them now."

"Mr MacAlpine, have they not earned a bit of spoiling?"

He looked up sharply.

"Aye Matron, indeed they have. Well done boys, sleep sound. If anyone else should come calling Matron and I will sort them out, right Matron?"

"Right Sir," and added in a tone of uncharacteristic menace. "I would welcome the opportunity."

Pitmeddan Castle School,
PERTH, Scotland.
27th Nov. 1940

Dear Sir James
This is an initial report concerning the incident on
the 13th, pieced together by myself and Matron from
the evidence collected on the following day, Mr
Wilson's account given to me in hospital and the
report from your grandson James and his friend
Peter.
The squad of eight enemy soldiers arrived at the gate
lodge at 3.00pm. They bore the uniform and arms of
the Home Guard and carried the correct papers which
the guard on duty examined. Small details alerted his
suspicions, so he phoned the office and the
Headmaster told him to let them in as normal. The
Headmaster sent Matron to warn James and Peter
before informing Mr Wilson of the situation.
The enemy squad divided themselves into two groups,
six to secure the airstrip and two to search the
school. Matron somehow rendered the two in the
school harmless as James and Peter made their way
to the observer post and raised the alarm enabling
help to be sent from Leuchars through your own
office and warning the real Home Guard to stay out
of sight. I believe the Headmaster then armed himself
with a pistol, crossed the bridge and was surprised by
one of the soldiers who shot him. Though mortally
wounded he managed to get off two shots killing the
soldier before he could reload. Those were the shots
heard at the observer post and served to kick off the
whole battle. In the ensuing confusion, the enemy
could easily have shot each other.
It may be significant that on that day Mr Wilson was

teaching while dressed in black. I'm certain he was carrying the pistol that disappeared during the first kidnap attempt, but I have no proof. I think he was expecting the Dornier 17 to land that was shot down over Northumberland. When the Anson arrived instead, he had to change plans and sides. He admits to dispatching a soldier with his throwing knife and taking his rifle which he calmly used to pick off the remaining kidnappers as they passed between him and the runway lights. It's rough justice that he copped one of the bullets from the Anson's Lewis gun. There's also the matter of the radiogram discovered by James and the large aerial in the loft space discovered by James and Peter. It could all be quite innocent, but I'm keeping a close eye on it. I must stress that I have no proof concerning my views of Mr Wilson and he may well be the hero as hailed. The soldier who attacked James and Peter was indeed 'hoist with his own petard'. Peter's first missile, which turned out to be his gobstopper, hit the soldier's helmet, tipping it over his eyes and so causing him to trip over the rope. He lost control of his rifle which twisted round so the bayonet caught the side of his neck.

I'll send on a detailed report later, with diagrams showing the positions of the various items of evidence.

Your obedient servant,
George T. MacAlpine, Headmaster.

Chapter 27

Matron's care and tasty food worked wonders, so by Thursday we were allowed back to our dorm. Cuts and bruises were still in evidence, but they didn't bother us. On the contrary, there was an un-stated feeling we were rather proud of them.

The funeral of our late Headmaster took place on the same day. It was as he wished, a simple ceremony for family and close friends, after which he was interred beside his ancestors in the crypt beneath the school chapel. Family consisted of a distant elderly uncle who sent his condolences. Friends were many and varied, from regimental colleagues to all connected with the school.

Matron told Peter and I all about the ceremony, after which, in the privacy of the school office, the family solicitor had read out the will. It was short and simple, leaving the school and estate in Matron's care, to govern or dispose as she saw fit. She spoke to us later.

"I have informed parents and staff that the school will continue without change, as I'm sure the Major would have wished."

The following Sunday there was no service, so Peter and I were allowed in to the chapel to see the Headmaster's memorial stone, carved in granite and set into the floor.

Major John Kenneth Harperson, M.C.
Born 26th May 1895. Killed in action 13th November 1940
....

The closed door of Mr Wilson's room was a constant temptation, so we decided to have a look, only a look without touching anything, but it was locked. If we entered through the roof hatch, it would mean disturbing the copper aerial which would be impossible to get back in the original position. Taking courage and a deep breath we approached the closed door of Mr MacAlpine's study. Peter knocked.

"Come."

We entered and stood in front of his desk.

"Well?"

Peter, as usual spoke for us both.

"Sir, we were thinking."

"That's always a good start, so what were you thinking?"

We were standing on a level with those impossibly green eyes; utterly hypnotic.

"Sir, with Mr Wilson in hospital we thought it would be a good opportunity to have a look inside his room."

"And have you?"

"No Sir, it's locked."

He turned round and grabbed a ring full of keys from a hook on the wall.

"So let's unlock it."

We followed in his wake as he took the stairs two at a time until we were standing outside the door of Mr Wilson's room. He looked at the lock and selected a key which unlocked the door, foreknowledge or luck, he didn't say. Before opening the door he turned to us.

"If Mr Wilson is a good agent he will have left some means of telling him if anyone has been in the room, so observe carefully."

He turned the handle and pushed the door open a few inches. A small piece of paper caught in the door jamb fluttered to the ground. He looked at us, winked and picked it up.

"Now we can have a look inside. Stand next to me and once more observe. Examine the whole room, walls, ceiling, floor and behind the door."

He pointed to a wire that snaked up the wall and round the edge of the ceiling hatch.

"That no doubt connects the copper aerial you observed in the roof space with what appears to be an unusually large radiogram. Hmm, I wonder."

He turned to look at the rest of the room.

"You see the carpet in the middle of the floor?"

"Yes Sir."

"Don't tread on it. Peter, go round the edge and take the corner. James you take this corner, now together, gently peel it back."

A slightly smaller sheet of paper lay beneath the carpet. Mr MacAlpine lifted a corner between thumb and forefinger to reveal a sandwich of more paper.

"What's it for Sir?"

"That boys, will record a print of whatever is placed on top of it, like our feet, which would give Mr Wilson a good clue as to who has been in his room, snooping round uninvited."

"Wow," said Peter.

"We have enough. Let's go," and he ushered us out. Before locking the door, he took the piece of paper from his pocket, wet it with his tongue and stuck it back in place.

"Right you two, my study, now and if you look as guilty as that, you'll never make good agents."

We followed him to his study and waited until he sat at his desk.

"Sit, sit," he said pointing to a couple of chairs, so we sat and waited.

"How old are you now?"

"Ten Sir."

"And it's my job to make sure you reach eleven," he mused, more to himself than us.

He opened a file, lying on his desk. He was wearing a pair of half moon spectacles which he alternately peered through at the file and over the top at us. He took them off and tapped the file with them.

"This is all about you, both of you. Your lack of size and strength has obviously been balanced by great resourcefulness and courage. I'm impressed."

He sat for another full minute staring at the file before coming to a decision.

"We shall make a pact. My part is this. I'll help whenever possible, to make you better agents. I'll hold nothing back. Any information which will be of help in securing your safety, I will pass to you. Your part is to do likewise and tell me everything you know. We shall have no secrets between ourselves and that includes Matron."

I was relieved to hear that, as we were fond of Matron.

"You will also," he continued, "give me no cause to find fault with either of you. Keep your heads down and never attract undue attention. Is that clear?"

"Yes Sir."

"Break this pact and you won't sit down for a week. Is *that* clear?"

"Yes Sir."

"Fine, anything else?"

"Yes Sir," I said. "When we were in Mr Wilson's room I remembered a dream I had. It would be about the time we first explored the roof space. You remember Peter, I told you at the time, but it wasn't a dream and I'd only thought it was because the noise had wakened me."

"A dream that wasn't a dream about a noise? Try and be more precise. What sort of noise?"

"Sorry Sir, it was the noise of a transmitter key sending a message in Morse."

"Are you absolutely sure it wasn't a dream?"

"Yes Sir, I'm certain."

"Can you remember the exact date?"

"I'm not sure of the date, but the first time was the night after I arrived at the school, then again the night before the rest of the boarders arrived."

Mr MacAlpine shuffled through the papers in the file.

"You arrived on the tenth of August and the next time would be, let me see, the thirteenth. It fits, damn and blast."

It was the first time we had seen him look worried.

"If you hear it again, you must let me know immediately, even if it's the middle of the night, you wake me. I'll probably bark your head off, but I promise not to bite."

"Yes Sir, we'll let you know."

"Good, now the boarders return on Sunday, school recommences on Monday and on Tuesday we have a memorial service for your late Headmaster, a fine officer and gentleman, who died defending his country.

I'll make enquiries and let you know anything else through Matron; dismissed."

When we left the study, he was staring with unfocussed eyes, at the file.

We knew the boarders would be curious about our involvement during the attack. The sound of gunfire and bullets pinging off walls wasn't the sort of thing you could hide from the rest of the school, so we would need an explanation for our absence and injuries. It was easier than expected.

Allan looked with disapproval down his long thin nose.

"Have you two been fighting again?"

"Sort of," said Peter. "It was dark and we got jumped, ended up in hospital and only got back on Monday."

"You look as if you came off worst."

"Oh, I don't know. You should've seen the other chap."

After that there were no more questions.

On Monday morning the whole school, pupils and staff, assembled before Mr MacAlpine in the main hall of the old keep. The area was divided in two with the juniors on one side and the seniors on the other, the aisle between leading from the door to a rostrum against the opposite wall. Something of his reputation had preceded his entrance, as the hall was noticeably quiet as he strode to the rostrum and mounted the two steps.

He was wearing a black cloak over a three piece suit in green tweed, a similar colour to his eyes which were ever moving behind narrow slit like settings.

"My name is MacAlpine and for the foreseeable future I will be your Headmaster. You will address me as Sir, as befits one who carries the King's Commission as an officer, though I have yet to be called gentleman."

There was some suppressed laughter, instantly quelled by his glare.

"My laws are simple, but rigorously upheld."

His voice rose to full volume as he thumped the lectern.

"I demand unquestioning obedience and the truth at all times. Orders given by me, or my staff, will be carried out promptly and to the letter. Failure to obey these laws will result in severe punishment."

Something at the back of the senior lines had caught his attention, as he continued in a deceptively friendly tone.

"I'm surprised I should have to bring this to your notice, but when I or any of my staff are speaking, you keep still and listen."

He stepped from the rostrum and ploughed unhurriedly to the poor unfortunate he noticed earlier, grabbed him by the scruff of the neck and frog marched him to the aisle.

"Heh, you can't do that."

"Oh no?" and he cuffed him round his head hard enough to send him sprawling on the floor.

"I suppose I can't do that either."

"You've made me skin my knee."

"That, my boy, is the least of your problems."

The senior pupil, a well built lad, got to his feet, waving his fists in rage, fear and frustration.

"When my father hears about this."

"Your father isn't the boss here," he roared. "I am and I can do what I damn well like. You will wait outside my study. By all means use the chair," he added sweetly. "It will be your last chance to sit for some time."

He stood still as the boy's footsteps receded to the other end of the school building. He returned to the Rostrum amid a silence broken only by the muted sobbing of one of the juniors. In five minutes, the school had changed.

"Miss McKay will lead us on the pianoforte as we sing hymn forty four, 'Little children wake and listen'."

From then on he was known simply as 'The Boss'.

The Boy Who Talked To Planes

From the confidential diary of Sir James Nettleton

Friday 29th November 1940

The report from Mad Mac arrived this morning. In general I agree with his conclusions regarding the attack on the evening of the 13th. I don't all together hold with his suspicions about Mr Wilson. One must accept, as with the first kidnap attempt that he saw off the enemy in a calm and business like manner. We have much to thank him for.

It's too easy to speculate the Dornier 17 shot down the evening of the attack, was preparing to land and pick up James as part of his kidnap. True there were only two of a crew found at the crash site, leaving room for two more. I still feel it's unfair to assume the other seats were meant for James and Mr Wilson. We must judge him on actions alone. With Mac's beady eye on him at the school, he'll have little chance of stepping out of line there and at the house, his work helping patients through recovery has been beyond reproach.

I couldn't be more pleased with the way James and Peter handled the situation. If the report from the CO at Leuchars referred to service personnel, their names would go forward for official recognition. As it is, no record can be made of the incident. However, I shall personally make sure Winnie knows all the details.

Chapter 28

The following day started with a short service of remembrance for our former headmaster. It was conducted by the same local minister who came every Sunday to the school chapel. He looked surprised by the silence in the hall, possibly due to the sadness of the occasion, but mainly the glowering presence of the Boss.

It may seem a contradiction, but I found the new regime strangely relaxing. I had enough stress in my life outside the school, so the removal of the rowdier element among the pupils was in many ways a relief.

Mr Wilson was allowed home to Ireland to recuperate over the Christmas holidays before returning to the school. He had talked to the Boss in hospital and filled in some of the gaps in our collective knowledge of what happened that night.

I can't say I was looking forward to Christmas. Would there be anyone at home that I knew? Papa, in spite of the many calls on his expertise, had managed to arrange a surprise.

On the last day of term, after the Christmas service, pupils and staff were bussed into Perth, to continue homeward in their separate ways. Alan's chauffeur driven limousine was waiting to collect him at the main door. He would have expected nothing less.

Travel by road or rail anywhere in the country was difficult and time consuming, so the Boss had made arrangements for the parents of children living some distance away, to stay overnight at the school. Peter's mother arrived in the afternoon to collect him, planning to take him home on the following day.

I understood, through a phone call from Papa, that I would be flying south the next day in one of the ATA Ansons. It was therefore with some surprise that I noticed a twin engined aircraft joining our circuit and preparing to land. It was late afternoon and the light was beginning to fade. I was standing with Peter and his mother near the door. The Boss and Matron were a few yards away when they looked up at the sound of the approaching aircraft. An understanding look passed between them.

"James!"

"Yes Sir?"

"Your transport has arrived early. Trot over and find out what's happening."

"Yes Sir."

Peter and I excused ourselves and hurried over the bridge and along the path. By the time we reached the airstrip, the Anson was parked near the Nissen hut and a group of RAF personnel were busy getting it ready for its overnight stay.

The pilot was walking towards us waving. Peter pointed.

"Is that not your Mum?"

"Yes, I think it is." It was my mother, her tall slim figure almost unrecognisable in the bulky flying gear. My feet reacted first, running towards her as I shouted,

"Mummy!" and fell into her arms. I don't know how long I stayed there, holding her as tightly as I could, the realisation of how much I missed her hitting me like an emotional flood. Papa, in his wisdom had known that I would need her now, when I was still recovering from our encounter with the enemy and had arranged her leave to coincide with the school holidays.

We walked back to the school, holding hands, Peter on one side and I on the other. As we passed the spot with its darker patch of gravel, we looked at each other, but said nothing.

Matron showed us to the room we were sharing with Peter and his Mum, where my mother was at last able to shed her padded overalls and leather helmet. She gave a twirl.

"How do you like my new dress?"

Only it wasn't a dress, but her ATA uniform. I felt so proud of her, my Mum, a pilot in the ATA. There was so much I wanted to tell her, but it would have to wait.

"I think you look wonderful," I whispered.

"Thank you kind Sir," she joked. "You may escort me to dinner."

I didn't enjoy the evening meal. Peter was sitting with his Mum and the chatter of voices passed over my head in a barely audible babble. I wanted to go home and feel safe in my own room. I needed time to heal.

The next morning we were ready for takeoff at first light. It was near the shortest day of the year, so every minute of daylight was important, especially as we had several stops to make on the way home, picking up ATA pilots returning to White Waltham. Fortunately the weather had been cold and dry, so we were able to land at our house, allowing one of the other pilots to fly the rest of the way. I noticed the fountain had been dismantled. Just as well with an aircraft the size of the Anson.

Papa had arranged to be at the house for Christmas, using his secure line to keep in touch with the Air Ministry. He spoke to me not long after we landed.

"James, I have an old friend staying not far from here who is rather keen to meet you."

I think he could tell from my lack of enthusiasm that I needed time without pressure, so he nodded knowingly.

"Perhaps we'll leave your visit until the better weather."

It was a strange Christmas. Small details stand out, but the overall memory is of being with my mother. It was like living in a cotton wool cocoon, in the world, but not of it.

I suspect our encounter with the enemy had left my hearing damaged, which added to the general effect. I would spend time at my bedroom window, looking into the far distance where misty hills and trees merged with the sky.

Cook would always find me a tasty morsel in her kitchen. I was happy to sit and watch her work. I was fascinated by her economy of movement, an efficiency born of long experience. She called me her little hero, though I can't say I felt particularly heroic.

In spite of our attempts at security, rumours of our encounter had spread through the hospital staff and like all good stories, had grown in the telling. If some were to be believed, I'd disposed of a whole platoon of enemy storm troopers single handed, using only an ancient oriental technique known to an elite few.

Apart from distributing the Christmas presents, I tended to avoid the hospital wards. It was too embarrassing. The stories became so outrageous and unbelievable, that they eventually dissipated like smoke in the wind. By Easter, everyone had forgotten, much to my relief.

At the end of the Christmas holidays, my mother and I both returned to work. An ATA aircraft collected us as part of the ferrying process, dropping off and picking up pilots at maintenance units, factories and airfields. I felt much refreshed and was happy to return to school, which I was surprised to realise, I had missed.

It was good to get back with Peter, as there was no one else of my own age who could understand what we had been through. The other pupils looked on us as alien beings, to be feared and avoided. It wasn't a pleasant situation.

As the next two terms passed without incident, we were gradually accepted once more as normal class members, well, almost normal. There would always be the furtive whispers and concealed looks, reserved for those who are different. It was something to which we had to adapt. We were changed and could never again be children in the commonly accepted sense.

Mr Wilson came home with me for the summer holidays. The plaster cast on his leg had been removed and with the aid of a couple of sticks, his mobility was almost back to normal. Though his physical work was of necessity reduced, he was ever willing to sit and listen to any patients wishing to unburden themselves of worries, fears and guilt. His small room had become unofficially a trusted place of confession. To my knowledge, that trust was never broken, at least not to anyone in this country.

My father had been granted some leave, so we were able to spend time together, going for long walks and getting to know each other again. I can't remember what we talked about, if anything. Being together was enough.

Our enemy had now turned his attention to the east, which may have had a bearing on Papa once more asking me if I felt able to visit his friend who stayed a short distance to the southwest.

"You remember I told you about an old friend who would like to meet you."

"Yes Papa."

"He's taken up painting."

We were standing on the terrace looking out over our precious sunlit countryside. That, at least, was so far unchanged.

"Your teacher tells me you're good at painting. Perhaps you could give him a few tips."

"I'll try Papa," and so arrangements were made for a visit a few days later.

I travelled with Papa in the back of a large chauffeur driven limousine. I remember it had a flag on the front and policemen stopped the traffic to let us pass.

When we reached the house, we were taken through to a large terrace. At the far edge, a parasol had been set up, shading an easel with canvas attached. A small rounded man sat in one of two folding canvas chairs. He was wearing a straw hat and the most colourful shirt I had ever seen.

Chapter 29

Papa and I walked over to the man at the easel.

"Good afternoon Sir."

I looked up in surprise, as I'd never heard Papa call anyone Sir. After all, he was a Sir himself. I would really have to watch my manners. The man looked up and raised a hand in acknowledgement.

"Sir, this is James, my grandson. James, you can speak freely about your abilities. Our friend is the keeper of all secrets."

He turned to look at Papa and they both smiled.

"I'll leave you to talk."

Papa walked slowly back and sat down on a long bench beside the door. I was left standing beside this strange little man, who positively radiated energy and appeared to be even more important than Papa.

"Come round where I can see you."

I stood next to the empty chair and we looked at each other.

"So you're James, the boy who can talk to planes."

I smiled and nodded, completely tongue tied.

"Sit down. I had the chair put there especially for you."

I sat down.

"Would you like some lemonade? We need something to drink on a hot day like this."

"Yes Sir," I replied. "I'd like that."

"Good!" He nodded and waved to someone near the door, making an almost imperceptible sign with his hand, indicating a drink.

Immediately a small table was placed between us with two glasses of lemonade within easy reach. Whether from memory or hindsight, I can't be certain, but I'm sure his had a golden glow about it.

"Good health to you young man," he said and we touched glasses.

"Thank you Sir and good health to you," I replied, thankful that my voice had returned.

We sat together, youth and age, enjoying the warm afternoon sun. I felt it polite to wait for him to speak, which eventually he did. He turned in his chair to look directly at me.

"James, your grandfather has kept me informed of your activities, including your latest brush with the enemy, from which, I trust, you have fully recovered?"

"Yes Sir, thank you."

He looked at me for a few moments, before continuing.

"I feel obliged to tell you that your ability to understand what you call, plane talk, has been of immense value to our country. In fact, I would go so far as to say that it played no small part in saving our country from invasion."

He nodded in thought.

"Allow me to offer, on behalf of the nation, my grateful thanks, as you must know that history will make no mention of it."

He smiled.

"I know, as I will be writing the history."

Now we both smiled. It was our secret.

He turned back to the canvas which was new and unmarked.

"Your grandfather tells me you are good at painting. What do you think of this one?"

He gave me a mischievous sideways look.

"But Sir, there's nothing there."

"I thought you might say that. True, there's nothing on the canvas, but I've been watching and thinking, so in a way I have started, in here," and he tapped his head. He turned to me again.

"Tell me young man. Have you ever been in trouble for day dreaming?"

"Yes Sir, quite often."

"From you parents?"

"No Sir, just my teachers."

"You have wise parents."

I nodded and we both took another sip of our drinks.

"Let me tell you something young man. One should never belittle or underestimate the value of silent thought, often referred to as day dreaming. It is the necessary forerunner of effective action. You can tell your teachers from me. It's important and I'm a very important person."

"Yes Sir," I said, but of course, I never did tell my teachers.

He looked back at the canvas.

"However, the effective action eludes me for the moment. Where do I start?"

"Sir, when I'm painting, I usually start with the sky."

"The sky, you say? Yes, I see. It makes sense, then what?"

"The bits that stand out and look more important than the rest, like the big tree standing on its own and the lake and those trees over there and there and the boat house, then all the bits in between."

I had become quite animated, forgetting for the moment how much older he was than myself. It looked as if he had forgotten too and we were simply two people trying to capture the beautiful sunlit scene in front of us, or so I thought.

"Let me get this straight young man. First we conquer the sky, then the key points, the important bits and then the land in between. Is that right?"

"Yes Sir, I think that's how I would do it."

"James, I like your analysis. You have a good brain," he said, and laughed.

"I should have you in the war cabinet."

I thought at the time he had a strange way of describing the painting, but realise now that he saw it as an allegory of the war as a whole.

"Off you go now young man and let me get on with the, with the painting."

I slid out of the chair and started walking back to the door.

"Tell your Papa you've been a great help," he called over his shoulder, as he attacked the canvas with great gusto. I remember saying to Papa, in all innocence.

"I think he knows what to do now."

Chapter 30

After the Summer Holidays we moved to the qualifying class, the last one in Primary. In December the Americans became our official allies, joining us in the fight against our common enemies, both in Europe and the Pacific. I knew nothing of this at the time, only meeting my first American airman the following summer when he was admitted to our hospital wing. He gave me some chewing gum, something I'd never experienced until then. It was interesting but I can't say I ever took to it.

During our summer holidays Papa arranged the hoped for visit to Duxford to see Crystal playing her part in the film 'In Which We Serve'. The deck and masts of a Royal Navy destroyer had been built at the side of the airfield. I was told that it was all wood, painted with great skill to look like rust streaked steel. It was exciting watching Crystal fly lower and lower, until she almost scraped the top of the mast.

I spoke to her later. She was understandably full of her latest achievement.

"Did you see how low I was flying, did you?"

"Yes Crystal, you were great."

"Yes I was. Did you see the steep turn at the end when I was right over on my left wing tip. Did you see me, I was brilliant wasn't I?"

"Yes Crystal, you flew with great skill. I think I hear Papa calling me. I'll maybe see you later."

I excused myself, disappointed she should be so boastful. It wasn't the way I had been taught to behave. I was also aware of the danger of believing what others thought you had done. I feared for her and hoped she wouldn't push herself to perform beyond her capabilities.

Later I saw the complete film and was once more impressed by her performance. Even though I knew the truth, it was difficult to accept that it hadn't been filmed in the Mediterranean, but a muddy field near Cambridge. It was another reinforcement of the fact that much of what is fed to us through the media, is illusion.

Whenever possible my parents would arrange for their leave to be taken during the school holidays. Unfortunately, as they were both at the same ATA ferry pool, they seldom managed leave together. In some ways this suited me as I was able to enjoy their exclusive company, one at a time. The staff still looked on me as a pint size slayer of storm troopers, which I'm ashamed to admit, I did occasionally use to my own advantage. At least I knew the truth and the truth would be allowed to emerge in its own good time.

My twelfth birthday was a muted affair, as there wasn't a great deal to celebrate as far as the war was concerned. However, in October the Boss announced a great military victory in North Africa. Our enemy's advance had at last been halted. It was all so far away that its relevance was not immediately apparent, but it was a turning point and worth celebrating.

Peter and I had now moved to the first year of the Senior School. Instead of one teacher for all subjects, we now moved around the school to different departments in places even I had not visited. My work outside the school still continued, much as before but lessons in school normally took priority. It wasn't until the following April that I had any meaningful contact with an aircraft. It was worth the wait and turned out to be the most pleasantly exciting encounter I can remember.

It was shrouded in even greater secrecy than usual. With the Boss' blessing, Mr Wilson and I were flown on the Saturday to my family home in the south. The Pilot of the RAF Dominie had been given orders to take us to Hatfield early on the Monday morning and forget anything else he saw or heard.

Papa joined us at our home, but his response to my questions was always the same.

"Patience James, wait and see. It will be worth it."

We took off at first light on Monday for the short hop to

Hatfield. My last visit was with Midge when she was at the de Havilland factory for a service. I found myself wondering where she was and what she was doing.

Security at Hatfield was rigidly enforced. Even Papa's papers were checked along with profuse apologies from the officer in charge. I thought Papa would be annoyed, but he commended the officer for his diligence in carrying out his orders to the letter. I hoped for a word with old DH4, but with so many armed guards about, I was in danger of getting myself shot if I wandered off on my own, perhaps another time.

We were escorted to one of the hangars which we entered by a small side door. Inside was the strangest small aircraft I had ever seen. It had no propeller and a hole where the engine should have been. It seemed far too close to the ground with a wheel under its nose instead of the tail. Papa stood smiling, his head tilted to the side waiting for me to speak.

"Papa, it has no engine. It has to have an engine so I can hear what it's saying, even if the engine isn't running."

"Ah but it has an engine James. It's behind the cockpit."

He signalled to a mechanic who opened a heat blackened panel to reveal a bunch of large pipes. If this was an engine it certainly wasn't like any I had seen and it smelled different, all very strange. I turned to Papa.

"Can I talk, you know, plane talk?"

I was worried about the presence of the mechanic, but Papa nodded.

"As long as you stay out of the cockpit, try the other side."

I moved round the nose, out of view, sliding my hands gently along her side. She was definitely a she. In fact she sounded remarkably like my mother.

"I'm James," I whispered. "What can I call you?"

"Call me Eve, for I am the beginning and the future. Remember me when you are rich in years, as my kind will be legion and carry you to the ends of the earth."

"I don't understand Eve, but I will remember. Can you fly?"

"Stay and watch. I'll carve my name in sound. Please remember this day."

"I'll remember Eve. Now I must tell Papa. Good luck."

I backed away from this strange aircraft and quietly took Papa's hand. Once we were outside, my grandfather asked.

"What must you tell me James?"

"Can I tell you later Papa? I have to think about it. It's not urgent."

He nodded.

We found the factory canteen where my grandfather could have a seat and a warming drink.

"Papa, it has no propeller. How can it fly?"

"James, before I tell you, please remember that this is absolutely top secret. You must tell no one about it, until it becomes public knowledge."

"Yes Papa."

"Now, let me think. Do you remember before the war when we celebrated Guy Fawkes Night with rockets?"

"Yes Papa."

"This new engine works in much the same way as a rocket, except it doesn't use gunpowder, because that wouldn't last very long. It uses paraffin which mixes with the air sucked in through the big hole in the front. When that burns, it pushes a big jet of hot burning gas from the pipe under the tail and that's what drives it along."

"Papa, did we use paraffin in the picnic stove?"

"You're absolutely right James. That's exactly what we used."

"I thought the smell reminded me of something nice."

Several large black cars were making their way on to the airfield.

"Come on James, with any luck that little aircraft will show us how flying is going to change."

The cars parked near the runway where a small covered stand had been set up with seating for the important visitors, one of whom looked familiar. He was more formally dressed than when we last met.

The hangar doors were rolled back and the small propellerless aircraft I knew as Eve was pushed out on to the apron. Her pilot and mechanics were fussing round her, making sure everything was ready. There was a feeling of expectancy, of something new, a beginning. A low whine, building in pitch to an almost unbearable degree was joined by a deep roar, not unlike our picnic stove, but many times greater. Small spurts of flame appeared at the tail. Moments later the flames turned to a steady roaring transparent blue. Puffs of smoke escaped from the edges of the engine panel. It looked as if it was about to explode, but the mechanics looked unconcerned and they were much closer.

The chocks were pulled away and she started moving to the end of the runway. She stood, as if gathering strength, the heat from her exhaust making the trees at the edge of the airfield blur and shimmer.

With a gathering of sound I had never before experienced, she moved with increasing speed along the runway, lifting off before reaching the assembled dignitaries. With wheels tucked up she passed us flying level building up to a safe climbing speed.

I put my hands over my ears as the small aircraft soared into the steepest climb I had ever seen. This was followed by a most accomplished display of aerobatics. I was impressed. My old painter friend had moved out from the shelter of the stand, a supporting stick in his right hand leaving his left to shield his eyes from the bright sun. I think he was impressed too.

There was such grace and beauty about the display, I was sorry when it ended. After landing, she taxied and stopped in front of the stand, her engine winding down to a faint sigh, followed by the metallic sounds of cooling.

"Did you enjoy that James?"

"Yes Papa, it was great."

I wanted to say more but couldn't find the words. Along with what Eve had said, I found the day strangely moving.

"Have you thought about what you wanted to tell me?"

"Yes Papa."

I told him, as far as I could remember, word for word what she said while standing in the hangar. Papa frowned in puzzlement, but it was Mr Wilson who spoke.

"Why would a modern revolutionary prototype aircraft use such biblical terms? Could it be a reflection of the prayers of those who built her, I wonder?"

Papa nodded, but made no comment.

I had to give voice to my thoughts.

"It was almost as if she was saying goodbye."

"Well I hope not James. There's a great deal more development work to do. You should see the design Mr Geoffrey is working on. It's nothing short of brilliant.

Now, I must get back to the Air Ministry. I'd like you to be back at school before dark if possible. Mr Wilson, you can see to that."

"Yes Sir, we should manage if we leave now."

Three months later Eve fell out of control from a great height and was completely destroyed. The wrong grease had been used on her ailerons and they froze. Fortunately her pilot managed to parachute to safety.

It was one of the small tasks Mr Wilson had talked about, that proved to be more important than anyone could have imagined.

Chapter 31

Three weeks after our visit to Hatfield the school received an urgent phone call asking if I could come to Dyce airfield near Aberdeen as soon as possible. It was Sunday evening and I was in the dorm sorting out my school things for the next day when Mr Wilson looked in and whispered to me.

"Warm clothes, meet me downstairs."

I nodded, grabbed my winter coat and cap and made for the landing, followed by Peter.

"It looks as if it's urgent. I don't know when I'll be back, so could you keep an eye on things?"

"Don't worry, I'll look after everything, see you later."

I met Mr Wilson in the hall. As we hurried out across the bridge he explained what was happening.

"There's an aircraft coming from Leuchars to pick us up. I've been in touch with your Papa through the secure line from the observer post. An enemy aircraft has landed at Dyce intact. The crew have defected and your Papa wants you to have a word with the aircraft before the scientists get their hands on it. I expect he has his reasons."

We were hurrying along the path to the airstrip.

"Sir, do you know what kind of aircraft it is?"

"I'm guessing, but as it's almost certainly from Norway, it's most likely another Junkers 88."

As we reached the Nissen hut, the Anson was turning on to the approach path. Moments later it touched down and taxied to where we were waiting. I scrambled through the small access door, followed by Mr Wilson whose injured leg demanded a slower pace. We strapped ourselves in as the Anson taxied to the end of the runway. One of the crew bent down and shouted in my ear.

"You couldn't manage that on your own the last time I saw you three years ago."

I looked up and smiled. It was the pilot and gunner who had rescued us after our near fatal encounter. We were in good hands.

Thirty minutes later we were touching down on the main runway at Dyce. I picked out the Ju88 immediately, even though tarpaulins had been draped over the insignia on fuselage and wings. We made ourselves known at the main office where our papers were scrutinised in detail. It would have been most unwise to just stroll over to have a look. However, Papa had been in touch with the CO and that made all the difference.

Mr Wilson having had experience of the Ju88 was able to open the hatch and using his stick, haul down the access ladder. This was a very different aircraft to Crystal. Instead of transparent panels, the nose was filled with guns and radiolocation equipment, the strange part being that neither showed any evidence of use. I heard him grumbling away as soon as I set foot on the ladder.

"I want to go home. It's cold and wet here and my nice wheels are all muddy."

I settled myself in one of the seats. Once again I hadn't been told the real reason for my urgent summons. I would have to search and hope I found something useful.

"I'm sorry about the weather, but I'm sure we can get your wheels clean again. I'm James, what can I call you?"

"My my, so you're James. My pilot told me about you. He *will* be pleased to see you"

This was the first time I couldn't tell by the voice, whether the plane was a 'he' or a 'she', so I bumbled on, feeling my way in the mental darkness.

"How does your pilot know me and what is your name?"

"Don't you remember, the poor dear was in hospital and you were at his bedside? He showed you a photo of his son, a lovely boy, not unlike your good self."

"I remember, so long ago. He seemed to know that I could understand plane talk and I wondered how he knew. I still don't know your name."

"My name, dear boy? No name, only a number. Anyway, what's in a name? A rose by any other will smell as sweet. Oh well, if you insist. I'm a Jerry plane so you better call me Jerry, plain Jerry ha."

Jerry or Jeri, I was as wise as ever, not that it mattered, so I decided to think of him as a 'he'. It simplified the thought process.

"Thank you Jerry. Did you come over from Norway?"

"Ooh, you *are* a clever clogs aren't you. Yes we did and we were flying so low I was picking up spray from my propellers, what fun."

"Your guns look very clean. Have you fired them recently?"

"Fired them, oh no, not for ages and that was only at a target drogue. Have you heard the noise they make, absolutely hideous, can't stand it."

"But what do you do when you find one of our bombers?"

"Oh we just creep up behind them and give them a fright. Then we chase them all over the sky. It's great fun. Sometimes they shoot back, not fair really when we only want to play. Guns are dangerous. They can cause harm."

I looked down at Mr Wilson who was leaning against the access ladder.

"Sir, he doesn't like guns."

Mr Wilson looked up.

"That's odd for a fighter. Ask him about his crew."

"Yes Sir. Jerry, are all your crew friendly towards us? I know the pilot is."

"Afraid not dear boy. One of them is a Nazi."

"Do you know which one?"

"Couldn't say, but the goose step and Nazi salute should give you a clue, just joking. Seriously, you'll be able to tell as two of them will be only too willing to co-operate, while the other one won't."

Another RAF transport was approaching to land. Mr Wilson called up to me.

"James, I think we should make ourselves scarce as this could be the scientists arriving."

"Yes Sir. I'll need to go now Jerry. Don't worry; you'll be given the best of attention. You're a most valued visitor, though I'm afraid no one else will be able to hear you."

"Bye bye dear boy; it's been a delight talking to you."

I scrambled down from the seat, through the hatch and down the ladder which Mr Wilson was holding. The hatch was closed and locked by the guard in charge. We reported back to the main office to say thank you and find the crew of the Anson. The enemy airmen were sitting in the office under guard when we walked in. I recognised the pilot who smiled broadly.

"Good to see you James."

The guard scowled.

"Quiet you!"

The other crew members smiled too, though in one there was a flicker of surprise and fear about the eyes, though I couldn't tell whether the expression was directed at me or Mr Wilson.

Forty minutes later we were stepping down from the Anson, leaving it to make the short hop to Leuchars. Mr Wilson walked in silence as we returned along the path past the walled garden.

"Sir, do you think being seen by the enemy airmen will put us in more danger?"

"I shouldn't think so James. Forget it."

The wind had dropped and the light in the western sky gave promise of a fine start to the week. It had been a busy evening.

The next morning I was able to phone Papa. Even on the secure line, I had learned to be guarded in what I said, referring to the Ju88 as 'our visitor'. I told him what the aircraft had said and he seemed quite pleased. I gather that what I had learned, confirmed information gleaned from other sources. It was worth the odd hour of missed sleep.

Chapter 32

A month later I was back home for the summer holidays. My mother and father both managed a few days leave during that time, but unfortunately due to pressure of work, not together. It was great to see them. Dad and I went for long walks across the estate. We usually managed to bag the odd rabbit which helped cook to eke out the rations. When my mother was home she preferred to sit on the terrace reading, if the weather was good, or talking to the convalescing patients.

I enjoyed listening, as they were without exception, people of courage, heroes with amazing tales to tell, albeit unwillingly. Even then with my own limited experience, I could appreciate why they were reluctant to bring to memory their fear and pain. I took it as a compliment that they should be willing to relate, even in part, what they had endured.

I remember chatting to Papa in one of his rare free moments. I found through experience, when he was sitting staring at the wall doing nothing, he was wrestling with some complex problem of state and so I didn't disturb him. If he was scanning the newspaper, it was all right to interrupt.

"Papa, are we winning the war?"

"Come and sit down James."

He rarely answered a direct question with out giving it proper consideration.

"We have certainly had more successes since the Russians and the Americans entered the war on our side. We've retaken large areas of enemy occupied land, so, in a sense, you could say we're winning but, we haven't won and it would be foolish to assume that we will."

"But Papa we've got that new engine that makes the aircraft fly faster. That'll help, won't it?"

Papa suddenly looked sad and tired.

"Oh yes, it'll help, certainly it'll help and James, you've been a great help too. You are indeed a weapon the enemy can't match, though I fear they may match everything else. You know you mustn't repeat any of this, but in the course of my work, I hear talk of weapons the enemy are developing. If even half the rumours are true, we still have a terrible fight on our hands. I only hope and pray that the war is over before any of them come to fruition."

"But Papa, we *will* win, won't we?"

"Oh yes James. I certainly hope so."

I nodded and left him to his many problems. If Papa with all his knowledge and power was so uncertain, who would be able to give me some reassurance?

I found Mr Wilson in the hospital wing. He had stopped for a rest, leaning on his stick for support. He too looked tired.

"Sir, do you think we will win the war?"

"I don't know James. What I do know is that whoever wins, many will lose. Why do you ask?"

It was difficult trying to put my thoughts in to words.

"When we were in Aberdeen, at Dyce, the Ju88 didn't seem bad. Neither did the airmen. I wouldn't think of the pilot as being evil."

"James, when you're playing football, do your feet run about and kick the ball by themselves; or does your brain tell them what to do?"

"I suppose it's my brain."

"Exactly, so if your feet kicked another boy in the shin, would you blame your feet, or the brain that told them to do it?"

"I see what you mean Sir. It's the brain that gives the orders, so if the brain is evil, so will be the orders."

"That's right, but if evil orders are given to good people, they risk severe punishment if they don't carry them out and mental punishment from their conscience if they do."

"Sir, do you think the enemy plane and crew at Dyce defected because they didn't want to do evil things?"

"Yes James, I believe that may be the case."

"I'm glad they came here, Sir."

His leg still gave him pain and he no longer radiated his former glow of health.

"Yes, I believe in the end they did the right thing."

Shortly after starting my second year in Senior School, Mr Geoffrey's revolutionary aircraft with the new engine was test flown at Hatfield. I didn't see the flight, but was able to talk to the prototype about a week later. Mr Wilson and I were flown down to Hatfield, as usual in one of the ATA aircraft.

The new fighter called himself 'Spider', but to me, he looked more bat like. I thought at the time, 'this aircraft could win the war', but in fact it was some time after hostilities ceased, that the development process was completed and the aircraft started reaching the squadrons.

At Hatfield I was asked to talk to a Mosquito that was in for service. It was one of the early bomber versions used by the Pathfinders and successive post service test flights showed little improvement. Large areas of her wooden structure had been replaced, patched and hurriedly repainted.

A set of steps had been placed under the access door, allowing me to scramble up to the pilot's seat. Usually I could hear aircraft talking as soon as I was in physical contact, but this time all was quiet and I had to rely on the feelings through my own body. They were unpleasant and frightening. Every joint in my body ached. My chest was sore. Even my skin felt itchy, but worst of all was an overwhelming feeling of despair.

It was scary. I scrambled unsteadily down the access ladder and found a packing case on which to support myself. I could feel tears welling up in my eyes, but was determined not to show any weakness in front of Mr Wilson. This was something I had never experienced before. It took several minutes of deep breaths to steady myself. Mr Wilson was studying me in a rather clinical manner.

"You learned something today, didn't you James."

I nodded and mopped my forehead with a hankie. Later back

at the house, I gave a detailed description of the feelings from the Mosquito to Papa. He understood immediately.

"James, you have just given a very accurate analysis of extreme age. The old plane is worn out, tired, had enough. I know how she feels. We're all tired and battle weary, men, machines, the whole country, but we have to keep going."

"Yes Papa."

"You could do with a rest yourself James, if you can call school a rest. I'll make arrangements for you both to return there tomorrow."

"We'll be all right Papa."

"I'm sure you will."

He nodded and sat down at his desk, immediately absorbed in his next problem.

The following day we flew north in one of the ATA de Havilland Dominies. I liked the Dominies. They had the same feel as our Puss Moth, Midge. There was a family resemblance.

We soon settled in to our normal school routine of lessons, sports and leisure. Now in the senior school, Peter and I were given more time on the twenty five yard range in the walled garden. We practiced with a .22 rifle and a small pistol, part of our late Headmaster's collection. Surprisingly, our tutor in this activity was Matron who was well known in the farming fraternity for her ability to dispatch a moving rat at twenty paces. She made it known to us that any rats of the two legged variety, masquerading as Home Guards, would get the same treatment. Our kind Matron had a core of steel.

Mr Wilson came home with me at Christmas. His wound had curtailed some of his physical activities, but generally he managed with the aid of a single stick. He never was one to chatter on without reason, but recently he had been noticeably uncommunicative. His face showed signs of stress, wearing a haunted look.

The New Year saw an increasing movement of army vehicles, many parked in barns or under trees.

Several months later on the 6th of June 1944 the greatest seaborne invasion in history successfully put allied armies ashore on the beaches of enemy occupied Europe. A week later, the first of the revenge weapons my Grandfather had heard rumours about, exploded in London.

From the confidential diary of Sir James Nettleton

Wednesday 14th June 1944

Yesterday, what we refer to as a V1 crashed here, creating a large area of destruction. It's a primitive flying bomb carrying, I believe, a ton of explosive. It was expected and defences have been put in place to reduce its effectiveness. The good news is our armies are ashore in France and should even now be closing on the launch sites. I fear much damage may be wrought before they are neutralised.

I hope this wretched war is over soon. I'm so desperately tired all the time. Even Mr Wilson is showing signs of fatigue. I suspect his leg wound is still giving him pain, though he never complains. His face looks drawn and grey, a sad contrast to when we first met.

James continues to make a contribution to the war effort out of all proportion to his years. Winnie was obviously delighted with their meeting, but wouldn't divulge what passed between them. I must say Peter Anderson has been a good friend to James. I had to laugh at the report from Leuchars describing his downing of the stormtrooper with a catapult and gobstopper. If we can keep that measure of aggression, resourcefulness and luck, we may yet prevail.

Chapter 33

Mr Wilson was home with me for the Summer Holidays. A few days after my fourteenth birthday, he spoke to me at breakfast.

"How do you fancy a trip to France?"

"Great, do they want me to talk to an aircraft?"

"I gather the army have captured one of the launch sites for the revenge weapon, so yes, anything you can find out from the aircraft could be of use in combating it."

"Isn't it more a flying bomb than an aircraft? I mean, will it talk to me?"

"There's only one way to find out. The Dominie should be here any moment. We can wait for it on the terrace."

We walked out to the balustrade by the steps. A watery sun shone faintly as a morning mist rose from the valley. Small sounds carried on the still air, so we heard the Dominie as it approached up the river from the south. Visibility was only a few miles, so we first saw it above the lake on finals before landing. It taxied to the area below the terrace and turned to face the lake, the engines ticking over at idle.

I trotted down the steps ahead of Mr Wilson, hopped onto the lower left wing and through the open door into the arms of one of the pilots, except he was a navigator, an enemy navigator. As soon as I touched the aircraft Dom the Dominie was screaming at me.

"It's a trap. I was captured at Dunkirk. Try and escape."

But there was no escape. Mr Wilson threw his stick in, which he followed, closing the door behind him. I was shocked into immobility. The Dominie accelerated towards the lake, lifting off into the mist and low cloud. Mr Wilson signed to me to fasten my seat belt. I found it difficult to believe he was a traitor, after so many years as my protector, but with Dom rattling on between my ears about being captured inland from Dunkirk, what else could I believe.

The navigator had calmly returned to his map table and was handing a note of course to steer to the pilot.

"Sir," I shouted to make myself heard above the noise of the engines. "What's going on? Have we been captured?"

He couldn't look at me, but gave a slight nod. I saw red. Anger, fear, frustration and despair mixed in a cocktail of uncontrollable emotions.

"Traitor," I yelled and launched myself at him. The back of his huge hand caught me round the side of the mouth and sent me sprawling in the aisle. The navigator looked round, shook his head and wagged his forefinger. A drop of blood spotted the dusty floor as I was picked up and plonked in one of the seats.

"Try that again and you'll be tied and gagged," he shouted in my ear. "You don't understand."

That was certainly true though I should've known that stupid displays of temper would be counter productive. What did Midge say? Act when the time is right, well now was obviously not an ideal time. However, I did have a sympathetic friend in Dom the aircraft, so I fastened my seat belt, sat with my head resting on my hands, and listened. Being tied and gagged was going to limit my options, so better behave. Perhaps an apology would help.

"Sir."

"Yes?"

"Sorry about that."

"All right."

"But I would like an explanation."

"Which you will have when we reach our destination."

What wouldn't I give for Peter's catapult, or the Headmaster's pistol? That would be even better. I casually put my hands in my pockets, hunting for something useful. Let's see, still have the conker, penknife, a small pencil that Mr Wilson gave me in happier times when I was talking to Crystal the Ju88, a hankie, now blood stained. That blow, I intend returning with interest, when the time is right. Tuppence for the phone; can't see that being of much use. Bribe the navigator to radio home; tell cook I'll be a little late for lunch?

My mind was wandering, looking for escape ideas, but I could think of nothing. We droned on, about two miles per minute if memory served me right. I had to admire the pilot in his use of cloud cover. He used every scrap and wisp of the overcast. Holes in the cloud revealed a patchwork of fields surrounding towns and villages.

Did anyone at home realise that I or we had been kidnapped? Questions would be asked first at lunch and checks would be made on the orders given, so alarm bells would ring early afternoon, by which time, who knows?

Water replaced fields as glimpsed through the odd break in the cloud, followed by stretches of wet sand and a shore line producing welcoming lines of tracer. So what, I was past caring.

The navigator moved forward, slid open a window, pushed out a Very pistol and banged off what I presumed were the current recognition colours. They worked after a fashion, as there was a reduction in fire, though some maintained the odd burst, as inaccuracy was the lesser sin. The pilot dropped full flap and side slipped to lose height. I could see the airfield he was heading for, rather close I would have thought, but he was the pilot, not me.

As we touched down, taxied and parked, a depressingly large number of uniforms in field grey encircled the aircraft, weapons at the ready.

"James," said Mr Wilson. "Tell them what they want to know and you'll be treated well. I can't see this war going on much longer, so what you say will make little difference."

"Yes Sir," but I had no intention of telling them anything.

"Sir, I still want an explanation."

He nodded, opened the exit and using his stick for support, stepped down from the wing. He was immediately surrounded by a group of enemy officers, smiling and slapping him on the back. I felt betrayed.

The navigator helped me down from the wing, not that I

needed any help but appearing helpless could work in my favour, given the opportunity. I had a few words of his language, so I said 'Thank you' and he smiled and patted me on the shoulder. I was led to a large open car and sat squashed between two hefty infantry types.

We travelled for over an hour to the south east, judging by the sun. The larger part of the journey was along a river valley with the river to the right of the road. I hoped memorising the geographical location would help if I had the chance to escape, but even easing my sitting position was met with a restraining hand pushing me back into the seat. It was obvious I wouldn't get more than two steps from the car without being shot. We eventually drove through the guarded gates of a walled garden surrounding a French chateau, marred somewhat by banners bearing the sign of the broken cross.

The Boy Who Talked To Planes

From the confidential diary of Sir James Nettleton

Saturday 5th August 1944

I've had some bad days in my life, but this must rank amongst the worst. James has been kidnapped. Out of the blue, I just didn't see it coming. I should have given more credence to Mac's suspicions regarding Mr Wilson. I'm guilty of falling into the trap I've warned others about, of only seeing what I expect to see. At about midday I received a telephone call from Mac on the secure line to say he and Matron had given Mr Wilson's room a thorough search and found under the floor boards an Enigma coding device, along with settings in books bearing the sign of the eagle and broken cross. I admit to feeling physically sick with fear.

Our local police were alerted and sent to the house to arrest Mr Wilson, but he had already left. One of the gardeners had seen him and James leaving in an aircraft with RAF markings but couldn't say what type, other than it had two engines. Enquiries show no such flights have been authorised. What can anyone do? By now James will be in occupied France. I've sent all the information I can by the usual channels to the French Resistance, so now we must wait.

What on earth am I going to tell his parents? It's a dreadful situation. Who do I turn to, Bomber Command? I feel so useless.

Chapter 34

I was escorted to the door where another soldier took me to a large airy room with French windows. Once alone I tried the handles, but they were locked. A guard appeared outside. He looked at me and pointedly eased the pistol in its holster, turned his back and stood motionless. Seconds later the door opened and a tall grey haired man walked in and waved me to an easy chair beside the unlit fire.

"Good morning James, please be seated. My name is Her Ehrlichmann."

He eased himself into a similar chair on the opposite side. A low table sat between us on which he placed a large folder.

"I've been looking forward to meeting you for some time. This folder is about you and your life to date, most impressive so far."

I looked but said nothing.

"Whether this folder continues to grow, or stays the same and is filed, depends on what you do and say. Believe me, I wish you no harm, but there are others shall we say, of a less patient temperament."

He hesitated, leaving the words hanging in the air like a dark cloud. I could feel the anger boiling up inside me, must control it.

"May I ask a question?"

"Certainly."

"Why have I, a civilian non-combatant and legally a child, been taken from my home? My home, which you must clearly understand from your knowledge of English, is my castle, a place of safety never to be violated in any way. Why have you behaved in such a disgraceful fashion, in contravention of several of the articles of the Geneva Convention?"

He sighed and sat back into his seat. He had brown eyes of an unusual depth which examined me with something akin to sadness. He had clearly been down this road before.

"Because you have knowledge which we want and we're not too fussy about how we get it."

I tried to wrong foot him, but I doubt if it worked.

"If I have knowledge that will bring this silly war to an end, you can have it with my blessing. You only have to ask."

To give himself time to re-frame his question, he asked.

"Would you like a cup of tea?"

"A cup of tea, of course that's the answer, a nice cup of tea. We'll all have a cup of tea and the war will end. Why didn't we think of that?"

"Enough," he bawled. "You make light of a serious situation. My patience is not endless."

I'm being stupid again, annoying them without reason.

"I'm sorry Her Ehrlichmann. I apologise. It's all a bit scary and I get nervous. Tell me what you want to know and I'll try and help."

"That's better."

He opened the folder and lifted a piece of paper from the top of the pile.

"I am reliably informed that you talk to aircraft."

"Yes."

"And that they talk to you."

I opened my mouth to protest, but he waved me to silence.

"There's no point in denying it. Your whole life is here, so let's deal with what we want from you. Help us and your life will continue, don't," he clapped the folder shut, "and this folder, like you, will cease to grow."

I had that feeling in the pit of the stomach when the Boss sends for you, only this was much much worse. I wish he was here now. He'd have this one for breakfast, grey suit an' all. Mr Wilson said it would make little difference to the outcome of the war, whatever I told them. Perhaps he's right.

"I'll tell you all I know," I whispered.

"Good, then let me explain. Our latest rocket powered fighter is experiencing compressibility problems as it nears the speed of sound. Controlling pitch is the factor which gives most difficulty and we know you have the answer."

I'm dead. I haven't a clue what he's talking about and no way of convincing him this is all way beyond me.

"You're having me on aren't you? Rocket planes, that's comic book stuff and the sound barrier is just that, a barrier. An aircraft would break up if pushed beyond the speed of sound."

"You disappoint me James. All you have to do is tell us the principal and we'll take it from there. You can have your own apartment with service, where you'll be safe until hostilities are over."

"Really Her Ehrlichmann, please believe me. I know nothing of the sound barrier or how to break through and if a scientist did tell me I wouldn't understand. I'm only learning basic maths and I'm not good at that."

He sighed and looked at the sunlit grounds beyond the windows and portico.

"You're wasting my time. You know what you have to do. By all means take time to consider, but your time is limited."

He pressed a button on the wall and walked to the door. He didn't look back. Two soldiers entered to escort me downstairs to a foul smelling cell. Before leaving, they removed my tie and shoe laces. The cell had a small barred window, too high to see through and a single light behind a wire grill. The walls were smooth greasy cement with words in languages I didn't understand, most likely casting aspersions on the ancestral lineage of our gaolers.

The words gave me an idea. I could leave a message. Our armies must be coming this way, if they haven't been pushed back; but too late to save me. The cell was furnished with many sheets of thin paper for toilet purposes. They were impaled on a hook attached to the wall. I remembered our old Headmaster's words, 'something hidden in full view is invariably overlooked'. I would write my report in pencil on the paper provided, but I would need time.

I was good at drawing. Perhaps I could fool them with some of the imaginary designs scribbled during some particularly boring lesson. He talked of a rocket plane, so I drew a spaceship like one I'd seen at the cinema in a Buck Rogers film. That wouldn't fool him. He's probably seen the same films. It has to be different, something I've made up myself. Let's see, if I draw a fuselage without wings and the tail fins like a rocket. No that just looks like a bomb. Right, I'll move the fins forward and make them bigger like wings and angle them back a bit. That looks better. I added a few angle measurements to give some technical realism, lay down exhausted and fell asleep. Next morning I awoke to find the drawing had gone.

The next day Her Ehrlichmann entered the cell. He was holding the drawing.

"Do I detect some co-operation James?"

I gave a non-committal shrug.

"Some of the angles need clarification, like this one here," he said, pointing to the leading edge of the wing.

"It should be forty-five degrees," which was the first number I thought of. I hoped he wasn't a scientist, as I was floundering now, trying to think on my feet, so I kept bumbling on.

"That's relative to the centre line," pointing vaguely at the drawing, "and you may have to adjust the centre of gravity to the areas of lift."

I hadn't a clue what I was talking about; just stringing together terms I had heard at various times in the past. He nodded sagely and wandered out. The door banged behind him and I collapsed on to the hard bed. Beads of perspiration were rolling down the side of my nose and I was shaking like a leaf.

At regular intervals food was pushed through a slot in the bottom of the door. I've managed some of it, but haute cuisine it's not. 'The condemned man ate a hearty meal?' Not if that was the quality on offer. However, later in the day the food took a turn for the better. It was almost edible. I wondered how long I could keep up the pretence, before I was rumbled.

I divided my time between writing my report, which was kept on the wall hook and drawings which I left lying on the floor where they could be seen. I worked day and night, thanks to the twenty-four hour light. I've tried to put down everything I can remember of my past fourteen years. If nothing else, it will give my own view of events.

I was surprised my imaginary aeronautical designs fooled them for so long. The deception ceased with a bang as the cell door crashed open revealing Her Ehrlichmann with a face the colour of puce.

"You think we're fools? You've made a deliberate mistake in the calculations."

I cowered in the opposite corner of the cell

"I told you I was no good at maths."

"It's time we took you on a little outing," he whispered in a voice full of menace. He left and the cell door slammed shut.

A few days later, I was taken out and driven several miles to witness an execution. It was a ghastly example of man's inhumanity to man and designed to show what lay in store for anyone who displeased the regime. I wasn't the only witness. Lines of young recruits, some little older than myself, had been paraded in a position from which they could view the spectacle.

It took place in the remains of a Roman amphitheatre, a location well suited to blood sports. A large mound of sand bags had been placed at one end to protect the stonework. After all, they weren't barbarians. In front a wooden post had been set up. Soldiers marched out carrying rifles and took up position facing the post. I estimated about thirty in all, in two ranks. As the first glimpse of the sun appeared over the horizon, the unfortunate victim was led out and tied to the post. The firing party took aim and on the order, fired.

I feel it's only fair to all concerned to describe what happened fractions of a second later. Don't believe the Hollywood version where the victim sags into an artfully contrived 'S' shape. He didn't sag; he disappeared, disintegrated along with the top half of the post. There was nothing left remotely resembling a human, alive or dead and without doubt, he was dead.

My attendance was a rather unsubtle hint that I could go the same way if I didn't come up with the information needed, information I don't have. Strangely I find it comforting. It's quick, without suffering. I won't even hear the bang.

Yesterday Mr Wilson visited my cell. I could hear the metallic tap of his stick as he approached, down the stairs and along the corridor. He stood in the doorway and asked if he could come in.

"You're not going to attack me are you?" he asked.

I found I no longer felt any anger towards him. I wasn't going to leave this world in a state of hate, so I patted the hard bed beside where I was sitting. I was tired, but at peace. I know I had lost weight as I had to take in my trouser belt a couple of notches.

"No, I'm not going to attack you or anyone else."

He sat and turned to face me.

"You asked for an explanation. It's quite simple. My family are no longer in Ireland. I was told they were moved for their own safety."

I turned to him.

"I see."

"I had to do their bidding if I was to see them again."

"And have you?"

He shook his head and looked at the floor.

"I've been a fool James. Beware of idealism."

"I shall if I get the chance."

"I'm sorry the way it's turned out. You're a good lad. I've tried to convince them that you could not possibly know anything of the latest advances, but once they get an idea in their heads, they won't move."

"Sir, if you get back, tell them. You know."

"I can never go back James. I'd be hanged as a traitor and rightly so. I don't know what will happen to me and they don't care," he said, looking towards the door.

We sat together in silence, pondering our separate fates.

"You'll have met Her Ehrlichmann."

I nodded.

"Do you know what his name means?"

"No Sir."

"Honest man."

We both laughed hysterically until the guard barged in and pushed Mr Wilson out. The cell door banged shut and my laughter turned to floods of tears. I had little chance of survival. That was yesterday. Now there's the first light of what may be my last day and I can hear someone coming.

I never did get that cup of tea.

Part 3

France, the way back

Chapter 35

The cell door opened. A tall officer in black stood looking at me, the dark angel in a Nazi uniform. He was about to enter when the siren started screaming its warning of an impending air raid. He scowled, hesitated a moment, slammed the door shut and marched off.

I recognised the approaching aircraft, Mosquitoes powered by two Rolls Royce Merlins in fine pitch, flat out, what a glorious sound. A group of fighters first to keep the gunners' heads down, then the bombers to pinpoint the target. It was only when the bombs whistled down, thudding on the ground and crashing through the building, I realised I could be the target, not a nice feeling. I flung myself into a corner of the cell below the window. The engine sounds receded and as the delayed action bombs ticked away, I tried to protect my ears.

"Ooooooooooh," the world collapsed as the ground heaved and shook, explosions coming like a fast drum roll. I felt rather than heard the last one. As if from a great distance, wood, stone and glass crashed and tinkled to an amorphous mound of silence, broken by a faint scream of pain. It was pitch black. Deaf I felt I could handle, but blind, please not blind. The salt taste of blood was in my mouth and every muscle and joint ached. I think I'd bitten my tongue. If I felt this bad, I had to be alive.

I tried to stand but my head bumped against something hard, roof or wall, I had no way of knowing. I crawled over the rubble strewn floor, trying to find the limits of my available space. So weak, hungry and in pain, I sat with my back to the remains of the wall and howled until I was too tired to even cry. I wiped the tears and dirt from my eyes as several minutes passed trying to recover my senses. As the sun rose and the dust settled, I could see shapes, bits of concrete and stone, wooden beams and the broken remnants of a once lovely building. Oh blessed light, what a relief.

I found my shoes and cut the string from the conker to serve as laces. Now I could move. If light could get in, I may find a way out. I found the wall hook with its precious sheaf of paper which I removed and stuffed into a pocket.

Fiery orange light flickered through the debris. Did I survive the bombs, only to be burned to death? The question was answered as gallons of water cascaded through the rubble and pooled in the remains of the small cell. Life was certainly interesting. Within the space of half an hour I faced being shot, blown apart, burned to a crisp or drowned. What's next, devoured by a passing pride of lions? Reality was almost as bad, as the movement of figures seen through gaps in the chateau's remains reminded me the firing party was still on call.

Fortunately the water flowed out of my broken corner as quick as it entered, but by then I was soaked to the skin. The cell had been next to a shallow dry moat, now draining the water from the firemen's hoses. I lay still, hoping that if any part of me was seen, I'd be taken for one of the many bodies. Was Mr Wilson one of them? I hoped not. We were both victims.

The cold seeped into my bones and my teeth chattered uncontrollably. It was all I could hear, as the concussion of exploding bombs had rendered me deaf, temporarily I hoped. I could see no more movement, so assumed the rescue teams had moved to another part of the ruin. I risked slipping out of my soggy clothes and wringing out as much water as I could manage in the confined space. Small pools of sunlight offered warmth and gradually turned me from a state of saturation to merely damp.

Shelter, a place of safety, food and rest were so vital that I had to assess the next move with care. Providence had given me a second chance. It would be unreasonable to expect a third, yet I would need all the luck and then some, to reach the security of home. By the time darkness fell and the moon rose, I had worked out my escape route through the maze of broken wood and stone.

I used the rubble from a protective balustrade to climb to the edge of the moat and look over. Part of the roof was lying within crawling distance and provided temporary cover. Bomb craters and debris allowed me to crawl unseen to the shelter of trees along the edge of the estate.

I shook with fear and exhaustion. My deafness was almost total and I jumped like a frightened rabbit at every movement. A small gap between thick bushes and the perimeter wall served as a temporary hiding place. Though I couldn't hear, I could feel vibrations through the ground when something heavy passed along the road on the other side. The rescue parties were replaced by curfew patrols, but none came near.

I judged it time to move, though I had only a rough idea where I was. I tried to think. We landed close to the coast and drove south east for about an hour, say about forty miles. The Allied forces landed west of the mouth of the Seine, so the airfield would be somewhere between that and Calais. A river flowed to the right of the road, so if I could find that I could follow it to the sea. If I headed south west I should find it. Then what? I was already suffering from hunger and exhaustion, so I needed to get my priorities right as I was in no fit state to go anywhere. I needed to find help, but who could I trust?

At least it was dry with a clear sky, a sky full of moon and stars. I could even pick out the Milky Way. I remembered Mr Davies all those years ago telling me about the stars in their constellations like the great bear. The great bear which points to Polaris, Polaris the North Star. If I could find that I would know which way to go.

I climbed onto the wall coping and lay still, checking for movement. On the opposite side of the road were houses and a narrow lane. The lane looked the best bet as it provided shade from moonlight. My big fear was danger creeping near with no audible warning. Now I could hear nothing and had to rely entirely on my eyes.

I was about to drop to the road when I saw the lights from an approaching vehicle. The army lorry stopped and two soldiers jumped from the back to start their patrol. I gave them time to get well away, dropped to the pavement and started crossing the road. I had no idea how much noise I was making, so couldn't hear their warning shout to stand still.

A torch moving and the muzzle flash of a warning shot sent me racing for the alleyway. Stand still? Not likely as I knew what would happen if I was recaptured. Rather risk death now than face its certainty later. A flying sliver of stone sliced my cheek as I reached the darkness of the alley. Fear and the instinct to survive drove my legs to greater effort. As the soldiers reached the alley, they let off a volley of shots, firing blind into the shadows. I saw flashes and sparks as the bullets hit stonework and metal posts. A bullet tugged my jacket as it flapped loose.

I swerved at right angles into a narrow opening between houses. As I reached the end of the house, the moonlight showed a high wall. I vaulted to the top, rolling over with little thought of what lay on the other side.

I was dead wasn't I? It was heaven complete with celestial blue sky and welcoming angels. I could smell bread baking. It must be the bread of heaven like the hymn we sang in church, but my understanding of heaven didn't include hunger and pain. I had the worst headache ever, with flashing lights and blurred vision. I tried to sit up, but felt sick and lay back down.

The angels coalesced into a single entity. Short dark hair framed brown eyes gazing at me with some concern. Her mouth moved but I could hear no words. I tried to speak but she put a finger to her lips and signed to keep still.

A larger version of the angel swam into vision, knelt down beside me and examined the bump on my head, then my arms and legs searching for breaks which thankfully I didn't have. She sat back with her head to one side. I thought of Matron and had to fight back the tears. She said something to the smaller angel and laughed, waving her hand in front of her face and holding her nose; sign language in capital letters, 'YOU SMELL AWFUL'.

She became serious and her mouth moved framing a question which I couldn't hear. I put my hands out palms up and pointed to my ears. She nodded in understanding and made signs asking if I could stand. I managed but every muscle and joint were crying out in pain. Perhaps I cried out too as she put a hand to my mouth and pointed to the wall I had tumbled over earlier. I nodded and managed with their help to reach the house door which they closed behind us.

She sat me beside a table and brought a bowl of warm water. With cloths and a small cake of soap she set about cleaning up my hands and face as if I was a small child unable to do this for myself. I sat gazing at nothing in particular; revelling in the first act of kindness I had been shown in weeks. She put a bowl of soup in front of me and a plate with new bread. It was a banquet. I couldn't ask what the soup was made from and didn't care. It was hot, wet and tasty. It also reminded me sharply of Matron's broth and again I had to choke back the tears.

Water was running into a bath. When did I last have a bath, or wash, or change my clothes? I couldn't remember. The lady slid my jacket off and noticed the strange label, in English. She pointed at the label and at me. I nodded. It was rolled into a bundle and stuffed into a drawer under other clothes.

She made signs asking 'can you wash yourself' and I nodded a 'yes', after which I was taken to the room with the bath, now half full of warm water. Oh bliss, the healing balm of soap and water. A small mirror hung on the wall. It revealed a shocking reflection of my weeks in captivity. I had never ever been in such a state of unkempt filth. I washed every part of my body. Even though the cuts and bruises were painful, they were given a good scrub.

She entered with a towel held in front of her so I could climb out and wrap it round my body. She left and returned with a man's shirt which I slipped on. My cheek wound was bandaged to absorb the ooze of blood and I was helped up narrow stairs to a bedroom of spotless cleanliness. There I slept until the next day. I woke with the lady gently shaking my shoulder. Even then, I jumped in panic before realising I was in a comfy bed and relative safety.

She was smiling and pointing to a tall bald headed man puffing his way up the stairs. He was wearing a suit and small glasses that kept sliding down his nose. He was smiling too and waving a stethoscope. I gathered from that, he was a doctor here to check on my state of health. He knelt in the narrow space between bed and wall and gave me the most thorough examination since being in the sick bay at Leuchars. He paid particular attention to my ears and eyes. He wrote out a page of instructions which he explained to the lady with many gestures indicating a small bottle containing a clear liquid and several small paper packets. As they made their way downstairs, the lady patted some clean clothes draped over a small chair and pointed to me. I understood. They were French, the first step on the road to invisibility. I remembered the lessons taught by Peter's Dad and the Boss. The lessons were fun then, now they were deadly serious and I mean deadly.

I dressed and descended to a kitchen filled with the aroma of fresh baked bread. French bread was a culinary discovery on a par with Matron's broth, but I could wish for happier times to enjoy it.

After I had eaten, and the table cleared, the lady put a piece of paper in front of me. On it was written, 'Madame et Yvette Jomaron'. She pointed to the names and themselves in turn. She handed a pencil to me and pointed to the paper, so I wrote 'James Edwards'. She examined it, smiled and wrote underneath, 'Jacques Edouard Jomaron' and pointed at me. I had been temporarily adopted, this was my new name and our lives now depended on me playing the roll to perfection.

The Boy Who Talked To Planes

From the confidential diary of Sir James Nettleton

Saturday 26th August 1944

James is free. I've heard through the Resistance, he is alive and with friends. I know he's still in danger, like all the inhabitants of occupied Europe, but now there's hope we may see him again alive and well. I know the Resistance will do their utmost to help him escape to this country. I can only pray that they have success in their efforts.

I've told Vicky he's safe. She hasn't slept since his kidnap, save through exhaustion. I've offered to arrange unlimited leave, but she won't hear of it, claiming she's better working and feeling useful. Feeling useful is something I haven't enjoyed these past few weeks, but now there's hope.

Mac blames himself for allowing the kidnap to happen and not properly protecting James. He even offered his resignation, but I told him he wasn't getting off that lightly. He's the most fiercely loyal person I know. I would fear for his well being if he wasn't kept busy. A return to his old ways would be in no ones interest.

I may sleep tonight.

Chapter 36

Madame Jomaron's bread, the company of Yvette and the doctor's medication all combined to speed my recovery. I felt safe and secure behind their door, beyond which, lay a dangerous world I would have to face.

On the fourth day after I had fallen into their courtyard, the doctor called in with a smile even larger than usual. Madame and Yvette were jumping around hugging each other. Maybe it was good news. The doctor bent slightly to talk in my ear and for the first time in days, I heard.

"Paris is free." Even the French I'd learned at school allowed me to understand. No wonder they were happy, but could only show it in the privacy of their home, quietly. Our allied lines must be spreading this way, so I would have to consider my next move soon. I tried to ask the doctor if he knew when my hearing would be fully restored. I took the Gallic shrug to mean, 'I don't know when,' though speaking in bad French with a bitten tongue it was probably, 'I don't know what you're talking about'.

To be honest, I was scared stiff at the thought of leaving the security of Madame Jomaron's home before my hearing was back to normal. I was haunted by memories of the patrol materialising suddenly from the darkness and having to force already weakened joints and muscles to do the impossible. However, the impossible had become the norm in our war torn world.

I was debating in my mind whether to make my way south towards the Allied lines, or north and west to find a boat, or simply stay and wait to be freed. The decision was made for me on the following day when a swarthy individual climbed over the back wall during the hours of darkness and let himself into the house. He spoke understandable English when I met him and was able to shed light on my situation. His brother was Madame Jomeron's husband who had escaped to England during the evacuation from Dunkirk in nineteen forty and was now chief liaison officer in London. I was facing the local organiser of the resistance, a veteran and survivor of many years of conflict.

"You are James Edwards?"

"Who wants to know?"

He looked at me sideways and smiled.

"You learn fast. No matter, it's enough to know that Papa has asked me to find you and send you back.

I sat weighing him up. Madame and Yvette were obviously happy in his presence, so I felt I could trust him. I certainly wouldn't want such a battle hardened character as an enemy.

"Well, you've found me. How do you send me back?"

"Can you fly?"

"Fly, why do you ask?

He didn't answer. I was being too cautious with a man who had risked his life daily to defeat our common enemy. I had to tell him the truth as I saw it.

"I've been flying since before I was born. I know how, but I've never been big enough to reach the controls, until now."

"Stand up."

I stood as he looked at me, considering the variables.

"It's a small aircraft," he said. "I think you could manage. We take you to it and you decide then. The priest will arrange things. We meet on Sunday at chapel."

Early the following Sunday I collected the written report from my jacket and stuffed it into my trousers. Only then did we leave the safety of the house for the short walk to the chapel. I was terrified, feeling the eyes of every enemy soldier boring into me and steeling myself for the shout to halt, but we were ignored. I was introduced to the priest as Jacques.

He greeted me with "Bonjour frère Jacques," and they all laughed. The ceremony was unfamiliar but I tried to move in unison with the family and mouth what little French I knew in time to the music. After the service we were taken to a horse drawn cart and together with others I didn't know, climbed aboard. I understood from the baskets of food and bottles of wine, that we were going on a picnic. Fortunately my hearing was returning in French which I was able to translate, though with my best efforts and a damaged tongue, my speech caused more hilarity than understanding.

The horse had one speed which it stuck to for mile, pardon, kilometre after kilometre. There was no rush. Bottles and pieces of fruit were passed round amid chat and laughter. On two occasions we had to pull into the side to let a convoy of army vehicles pass. We came to a check point and were waved through. As we passed a couple of bottles were handed down to the soldiers. It was a regular Sunday outing and nothing out of the ordinary.

My watch had disappeared at the chateau, but by the sun's position I guessed we were heading west. We left the main road and after another half hour turned into a field bordering an area of forest. Blankets were spread on the ground; the horse unhitched and allowed to graze. There were several other horses in the field. They looked up at our arrival, decided it must be Sunday and resumed cropping the grass.

Monsieur Jomaron sat beside me with his back to the forest.

"Enjoying yourself James?"

"Yes, it's been a pleasant day so far. What happens now?"

"Behind me you see a track going into the forest. It leads to an old sawmill. The aircraft is in one of the sheds. We found it where we're sitting now, no one near it."

"I see the track."

"I am always told of these flights, but I know nothing of this one."

"That's strange. Does it have RAF markings?"

"Yes and daytime camouflage, not usual for secret flights."

"Are we going to see the aircraft now?"

"Yes, and if all goes well, you should be on your way tomorrow morning."

"Good."

"In case enemy eyes are watching, we'll do it this way. Madame Jomaron and I will collect a basket of food and walk slowly into the forest. You wait a few minutes, talking to Yvette and take her over to the edge of the field. That will give you a chance to look at your take off run, which should be downhill that way and in to wind, understand?"

"Yes," I nodded and looked at Yvette, who smiled.

"Good, enter the forest and cut across to meet the track. Follow it until you reach the saw-mill. We'll be waiting for you there."

I nodded. It was such a fine sunny day, yet tomorrow I could be only a memory. Monsieur Jomaron casually collected a few edibles in to a basket and strolled off with Madame Jomaron taking his arm. Yvette was looking past me watching them as they were gradually hidden by the trees. A couple of aircraft roared overhead, Typhoons or Tempests but too fast to be sure. They were ours, armed with rockets and looking for targets of opportunity.

Yvette stood and beckoned me to follow. As we walked towards the forest, she stretched out her hand which I took in mine. When had I last touched a person? When the back of Mr Wilson's hand struck my mouth? That hardly counted. When in kindness, I couldn't remember, it was so long ago.

"Yvette, I wish I could talk to you."

She looked up, smiled and said something about it being a good day. It certainly was a good day. I wished the forest was further away. I could happily have walked forever across this field, holding Yvette's hand. I was forgetting my task. The field had a firm surface, falling away in a gentle slope. That would shorten the takeoff run, my first takeoff. What am I thinking of? I have to be trained to pilot an aircraft. I can always refuse; say the risks are too great.

We reached the first of the trees. I looked back to the site of the picnic. The priest was leading the horse back to the cart as others collected food, baskets and blankets. Nothing must be left.

Once beyond the edge of the forest we turned and walked parallel to the field until we reached the track. It was wide enough for a lorry, but an aircraft? The saw mill consisted of several sheds; some open sided with roofs of rusting corrugated iron. Yvette's mother and uncle were waiting for us outside one of the smaller sheds.

"It is in here James. Come and see."

We entered by a small door set into the larger main doors and there it stood, a Puss Moth. Its wings were folded back, which accounted for it sitting in a shed more the size of a garage than a hangar. I'd flown in a Puss Moth so often I knew its feel, maybe I could risk it. I put my hand out to check on the state of the propeller. It was like an electric shock.

"Midge?"

Chapter 37

I jumped back in surprise and bumped into the main doors.

"Monsieur Jomaron, I must talk to you. There's much to explain. Can we go outside?"

"Yes James, who is Midge and what must you explain?"

We trooped out and found somewhere to sit. This could be difficult, as he would have to translate some rather hard to believe pieces of information.

"When you asked if I could fly, I said I'd been flying from before I was born."

"Yes, go on."

"That is the aircraft I was flying in."

"That," and he pointed at the shed, "is the same aircraft. How do you know?"

"She told me."

"You are making a joke?"

"No, seriously, she's called Midge and was given to my parents as a wedding present by my grandfather, Papa. My mother is a pilot too and I grew inside her when she was flying Midge. That's how I was born with the ability to communicate with aircraft and why I was kidnapped by the Nazis, because they wanted to use my knowledge and abilities, but I didn't know what they wanted and they were going to shoot me, but the chateau was bombed and I escaped. The rest you know."

They looked at me as if I had fallen from another planet.

"This is incredible. Can it be true?"

"It is the truth, so if I talk to myself, you're hearing my half of a conversation with Midge."

They talked to each other as he translated the whole story.

"Tell me James, does this make it more, or less likely, that you'll be able to fly."

"Oh more, much more, I may have no experience as a pilot,

but Midge won't let me down, I'm sure of that."

There followed a heated discussion between the three of them with Yvette leaning over and patting my hand before sitting upright with her arms folded in front of her. Monsieur Jomaron threw his arms in the air in disgusted resignation.

"Yvette wants to go with you, to see her father. Her mother says it's all right with her, if it's all right with you. I say it's crazy, mad."

He turned and looked away. I have to admit, I liked the idea of Yvette's company, though it was only fair to spell out the dangers.

"They realise I have never flown a plane before."

"Yes."

"And assuming I get it off the ground, there are still enemy aircraft about and we could be intercepted and shot down."

"Yes."

"And we don't know what state of repair Midge is in and how much fuel she has and the hundred other things that could go wrong."

"Yes and she still wants to go with you."

Now it was my turn to give the universally accepted Gallic shrug of resignation. I turned to Yvette.

"You know how dangerous it is and you still want to come with me?"

She nodded and turned to her uncle.

"She says she trusts you and you obviously trust Midge. Once these women make up their mind, there's no shifting them."

"Oh very well, she can come."

Her uncle didn't have to translate. She flung her arms about me and kissed my cheek. I blushed.

"I'll have to ask Midge and make sure she's in a fit state to make the journey."

"Naturally."

So we all trooped back into the shed. They stood watching me, waiting for the performance to begin. For some odd reason I experienced something akin to stage fright. I'd never had such a large audience. I opened Midge's door and settled myself in her pilot's seat, checking to make sure I could reach everything, which surprisingly I could. Midge was talking as soon as I touched her door handle.

"What was all that about? I was going to say 'hello James, nice to see you' and you all ran out. I'm not that scary, am I?"

"It was a shock. I wasn't expecting to see you, in a shed, in a forest, in France, surrounded by the enemy when I thought you were safe at home flying messages round the country."

"I could say the same about you. Shouldn't you be in school?"

"I was kidnapped."

"Kidnapped?"

"That's right and if these good people hadn't found me, I wouldn't be here. In fact I wouldn't be anywhere."

There was a pause before she added.

"They found me too, out there in the field. Please thank them for me. I don't think black crosses would suit me."

"Yes I will."

I leaned out from the door.

"Midge says thank you for hiding her here. She doesn't like the idea of black crosses all over her nice paintwork."

Monsieur Jomaron translated and they all laughed.

"We are pleased to be able to help Midge, and you James."

"Truly it's help we would be lost without and now Midge has to explain why she's so different to when I last saw her."

"Everything has changed James. You know that. All right briefly, I was requisitioned to work in the Air Transport Auxiliary, like your parents, which is why I'm in RAF battle dress."

"You've been given blind flying instruments."

"That's because I was moved from the ATA to the RAF as the personal transport of a Wing Commander and he needed to fly at night. You'll have noticed the lights and generator and there's a battery under your seat. There's an intercom through the flying helmets, so you'll be able to talk to each other."

"All useful additions, but it still doesn't explain why you're here."

"Simple, it's because Wingco is barking mad. He was running low on his favourite tipple, so he lands here and wanders off in full uniform and flying gear to find some. There's an empty crate in the back."

I looked behind the rear seat.

"So there is. I hope he's not expecting you to wait for him."

"No, I shouldn't think so. He's probably found some bottles and is holed up in a handy cellar checking the quality. I think we should go home."

"Talking of checking the quality, I should look you over to make sure you're all in one piece before my first solo."

"Wingco may be a trifle eccentric, but he makes sure I'm well maintained with the best of materials, so you should have no worries on that score."

"How about your fuel state?"

"I was topped up before we left, so there should be plenty to get back."

"Fine, so we're ready to go, or rather you are. I'm not so sure about myself."

"You'll be fine. If you were learning to fly you'd have a flying instructor shouting in your ear, which is what I'll do."

"Thanks Midge. Now I better tell them what's happening."

I told them everything Midge talked about, including the Wing Commander who Monsieur Jomaron had heard of. Monsieur Jomaron in turn briefed me on a course to fly.

"Take off down the field, stay on the same track until you reach a river, turn left and follow it to the estuary then head west for five minutes, turn on to a north westerly heading and keep going."

"Presumably until we find England's green and pleasant land," I added.

This, I thought, all assumes staying in the air, not bumping into anything hard or wet and avoiding the nasty planes with the black crosses. I can but try.

We ate from the picnic basket and bedded down for the night. The others went to sleep with no trouble, but I only managed four hours if that, my sleep fitful and broken by strange dreams.

At first light, I woke Monsieur Jomaron to make a start. There was no thought of breakfast as my mind was filled with other concerns. We manhandled Midge with difficulty down the rutted track to the centre of the field, pointing her along its length as it sloped towards the river. I tried to remember everything I'd learned from observation over the years, but there were so many variables. Had I taken on more than I could manage? I was about to find out.

Chapter 38

With the help of Monsieur and Madame Jomaron, Midge's, wings were unfolded and locked, control surfaces checked for free movement, fuel on and engine primed ready to start. Would the noise of the engine attract unwanted notice as it warmed up? The next few minutes would decide.

Madame said something and pointed to the back of the cabin. Monsieur translated.

"She says we should leave the empty crate in case Wingco comes back for it."

"Good idea."

I leaned into the back, pulled it out and left it behind the tail. The absurdity relieved the tension a little. Yvette and her mother made their goodbyes. I checked that she was securely strapped in and there were no other loose articles in the cabin. I signed to her to put on the leather flying helmet and made sure the intercom plug was in place. I shook hands with Monsieur and Madame Jomaron and thanked them for their help.

"One last favour, could you help to start the engine?"

"Certainly and I would ask a favour of you. Look after Yvette."

"I will, with my life."

Forgive the dramatic, but within the next hour it was clear we would either live or die together. I made sure the doors were properly closed, slipped on the leather helmet and slid open the side windows. Right then, here goes. Check fuel quantity, more than half full, primary magneto on and,

"Contact."

Monsieur Jomaron flicked the propeller; Midge coughed a couple of times until her engine settled to a fast idle. He gave the thumbs up sign, which I returned. Yvette waved to Madame, leaned forward and patted my right shoulder, pushing her fist where I could see it, thumb raised. She had such small delicate hands. I turned round and forced a smile, which she returned. What a warm smile. How could I ever think of failing them? Her mother and uncle were nowhere to be seen.

I had no more excuses, only a dry mouth and hands slippery with sweat. My left hand gripped the throttle, my right the control column and my feet were poised unsteadily on the rudder bar. I was shaking with fear.

"What do I do now Midge?"

"You take off and fly home, that's what you do. See the line of trees and the big one, taller than the rest? It's on the other side of the river. Aim for that. Keep it in the centre of the screen. I tend to swing to the right on takeoff so we'll need a touch of left rudder to keep me straight."

Yvette was yelling something in my ear. If only I'd paid more attention to my French lessons. She was pointing to something behind us, the lights of a vehicle. That was the jolt I needed to push the throttle open as far as it would go. Now we were racing across the grass cropped by the horses. The horses, had anyone checked to see if they were still in the field? Yvette was whooping and waving her arms in sheer exhilaration and Midge was rattling off a stream of instructions which I attempted to follow.

The wheels had stopped rumbling. We had left the ground and I was aware of that beautiful fluidity of movement associated with flying. As we gained height I relaxed.

"There's the river. Start the turn now Midge?"

"Yes James, try and keep it in balance. Keep an eye on the turn and bank, keep the top needle centred. Check your vertical speed. Bring the revs back; two thousand one hundred should be about right until we build up speed. Level out now, check your VSI again, and keep my wings level."

"Midge, I've got seven instruments to keep an eye on and I'm supposed to look outside. How many eyes should I have?"

"You'll manage. There's the estuary up ahead. Keep low. There are gun emplacements on the headlands. Perhaps they won't bother with small fry like us."

But they did and lines of bright tracer raised spouts of water up ahead. Soon we were well out over the channel, into the darkness and mist, as yet unscathed.

"You can start gaining height now. Ease the stick back until you're doing about sixty knots and hold it at that."

"How's that Midge?"

"Fine, now can you see what heading you're on?"

"No, not if I'm to fly you at the same time."

"Fair enough, try easing round to the right until the sun is shining over your right shoulder. That should do for the moment. Level off between two and three thousand feet and use the trim lever to ease the pressure on the control column."

"I never thought it was this complicated. How's that. It looks so easy when someone else is flying."

"You'll learn. You've wandered round to the right. Keep a bit of left pressure on the stick. Try and set the compass to three thirty. That should take us somewhere near Dungeness."

"I'll try."

I fumbled with the compass, managing to set it while wandering all over the sky. My parents made it look so easy. I would never criticise their flying again. After much concentration I settled on course, height three thousand ish. I'd managed to get everything in balance, height, speed and course, trimmed so Midge was almost flying herself; almost. I was mentally congratulating myself, dead easy this. No no, don't even think dead.

"James, how do you feel about some aerobatics?"

"What?"

"Something evil this way comes, but don't panic."

"Why, what else am I supposed to do?"

"You follow my instructions to the letter and we may, just may, survive. That's what you do."

"All right, I'm ready."

"I'm assuming it's an enemy fighter, a novice by the way he's flying."

"Oh good, perhaps we'll be friends."

"It's more likely he sees you as his first kill, easy meat. He's far too fast. His instructors will tell him we break left and climb, so we'll do the opposite. Start a gentle turn to the left, just to kid him along."

"How's that?"

"Good, he's following us, lining up for a deflection shot. When I say go, stuff the stick forward and right with full right rudder. Hold it; hold it, steady; 'GO'."

I rolled Midge to the right as a burst of fire shredded the patch of air we occupied fractions of a second previous. The yellow nosed Me109 shot past in a blast of sound as our nose pointed at the channel waters. Yvette was screaming the most vitriolic abuse at our attacker and Midge was screaming in my head.

"Close the throttle. Pull the air brakes. Don't let me go over a hundred and twenty or you'll have my wings off."

The air speed was closer to a hundred and thirty and I could feel Midge creaking in every joint. I eased the stick back, trying to shed speed as we plunged closer to vast areas of wetness. Yvette was pointing over my left shoulder. I caught a glimpse through the roof light of the 109 in a climbing turn to the left.

"Well done James. Hold the speed just below one twenty and turn left onto our original compass heading. Lose height until we're as low as you feel comfortable."

"Comfortable? I should wish."

"You're doing fine. Keep focussed. You can level out now. Close the airbrake and bring the engine revs up to what they were, speed about ninety. We're at about a hundred feet. Hold it at that. He's going to try a head on attack, but he's too high and close. He'd be straight in the drink if he tried."

A burst of fire over our heads churned the water behind us as the 109 flashed past in a diving turn.

"What do I do now Midge?"

"Keep going on course, straight and level. I've got an idea. It's a long shot, but worth trying. Our weapons lie within us. He has missed twice, so he's angry and liable to make a mistake. Let's encourage him."

"I'll try anything Midge, just to stay alive."

"I know. Ease the throttle until we're doing seventy, sixty if you can manage, but don't lose any height."

"Right, got that."

I managed to get the speed down to about sixty-five and re-trimmed to fly level.

"Now James we have one chance at this, so let's get it right. He won't be fooled a third time."

"I'm listening Midge."

"When I say 'go', close the throttle and pull the stick back until we're going straight up, then open the throttle and put the stick forward so we keep flying speed. He's behind us, too fast. He's dropped his flaps to slow down. Get ready, now 'GO'."

With throttle closed I hauled back in to a steep climb as the air speed dropped to zero, then throttle open and stuff the nose down. Why he didn't blow us out of the sky, I'll never know. Perhaps the closing speed was faster than he'd estimated. He tried to avoid us, pulling up to narrowly miss as he passed over our heads, fighting like mad to stave off a stall. He almost managed, but the aircraft and the laws of gravity had taken over. There was a sad inevitability about its last movements as the 109 lazily turned on its back and curved into a final vertical plunge. A few fragments bearing grey camouflage were left floating in a welter of foam.

Yvette was dancing around, waving her fists and cursing his soul to a place of eternal torment. She hated as only those from an occupied country can hate. I was almost in tears from a mixture of sorrow, exhaustion and relief. I was glad to get rid of the 109, which I regarded as a thoroughly nasty piece of aerial mechanics, but the pilot would be only slightly older than myself. It was a sobering thought that given different circumstances, we could have been friends.

"Well done James. Check your heading, increase engine revs

to normal and bring us back to three thousand feet."

"Yes Midge."

Chapter 39

I opened the throttle and settled the speed for a climb to our original height. I couldn't drag my thoughts away from the young pilot at the bottom of the channel. I hope he died quickly. Even Yvette had gone quiet. Once on course and trimmed, I spoke to Midge.

"Midge."

"Yes James?"

"When I saw the 109 I was scared because he had guns and we haven't, but I also wanted to avenge Sweetie and now I have. Why don't I feel any happier?"

"It's the war James and war forces good people to do things that in times of peace they wouldn't even consider. Would you rather *we* were all sitting at the bottom of the channel?"

"No, of course not."

"Well, there's your answer. It was necessary for the survival of you and those close to you."

I looked round at Yvette. She smiled, leaned forward and gripped my shoulders. She understood. How I wished I could speak her language and share with her my feelings, but that would have to wait for a later time.

Aircraft flew back and forth at various heights, all friendly. Why couldn't a flight of Spitfires come along when I needed them? The coast of England came closer with every minute, but we were still a long way off. At least no one was shooting at us. We were able to enjoy being at three thousand feet above a calm sea, and the morning sun shimmering with a thousand rainbows from the propeller arc. I was able to relax a little and point out to Yvette ships and aircraft I recognised.

"James, we have a problem."

"What's wrong Midge?"

"I'm sure we're losing fuel from the left tank. After what we've been through I'd be surprised if we hadn't collected the odd bullet."

"What should I do Midge?"

"Close off the right tank until the left one is close to empty, then we'll switch to the right and hope there's enough to get us to Lydd. I'll tell you when to change over."

"That's the right one closed."

"Good, now lean out the mixture, no more than half an inch."

"Right, got that, anything else?"

"Look out for a passing angel, we may need a lift."

"Oh, that bad."

I looked at the fuel gauges below the wings and the left one was much lower than the right. The mass balance on the left aileron was missing too, which would account for the difficulty in keeping Midge straight. The asymmetric drag would also use more fuel. Things were looking decidedly dodgy, but we had done everything we could to keep flying.

There was still a large stretch of water between us and the coast when Midge told me to switch tanks. Even the fuel gauge under the right wing looked close to the empty mark. Trying to avoid the 109 had used much more than normal cruise mode, so now every drop was precious.

The minutes dragged by as the line of the coast inched down Midge's cowling, reaching the bottom of her instrument panel, then the corner of the side window. I could see the airfield. As we crossed the coastline the engine coughed, picked up for a few seconds, coughed twice and fell silent as the propeller continued to turn until it too stopped.

"That's it James, not a drop left. We have become a glider."

"I prefer a glider to a submarine, which we nearly were. So what do I do now?"

"Hold the speed with the stick at about sixty and aim for the airfield. We may have to land short."

"I've never landed an aircraft."

"Think of it as making gentle contact with mother earth and

I would stress the gentle. I'll talk you through it."

I turned to look at Yvette, her face pale against dark hair and eyes. I forced a smile.

"Out of petrol," and pointed to the wings.

She nodded and put forward a small hand to hold my shoulder. I had to save her and Midge. To end now after all we'd been through was unthinkable.

I could hear fabric flapping. Several holes were now evident close to the left tank and a strip of linen trailed from the wing tip. I could see a railway track near the airfield boundary with a goods train stopped at a signal. The smoke from the engine indicated an onshore breeze which could work in our favour.

"James, we're cutting things a bit fine, but I can see our angel, in the form of a steam engine."

"Midge, please don't talk in riddles."

"Steam engines are hot and hot air rises, so aim to fly over the engine and it may give us a few extra feet."

"See what you mean. Good idea."

I eased Midge round to point at the engine, then a bit more to counteract the breeze. Oh no, the signal changed and the train started moving.

"Keep your heading, the heat will be in the same place."

As we passed over the track, an angelic thermal lifted us gently over the airfield boundary.

"Aim for the grass at the side of the runway. We don't want to get in the way of the boys in blue. Hold your speed steady."

I fought the urge to pull back on the stick as the grass flashed past ever closer.

"Ease back now, a bit more, hold it at that, hold it and we're down."

We were bumping across the grass, trying to hold Midge straight with the rudder and coming to a stop, the sounds of flight suddenly replaced by those of a busy wartime airfield. We were back on friendly soil. Even the sight of an RAF Regiment sergeant red faced and armed couldn't wipe the smiles from our faces. He ducked under the wing, opened the door and saw what he took to be a French boy and girl.

"Parleyvouzanglais?"

"Thank you sergeant, I parley quite good anglais, it's the French I have difficulty with, but mademoiselle would be grateful for your help, as she doesn't speak English."

"Fair enough, but first we have to get you and you aircraft to a safer place, then we can have introductions and explanations."

He was quite the gallant, helping Yvette out and chatting to her in French, to which she responded with enthusiasm.

"Learned the lingo during the last lot I did. See a bit of the entente cordiale here do I," he said, giving me a broad wink.

I didn't know what to say, so changed the subject.

"I'll give you a hand folding the wings."

A small pickup arrived with a couple of airmen and together we managed to tow Midge to a safer place in one of the hangars. Having said my silent goodbye to Midge, Yvette and I were handed over to the care of the Commanding Officer and the station Intelligence Officer.

"Well, young man," said the CO. "You have some explaining to do."

"Yes Sir, I have. Before I start, could I ask of you, two favours?"

"Go on."

"Could you please, as a matter of urgency, contact Sir James Nettleton at the Air Ministry and tell him that James Edwards, Midge and Mademoiselle Yvette Jomaron are back in the country and to tell her father, who is the chief liaison officer to the French resistance that his daughter is safe."

"And the second favour is?"

"Not to repeat anything I say, to anyone else who doesn't have the highest security clearance."

"Before I agree, why Sir James?"

"He's my grandfather. My mother is his daughter."

"I see, you're James Edwards and this is Mademoiselle Yvette so who is Midge?"

"She's the aircraft we arrived in."

The CO sighed and looked at the ceiling. I knew he was wondering what sort of loony he was dealing with.

"I will try and explain but Sir James will want to know as soon as we land and he may be annoyed if he's not told immediately."

"You better be telling the truth," he said with some menace. He picked up the phone and asked to be put through to the Air Ministry and the office of Sir James Nettleton. It was answered by his secretary but as soon as my name was mentioned, Sir James came on the line and spoke to the CO.

"Sir James asks what you call him."

"Papa."

The CO handed me the phone.

"He wants to speak to you."

From then on, a degree of trust was evident. I told Papa briefly about what had happened and asked if he could contact Yvette's father Monsieur Jomaron.

"Sir, he wants to speak to you again."

The CO picked up the phone, said 'Yes Sir' several times and wrote a page of notes before recalling the exchange. He then spoke to the De Havilland factory at Hatfield asking them to collect a special Puss Moth for repair. After replacing the receiver, he turned to us.

"You now have our undivided attention. Please continue with your report, after which I've been told to make sure you are both fed, because you are always hungry. Am I correct?"

"Yes Sir, but I have been learning through necessity to go without."

Starting on the morning of the kidnap, I recounted the whole story up to landing on the grass beside the runway. I even showed him the notes I'd made while imprisoned in the chateau. When I finished there was a long pause.

"Let me get this straight. You were kidnapped in a Dominie, taken to a chateau in France which was bombed, escaped and sheltered by this young lady and her mother, taken to an aircraft which just happens to be your own. This talking aircraft tells you how to fly, so well that you outwit a 109, causing it to stall and crash into the channel. Then you run out of fuel and glide into a near perfect landing, which I witnessed. You really expect us to believe this? I've never heard such nonsense."

The CO looked at the Intelligence Officer.

"Do you believe this?"

"Well Sir, I'm afraid I do. It fits our own information."

"You really did splash a 109 with an unarmed Puss Moth?"

"Yes Sir," I said, "but I had help from the Puss Moth. She talked me through it. Ask Yvette."

So he asked Yvette in perfect French and she did the most convincing mime of a stalled 109 turning on its back and diving into the channel, after which, as tears ran down her face, she shook her fists and stamped the floor in the imaginary spot where the 109 vanished. One could almost taste the hatred.

We were taken to the officer's mess for a meal but it wasn't just any meal. Oh no, it was precious bacon and eggs, flying rations for those recently returned from a mission. Later that day, a car arrived from the Air Ministry to collect us. I don't think the CO was sorry to see us go.

From the confidential diary of Sir James Nettleton

Monday 4th September 1944

I'm having difficulty seeing to write as tears of joy and relief are filling my eyes. I look forward to hearing the whole story from James, as the version I've been given is so bizarre, it beggars belief. James flew Midge in to Lydd this morning. Why Midge was in France and how James managed to fly her are facts yet to be explained. I was surprised to learn he was accompanied by Captain Jomaron's daughter Yvette.

I telephoned Peter and Vicky's ferry pool as soon as news came from the CO at Lydd. They promised to pass on the good news at the earliest opportunity. How am I going to face James? I feel I've let him down. I can find plenty of reasons, but no excuses. The best I can do is help finish this rotten war and let him live in a world at peace. A world at peace? I fear that may prove an unattainable ideal, but we must try. We must try.

Chapter 40

I had never seen Papa's place of work and had always imagined it as the centre of a web of telephone lines radiating out all over the country. In reality it was not unlike many rooms in our own home with the addition of a desk and telephone.

We were shown in by his secretary. I needed no introduction to Yvette's father as she rushed into his arms amid a torrent of words and tears. Somehow she managed to condense the last fortnight into a few seconds. I walked over to Papa who put his arms round my shoulders. We were now the same height. He whispered in my ear.

"We'll talk later. Glad you're both back safely."

Monsieur Jomaron was a tall dark haired man in the uniform of an officer in the French air force, though I couldn't tell which rank.

"Yvette says you are her hero."

"I'm not sure about that Sir. I was just trying to stay alive."

"That James, is what heroes do. Now I must kiss you on both cheeks as an acknowledgment and thanks for bringing my daughter back to me."

I felt embarrassed until I felt the wetness of his tears on my cheeks. It was a step in my understanding of a conquered nation, now liberated. What privations they must have gone through and humiliations we could never understand.

"I will always be in your debt James."

"Sir, I wouldn't have survived without the help of your family and your brother."

"So we are even and that is good."

He shook my hand formally and gave a slight bow. Yvette put her arms round me and kissed my cheek. I thought she would step back, but she kept holding me and laid her head on my shoulder. I should have felt embarrassed, but didn't, so I held her in the same way. If this was the 'entente cordiale' the sergeant mentioned I welcomed it. Sadly it was also goodbye, as we were unlikely to ever meet again.

Papa escorted Monsieur Jomaron and Yvette to the door, where they shook hands. Yvette turned to me.

"Au revoir Jacques Edouard."

"Au revoir Yvette."

I stood looking at the closed door for some time. In closing, it brought to an end part of my life, a part containing the worst and best aspects of humanity. I was learning that experience brings irrevocable change. Papa took me by the arm and guided me to an easy chair. I sat with the sound of paper crackling, my life story stuffed down my trousers. I retrieved it and handed it to him.

"I wrote this Papa, in the expectation of being shot. I hoped the approaching Allied armies would find it and know what happened. It records up to the morning before the chateau was bombed."

He held it as if it was the most precious of manuscripts.

"You may have created an important historic document. Would you like to have it typed out? My secretary could and she can be trusted not to breathe a word of it."

"Yes Papa, I'd like that. I hope she can read my writing."

He smoothed the crumpled sheets, put them in a folder and took them to the next room. Moments later he returned and sat beside me.

"Now tell me everything that happened from the morning of your kidnap to when you entered this room today."

It took several hours, due to a number of interruptions which were too urgent to wait. After I'd finished he remained lost for some time in silent thought, but made no comment on my recent brushes with the dark angel.

"I'll make arrangements for a travel pass so you can go home tomorrow by train. I should be with you next weekend when we can talk more. Then we should get you back to school."

That evening I dined with Papa at his club where I also slept. The next day I caught an early train to Buckingham, where a car was waiting to take me home. I was still wearing the clothes that Madame Jomaron had given me. Now I understood the suspicious glances from fellow travellers on the train. Apart from looking different, the clothes carried the aroma of France, a subtle mixture of garlic and the strong cigarettes that Monsieur Jomaron smoked. I washed and changed, storing away the clothes in a drawer with the hope that some day, in a more peaceful future, I would be able to return them.

The only person in the house I knew was cook, so I visited the kitchens to say hello. Once again she was peeling onions, or so she said, though none were to be seen, only the evidence in her eyes. From her I learned that my old tutor Mr Davies had been given the use of a small cottage in the grounds of the estate. It was years since I'd spoken to him and basked in the warm rays of his wisdom.

We sat on either side of a large fire. He looked even more like Father Christmas, but now he felt the cold, even in summer. As we talked, the hours and years rolled back. I stroked the silky fur of his spaniel and we toasted slices of bread on long forks, until recent events across the channel were no more than a bad dream vaguely remembered. We were having afternoon tea for the third time when someone knocked on the front door.

"My my, two visitors in one day, is it my birthday?"

It was my mother, still in her ATA uniform. Papa had arranged leave for her while I was at home. After excusing ourselves from Mr Davies, we walked with our arms round each other, back to the big house. We were both thinner for different reasons. She had been worried sick after my kidnap and had only started eating properly when news of my safety had filtered through the various channels of communication.

She was understandably angry with Mr Wilson, but I managed to convince her that though initially his traitorous intentions were genuine, over the years doubts crept in to his idealistic view of the 'master race' and the final act of treason was forced on him by the hold the Nazis had over his family.

Dad managed a couple of days leave towards the end of the week and Papa arrived late on the Friday night. Earlier that day the first of the enemy's huge aerial rockets had exploded in London. The media reported it as a gas explosion as the government was trying to keep from the general public the truth that we had no effective defence against them once they were in flight. The only way was to destroy them or their launchers on the ground and that required techniques still to be developed.

We talked a great deal that weekend. I tried to make light of my experiences, so they wouldn't be worried, but I doubt if they were fooled for a minute. My mother had to return to the ferry pool on the Thursday, but Dad stayed until the Monday when he flew me north in a Dominie to the school airstrip. I had always liked the Dominie, but after recent experiences and before boarding, I would grip one of the outer struts and ask it if all was well with the world.

I left Dad to continue back to his unit at the ferry pool and walked back along the path across the bridge to the school as if for the first time. It wasn't changed, but I was. I walked into the dining room to be greeted by a roar from the Boss.

"Edwards, you're a month late, my office now."

"Yes Sir."

I turned on my heel and walked out amid gasps of horror from the juniors. The Boss followed, caught up with me and in a much quieter tone.

"Have you had any lunch James?"

"No Sir."

"We'll head for the kitchen first and get you fed. There's some of Matron's broth on the stove. You fancy that?"

"Yes Sir, I'm always ready for Matron's broth."

The Boss was about to help himself when Matron walked in.

"Headmaster, will you take the lad through to the wee room and let me see to that. Do you want some yourself?"

"Yes Matron."

"Good to have you back James. You've grown." She looked at me closely and added, "in more ways than one."

After enjoying the symphony of tastes wrapped up in Matron's broth, we walked through the Boss' office, past his secretary in the next room and into his living quarters.

"See I'm not disturbed by anything short of a plague of locusts, understand."

"Yes Sir" and she smiled sweetly before resuming her typing.

He closed the door and indicated an easy chair for me, before sinking into its twin on the opposite side of a low table on which lay an envelope marked 'Registered Post'.

"This is a report from your grandfather concerning your recent activities and frankly, if it had been from anyone else, it would be straight in the bin. Am I supposed to believe this?"

I didn't answer immediately as it was slowly dawning on me that I no longer feared him. I certainly respected him and that was as it should be, but I also liked him. We were on the same side, fighting a common cause.

"Firstly Sir, I can neither confirm nor deny and as it's clearly addressed to you personally, I have no wish to know the contents."

The Boss sat up in his seat, examining me as if for the first time.

"Secondly, I must ask if your security clearance includes knowledge of my special ability, as I can understand the report making little sense if it doesn't."

He glared at me with his green eyes, but I was no longer intimidated and he knew it.

"The short answer is yes, but I always thought it meant a super sensitivity to engine and wind noise. It's more than that though, isn't it?"

"Yes Sir."

"They speak to you in words, in English."

"Yes Sir, inside my head."

"Well I'm damned. Taken that way, it does make sense."

He glared at me again in a last parting shot.

"You wouldn't lie to me would you?"

"I wouldn't dare Sir. In any case, we made a pact and I'm not about to break it."

"Tell me James, as one pilot to another, did you really cause an Me109 to stall and crash into the channel?"

"He made a mistake."

"He certainly did. In fact the whole damn lot made a mistake and look where it's got them."

He moved in his seat, as if trying to get comfortable.

"James, I have a confession to make and I would ask you not to repeat the information to anyone else in the school."

"Sir?"

"If I'd been quicker, I could've prevented your kidnap. You remember the time when you and Peter had a look inside Mr Wilson's room and I pointed out the carpet covering the sandwich of paper?"

"Yes Sir."

"I realised too late, it was covering something else, loose floor boards. Matron helped lift the boards and we found a Nazi coding machine with books of settings. It was the same day you were kidnapped. We contacted Sir James, but there was no time to save you. There now, I've told you. Doesn't show me up in a good light but it's best you know."

I sat for some time, thinking about what he had said. A day earlier and Mr Wilson would have been caught and no doubt hanged as a traitor. I'm glad that didn't happen. I wouldn't have met Yvette and I'm glad that did happen.

"Thank you for telling me. I appreciate your frankness. You may find this also hard to believe, but I'm happy it worked out the way it did. I've always wanted to fly Midge. Now I have."

"Talking about flying James, we should get you and Peter started on the glider at the airstrip before Midge teaches you any more bad habits. We'll make it Saturday weather permitting."

He picked up the report, changed his mind and put it back on the table.

"The school can manage without us this afternoon. Reports only give the bare facts. Tell me what *really* happened in France."

So I did.

Chapter 41

We talked until it was time for the evening meal. He told me many of his experiences in the Great War, told in confidence, with the unspoken understanding that they would go no further. It was a comfort to realise that I and this great bear of a man had suffered the same cocktail of emotions. His small sitting room had become a place of mutual confession, to be respected in similar manner. He was looking at the livid wound on my left cheek.

"I'll wager you didn't get that from the point of a sabre, like this one," he said, touching his own scar.

"No Sir, nothing as glamorous, but no less exciting at the time."

He nodded in understanding.

"Let's go to Tea and show off your battle scars, but if anyone should have the temerity to ask how, just wink and keep them guessing."

Later I spoke to Peter and though there are no secrets between us, I have to admit omitting certain aspects of the adventure. Someday I'll tell him everything.

The school now had a different games and gymnastics instructor. Every time I saw him I wondered what had happened to Mr Wilson. I hope he left before the chateau was destroyed, but where would he go with enemies on both sides of the lines.

Christmas at home was a muted affair. The country was holding its breath in the hope this would be the last Christmas of the war. My mother managed leave on Christmas Eve and Christmas Day, but father had to work on. It was a difficult time at their ferry pool, due to several recent fatalities. Hasty modifications, long hours and bad weather were taking their toll.

I had witnessed first hand the ruthless punishment meted out to those who broke the enemy's laws, but I had no idea of the monstrous evil that lurked within the Nazi regime. The evidence for this came in the New Year. Reports and pictures were coming from Europe, showing the depths of inhumanity to which our enemy had sunk. I saw images of our soldiers with cloths wrapped round nose and mouth to protect them from the stench as mounds of bodies were scooped by bulldozers into communal graves.

I couldn't take it in. This was unbelievable. An evil so great, had to be destroyed without pity.

Three months after this discovery, our Russian allies entered the enemy's capital. A week later the dictator was dead, resistance collapsed and an unconditional surrender was agreed.

The war in Europe was over.

A few days after my fifteenth birthday atomic bombs were dropped on two cities in the Far East, completely destroying them and everything within. With this act of mass destruction, World War Two finally drew to a close.

There were great celebrations and I knew I should feel happy. I was alive, as were my immediate family, so why this grey feeling of sadness. Was it because the world I had left to go to school in Scotland had changed beyond all recognition and would never return? But I too had changed. Shadows behind the eyes were recognised by Matron and the Boss. We had all faced death, but lived to continue the fight. The enemy was conquered, but evil was not. Yet in those seconds when life and death were in the balance, I had never felt so alive and in that memory lay danger.

It was something the Boss had warned me about. If you dice with death trying to recall that state of heightened awareness, eventually the little cubes fall in favour of the dark angel.

Though peace had been declared, one could never say the world was at peace, far from it. The armed services were still needed, though my parents were allowed home to rest and recuperate. Midge was restored to her former white, with the addition of a small black cross below her window. Papa decided to retire from government service and work on the restoration of the house and estate. Perhaps because of this I was no longer asked to talk to aircraft. I hinted in various quarters that my hearing had been affected by the bombing and couldn't be relied on to hear 'plane talk'. I was happy to be left alone without additional responsibility.

In talking to Midge, I found peace.

Explanatory Notes

Below is an explanation of the historical significance of certain parts of the book

Pronunciations: The Messerschmitt 109 and the Junkers 88 were usually shortened to Me 109 and Ju 88, but were pronounced M E 109 and J U 88.

Chapter 2: Tommy Tailwind is based on a Hawker Hurricane flown form Turnhouse, near Edinburgh to Northolt, London, on 10th February 1938. The distance of 327 miles was completed in 48 minutes, giving a point to point average speed of 408.75mph. Not bad for an aircraft with a stated top speed of a mere 335mph. The explanation, not initially released to the press, was a gale force tailwind. The pilot was Squadron leader John W. Gillan of 111 Squadron, for ever after known as Downwind Gillan.

Chapter 3: The story of the Wellington bomber with the erratic flight characteristics is based on a true case, which was only solved by chance.

Chapter 6: The tall masts near the East coast of Yorkshire were part of the Chain Home radar system. The Graf Zeppelin made a two day cruise along the east coast between the 2nd and 4th of August 1939 to investigate our radar defences. Fortunately for our country, they were searching in the wrong frequencies. It's sobering to think that a different history could hang on the slight twist of a radio knob.

Chapter 17: In November 1939 during the Battle of France, the French captured intact, a new Messerschmitt Bf109E. They handed it on to us and it was flown to Duxford for evaluation. The findings proved useful. I make no apologies for being biased. To me it was a nasty little beast intent on destroying our beautiful aircraft. On a good day, I would call it a worthy opponent.

Chapter 18: The naval victory mentioned was the Battle of the River Plate.

Chapter 21: I've listed the main shortcomings of our fighters, discovered by experience during the battles over France prior to the Battle of Britain. I've simplified, for the sake of the book, the problem with the compass, which was common to all aircraft with inward retracting wheels. It was realised early on that the steel wheels required degaussing. This worked fine as long as both wheels were degaussed in the same factory. The problem arose when the wheels came from different factories and one wheel was more efficiently degaussed than the other.

The problem caused by negative 'G' on the Rolls Royce Merlin aero engine was solved by a lady design engineer called Miss Shilling.

Chapter 22: Like chapter 5, this was another point where the Battle of Britain and therefore the war was turned in our favour. A Junkers 88 bomber was returning to occupied France from a reconnaissance flight and lost its bearings. Flying south over Wales, they mistook the Bristol Channel for the English Channel, landed at Chivenor in Devon and were promptly arrested. The aircraft contained the latest target finding device, disguised as part of the beam instrument landing system. Through Intelligence, the scientists managed to identify the device and cobble together a means of bending or interrupting the beam using in one case hospital x-ray equipment. This caused an enemy bomber to bomb part of London, which gave Churchill the excuse to mount a raid on Berlin. This so enraged Hitler that he ordered the target for his raids to be moved from the RAF airfields to London, so allowing Fighter Command to recover, maintain mastery of the air and compel Hitler to postpone indefinitely his invasion of Britain.

Chapter 30: The flying scenes in the film 'In Which We Serve' were filmed at Duxford using a captured Ju88. I have an old friend who worked on it and was there during the filming.

On the 19th April 1943 an experimental jet aircraft built by Gloster, was demonstrated at Hatfield in front of Winston Churchill.

Chapter 31: On the 9th of May 1943, a Ju88 night fighter defected with her crew and landed at Dyce, near Aberdeen. This aircraft has been preserved in the museum at Hendon.

The chapter endings in part 1 show the side view in silhouette of a De Havilland Puss Moth and in parts 2 and 3, a Supermarine Spitfire Mark 1X (9).

Glossary of Terms and Abbreviations

Bairn: A Scottish term for a young child.

Stushie: Described in a Scottish dictionary as a row or uproar, usually in protest against something.

REME: Royal Electrical and Mechanical Engineers.

CO: Commanding Officer.

MO: Medical Officer.

Sodium Pentothal: An intravenous anaesthetic, sometimes called the 'truth drug' and used as an aid to interrogation.

ATA: Air Transport Auxiliary.

MC: Military Cross.

Tuppence: Two old pennies.

Very pistol: A pistol designed to fire coloured flares.

VSI: Vertical speed indicator.

Deflection shooting: The art of aiming in front of a moving target so the missile and target arrive together in the same patch of air.

Acknowledgements

I am indebted to the following people for their help and encouragement.

All my family, especially Brodie my grandson, whose honest criticism, technical expertise and belief in my abilities, constantly renewed my creative energy.

To all who supported my endeavours I give my thanks, but Kathryn Fisher, Douglas Gilmour, Ellen Hayward, Kirsty Mc-Clymont, Joyce Orr, Suzanne Taylor and Elizabeth Tucker added that most precious of gifts, their time.

Lastly, my mother, who in the late 1930s, introduced me to the family with the beautiful white aeroplane.

About the Author

John Milne was born in 1933, about the same time as Hitler came to power in Germany. His family moved to Hamilton in 1939 and within a month of starting primary school, war was declared. His father served in a Pathfinder Squadron of the RAF and was a strong formative influence. After school he studied sculpture at the Glasgow School of Art under the guidance of Benno Schotz. National Service was spent in the Intelligence office of an RAF radar station in the north of Scotland. His father's untimely death was the prod needed to start writing his autobiography and learning to fly. He soloed after four and a quarter hours dual when the instructor stated he'd had enough and climbed out. Many of the experiences and characters met during his life have been used as models for large parts of this, his latest book.